I0554134

I knew I was taking a risk, but I had no idea how much trouble it could cause me...

I couldn't hide forever so I lathered more makeup on my face, hoped the darkness and smoke below would hide any traces left by Charley's fist. I left the empty dressing room and went downstairs. Nothing seemed different. Trixie was on stage. A few eyes were on her, but as usual most of the men were either drinking, masturbating, smoking, or all of the above. Yet, for me everything had changed. I lingered at the bottom step and looked for Charley. If I saw him, I would have Joe arrest the bastard.

I sat by myself in a corner under the stage, thinking what I needed was a stiff drink. Joe was busy with a group at the other end of the bar. While I waited for him to notice me, I kept busy imagining Charley behind bars. I knew that wouldn't happen. Not to Tony Corelli's partner. Corelli knew judges. He'd proven that with my case.

Tony wouldn't let anything interfere with his plans for Atlantic City. He made that plain enough. He was in trouble and I was the oil that would grease the kinks to smooth sailing. Once he found out I willingly went upstairs with Charley, he'd say I deserved whatever I got. He might even look at the incident as a betrayal. I'd gone behind his back and possibly made Charley a threat to his plans. How stupid could a girl get?

Joe noticed me after about five minutes. His eyes narrowed and his jaw tightened.

"Charley Rossino stormed out of here like the devil himself was after him. Never knew he could move so fast." He leaned closer. "Did he do that to you?"

"Let it go, Joe."

"No way," he said. "That asshole hit you. You can't hide the bruises with makeup."

After five years of being the traveling companion and lover of a secretive man thirty years her senior, Erin Matthews fears his increasing paranoia. At age twenty-two, Erin escapes to a new city, determined to survive with her limited skills and experience. She cannot run, however, from the dark act that facilitated her escape. Making one bad decision after another, she lands in the Philadelphia demimonde world of entertainers, hustlers, and thugs. But will her newly learned skills, native intelligence, and honed instincts be enough to keep her alive until she gains the redemption and forgiveness she seeks?

KUDOS for *The Flawed Dance*

In *The Flawed Dance* by Laura Elvebak, Erin Matthews is running from an abusive boyfriend who is connected to the mob. She takes refuge in Philadelphia, living with a friend of a friend. She finds a job and a place to live, but she can't seem to stay out of trouble. Making one bad decision after another, she ends up back in the same situation and has to dig her way out, one painful shovelful at a time, while struggling to survive in the underworld of entertainers, thugs, and organized crime. The story has a ring of truth that makes you feel like you're right there suffering with Erin. I was impressed at how real Erin seemed to me and how hard I rooted for her, even when she made the same mistakes again and again. It takes a really good author to do that. ~ *Taylor Jones, Reviewer*

The Flawed Dance by Laura Elvebak is the story of a young woman on the run from domestic violence. But it is much more than that. This is the story of life. Real life. Our heroine, Erin, leaves her abusive boyfriend and flees to a new city, trying to start a new life. But what she doesn't realize is that you can't run away from yourself. The bad decisions and mistakes she made that got her into trouble in the first place, she makes again. And again. Until she ends up back in the same bad place, with another abusive boyfriend, in trouble with the law, and struggling to survive in the shadowy world of dance clubs, bars, crime bosses, and the dreaded "room upstairs." Erin is naïve, inexperienced, and in way over her head. But she learns quickly. You can't help but cheer for her as she tries to change not only her life and circumstances but also herself. *The Flawed Dance* is well-written and, at times, seems almost too real, the pain and desperation too authentic. Either the author lived the story, or she did some first-rate research. The story is intense, thought-provoking, and well worth the time to read. This one's a keeper that you'll want to read again and again. ~ *Regan Murphy, Reviewer*

ACKNOWLEDGEMENTS

First of all, I thank my amazing editors, Lauri, Faith, and Joyce for their support and faith in me.

I will be forever in debt to my fabulous critique group members—Amy, Bob, Dean, Julie, Kay F., Kay K., Leann, and Millie for their invaluable insight and advice. Thanks also to the Soparker-Hairston family—Charlie, Susie and Isabella—for their continued support and for the use of their lovely home for our meetings. Thanks also to my Thursday Night critique group members— Anita, Clif, Devon, Doug, Gail, and Gene for their support and advice. Both groups have shared their writing and time with me for over fifteen years.

THE FLAWED DANCE

Laura Elvebak

A Black Opal Books Publication

DEDICATION

To Shawn, Brian, and Tanya

CHAPTER 1

The instant I landed the blow on Johnny's head, I knew he would live with me forever. I knew I wouldn't escape no matter how fast or how far I ran. He lived with me as I crossed borders to a new life, one filled with unfamiliar sights and smells. I was the same person as yesterday, yet different. I was free, but shackled with my past. What other choice did I have, but to go forward?

I took a deep breath and trudged up the dark, narrow stairs of the converted row house, following Jesse to the second floor. The smell of grease and stale cigarettes seeped from the walls. I hesitated, one foot on the next step. "I'll be the only white woman living in this building, won't I?"

Jesse looked over his shoulder. "You wanna turn around and go back?"

If only I could. But I didn't come all this way to change my mind at the last minute.

I stared straight ahead. "No."

Jesse's thick upper lip curled. "Didn't think so."

The door at the landing came into view. I clenched my hands to keep from shaking and reached for something to say to calm my nerves. "The radio said there've been riots in the city since Doctor King was killed." Not that I was worried. Street fighting no more affected me than the war in Vietnam. I was more scared of Johnny. Dead or alive.

"This is the west side," Jesse said, now sounding annoyed. "No trouble here."

I didn't know west from east. I'd never been to Philadelphia. What if there were riots? Maybe I should be worried, should have paid more attention to the news. No trouble for him, but what about me? I decided to keep my mouth shut until after I faced the stranger on the other side of the door—Jesse's brother and my new roommate.

Jesse rapped hard on hollow wood.

A stocky man, wearing a faded flannel shirt and tan trousers with suspenders, opened the door. The man looked old enough to be Jesse's father. His smile reached his eyes. Maybe he was the one with the nice gene.

"This be her. Erin." Jesse mumbled the words. With a furtive glance in my direction, he said, "This be Carl, my brother I tol' you 'bout."

Carl chuckled softly, dispelling the bad air between Jesse and me. "I suspect she guessed that already. It's a pleasure meeting you, Erin."

His voice had a musical, sing-song quality. Cocoa skin crinkled around warm dark eyes. Tight gray curls framed a pleasant face, but I suspected the map of wrinkles remembered a road traveled over many miles of ruts and potholes. I wondered if my own face reflected my journey. I pushed away the thought and gave him my best smile, wanting to make a decent impression, no matter what Jesse might have said about me.

Carl gave me a quick study. I tensed, thinking he could see right through my shell to the runny yolk inside. I thought he looked trustworthy, but my ability to judge men had not proved reliable.

I understood Jesse's motivation for driving me all the way from New Jersey, but how did he convince his brother to take a strange white girl into his tiny apartment and into his life? I'd give anything to have listened in on that conversation. The man had to be a saint in disguise.

Carl stepped aside. "Come on in. You made it in time for breakfast."

Jesse looked uncomfortable, a definite change in attitude now that he was in his brother's presence.

I wanted to be sure Carl understood. "You really don't mind if I stay here a few days? You probably didn't have a chance to think this through."

"How old are you, girl?" Carl's tone was soothing.

"Twenty-two."

Carl nodded. "Jesse said you were a decent person and needed someplace to stay. That's good enough for me."

Decent? Jesse called me decent?

"Hope you don't mind tight quarters. I only got the one room and one bed, but you be safe here."

A quick study of the efficiency almost changed my mind. To the left of the door, a stove and a tiny refrigerator squeezed in next to the sink and a narrow counter. A small dining table, two chairs, and a foldout sofa bed with an end table was the sum of Carl's furniture. One bathroom and a closet filled the rest of Carl's space. Where would I sleep? Did it matter? I didn't have anywhere else to go.

"You sure are trusting," I said.

You don't know Carl either, I thought, as I set my bags on the floor, felt my stomach tighten. My words spilled out like water. "Don't worry. I'll get a job right away. I'll pay you back, whatever you want, for rent, for food. Won't take me long to find my own place and be out of your way."

Carl gave me a fatherly smile, but didn't respond. Instead he spoke to his brother. "You're welcome to stay, Jesse. You must be hungry after your long trip. No sense in rushing out again."

"I gotta get back," Jesse said, not looking at me. "Phyllis will skin me alive if I don't get back in time for work." Phyllis was Jesse's wife and could be a bitch if she suspected Jesse even looked at another woman, let alone helped one who was running from another man.

Carl's tone stayed calm but firm. "You can at least have a cup of coffee before you go. Don't want you falling asleep while driving."

"Yeah, okay. I can do with a cup." Jesse lowered himself into a hard, armless chair, the type I remembered from school.

Jesse hadn't looked at me since we arrived. We both worked at the same restaurant. I was a waitress, Jesse a bus boy. Last night, I arrived late and gave him my tale of woe—omitting a few details.

To my surprise, he agreed to help me, even left work two hours early. His attitude had since changed. Guess he got scared I'd tell his brother about that cheap, smelly hotel room with puke green walls he insisted we stay at, arguing he was too tired to drive all night after working.

I couldn't even guess what Carl was thinking while he scrambled eggs and fried bacon.

He turned off the burner, poured boiling water into three cups, and mixed in instant coffee. He handed each of us a cup.

Jesse gulped his and stood.

"Thanks, Jesse. I won't forget what you've done for me." I meant every word. "There's no possible way Johnny will find me." *Because he's dead.* "Just don't tell anyone."

His eyes bugged and his back went rigid. "You crazy? You think I want my skin stripped from my bones and my neck stretched and hung from a tree? And that's just what my wife would do. Your husband would probably cut off my balls. Nobody knows nothing, and nobody ain't gonna know."

I sat on the bed and spoke as calmly as I could manage, which I could tell irritated the hell out of him. "Stop worrying. Johnny won't suspect you. If he shows up at the restaurant looking for me, will you let me know?"

I surprised myself sometimes. I could lie like a professional con man. Practiced the art while living with Johnny, who I knew wasn't ever going to show up anywhere.

Red lines streaked the whites of Jesse's eyes. "Are you kidding? How, without getting people suspicious? What I am supposed to say if they ask where I disappeared to same night as you? I ain't saying or doing nothing to make them look twice at me."

Carl chuckled. "My goodness, you sure are paranoid. Don't make this a big deal. You learn something might help our girl here, call Nettie. You still have her number?" He turned to me. "She's a good friend, lives upstairs, has the only phone."

Jesse gave him a sour look. "Yeah, sure." He moved toward the door.

Carl laid a hand on his shoulder. "Take care of yourself, Jesse."

"Little late for that shit," Jesse said, and shook him off. "Don't worry. This is the last time I go outta my way, be a Good Samaritan. What's in it for me, huh? Nuthin'."

His attitude pissed me off. I wanted him to go, but I still owed him. More than he'd ever know. I swallowed with difficulty. "Thanks again, Jesse."

He didn't look at me. "Yeah, don't mention it."

I knew he was thinking of last night and how he

missed out on that big thank you he was expecting for his trouble and didn't get.

"Are you all right?" Carl asked me after Jesse left. He handed me a plate with a liberal serving of bacon, eggs, and buttered toast.

I put the plate on the table and settled in the chair, still warm from Jesse. "I'm fine. More worried about you. Don't want to bring trouble to your door."

Carl shook his head slowly, the smile trembling on his lips. "You don't bring trouble, girl. Trouble was here before you was born."

I wanted to laugh before I burst out crying. What would he say if I told him the truth about me? How much trouble would that be?

I pulled myself together. So far, I'd handled myself pretty well, I thought, pretending to be normal. I almost believed the lie. *Just act like nothing bad happened. Take the bad stuff, roll it in a ball, and stuff it in a corner. Don't tell anyone.*

"Are you sure you're all right?" Carl's concern finally got through to me.

"Yeah, sure. Are you?"

He chuckled. "Don't you worry your head about me. You go ahead and eat."

He sounded so confident. Maybe I *would* be all right. Nothing I could do about the past. My life started now. I looked into his eyes, sensing a deep peace in them. I envied that look. My stomach rumbled as I gazed at my plate. "You shouldn't have bothered." I managed a smile and realized I was hungry after all. "But I'm glad you did." I drank half my coffee before tackling my food.

"It ain't nothing special. I have to eat anyway." Carl sat opposite me and dug his fork into the eggs.

I finished first and rinsed my plate in the sink. I had to be doing something. Too wound up to relax, I meandered to the window next to the bed and looked out over the gray day. Fog hovered over the tiled roofs of row houses that marched down both sides of the street.

Carl brought me a fresh cup of coffee. I wondered at his patience, felt a touch of envy at the mellow look in his eyes. He seemed too good to be true. "I'm really grateful for your taking me in," I said. "But I'm curious, what's in this for you?"

He frowned. "What do you mean?"

"All you knew about me is whatever Jesse told you and he didn't know much."

He said with a straight face, "What? Are you going to tell me you're a serial killer?"

I almost dropped my cup. "Why do you say that?"

He looked at me funny, and I held my breath. Then he laughed. "You look so serious. I'm kidding, my dear. Oh, wait. You think I have a hidden agenda? Honestly, I didn't know what to expect when Jesse called. He said you needed to get away, but had no place to go. I feel it, girl. Think you're the only one who's come from bad times?" He patted my arm. "Are you uncomfortable here?" He slapped his forehead. "What am I saying? Of course, you are. You come in to a strange city to move in with someone you've never met, a man of color."

He didn't get it. I put my hand up to stop him. "Uncomfortable? Carl, you have no idea what my life has been like the last few years. I don't think I could ever be that uncomfortable with anyone or anything again. Except maybe…" I looked down at the sofa that would pull out into a bed at night.

"Ah, yes, I can see where the sleeping arrangements might make you nervous, but you don't need to worry about me." He tapped his chest. "I have a weak ticker. When I go to bed, it's to sleep. I wish I could offer you something more, but this is all I have."

I wanted to take him at his word. Just in case, I still had my grandmother's hat pin, the one that kept Jesse away last night.

"I suppose you're curious. Why I left in such a hurry?" I said.

"That's your business. I figure if you want to tell me, you will." Carl took his empty plate to the sink.

I stood and moved him aside. "I can do the dishes. You've done enough. Sit and relax."

He looked startled, but then he smiled and sat on the sofa. "Thank you."

I filled the sink with soapy water. The silence stilled the room. I wanted to scream just to avoid listening to my own thoughts. Or Johnny's voice. My insides were quivering like jelly.

"Johnny's thirty years older than me." *Good one, Erin. Carl and Johnny are probably about the same age.* I scrubbed a dish so hard the painted flowers were in danger of peeling. "He's got lines on his face like yours. Used to be a hard hat diver for oil companies. Demolitions expert. Worked all over the world—before his accident. But our age difference was never a problem." *That's right. Keep talking like Johnny's alive.*

I steeled myself for Carl's question, but it didn't come.

I rambled on, unable to keep quiet. "I left him once when we lived in Key West. Hopped a bus to Miami. He found me the next day." I shot another glance at Carl, who sipped his coffee while he listened. "Talked me into going back with him. Said he needed me. Threatened to kill himself if I didn't. I was all he had, you see. That made him jealous all the time. We didn't stay in one place long enough to make friends."

I wiped my hands and turned to face Carl. "But this time is different. He won't find me. I've never been to

Philadelphia. Don't know anyone here. I was smart this time, didn't leave a trail. I don't know why I'm telling you all this." I blew out a shaky laugh. "I just don't want you to worry."

I didn't really lie. Everything I said happened. I couldn't tell him the rest. I couldn't tell anyone.

I turned my back to him and finished washing the dishes. I avoided Carl's eyes while I picked up the dish towel to dry them.

After a long silence, he said, "A lot of life packed into twenty-two years."

I squeezed my eyes shut for a second. *If you only knew the half of it.*

"I'm not worried," Carl said. "I'm curious about one thing, though. How did you get Jesse to help you?"

The question threw me. My laugh sounded brittle. "You know what? I didn't. I asked a few of the girls, the other waitresses. No one else wanted to get involved. Jesse volunteered."

Carl had taken another sip of his coffee, and he almost spit it out. A few drops hit his chin and he wiped it with his hand. "That crazy fool." His eyes narrowed. "But I never knew him to help someone out of the kindness of his heart. He'd want something."

I guess he knew his brother well. Jesse had a family, but fancied himself a ladies' man at work. He probably envied Carl's bachelor lifestyle, or the way he imagined how his brother lived. But regardless of what Jesse hoped to gain by having me to himself for the duration of the trip, I considered the man a hero for following through with his offer.

"Jesse did exactly what we had agreed upon," I said.

Still holding the dish towel, I sank in the chair.

Carl looked at me shrewdly. "What did he expect from you?"

I looked away, not wanting to rat out his brother.

Carl pressed on. "That boy always act like someone gonna beat him to death when he hiding something. He acts jumpy, too, eager to leave."

I figured he'd already guessed the answer. "He made a move on me," I admitted. "But I had my secret weapon." I pulled out the hat pin Grandmother had given me. I remembered Jesse's expression as he lay beside me in that hard bed with the gray sheets, reaching for me, only to get stabbed for his trouble. "It works."

Carl flung back his head and laughed outright. "No wonder that boy was pissed. Good for you." He sobered and gave me a knowing look. "You're not what I expected, Erin Matthews."

What had he expected?

"You won't be sorry, Carl."

I hoped those words were true.

CHAPTER 2

"Is the rain ever going to stop?" I tossed the question at Carl the moment he walked in the door at five-fifteen. After three days in the cramped apartment, my skin felt tight and my head pounded. While Carl worked during the day, I paced the tiny room, when I wasn't scouring the want ads in his stack of *Daily News* he kept in a corner. Besides the news bites about the war, race riots, and war protesters that Johnny never discussed with me because *I was too dumb*, there were the usual murders and high-profile trials that splashed the front pages. No one fitting my description was reported missing. No unidentified body found in New Jersey. I was safe. For now.

Carl met my words with his usual calm. He shook off his wet umbrella and shrugged off his coat. When he'd hung both in the overcrowded closet, he went to the sink and washed his hands. He looked worn and tired after the bus ride home.

I knew he did some kind of social work, but he never talked much about it. After listening to other people's complaints all day, he didn't want to listen to mine. I tried to minimize my growing desperation while he was around. I was used to hiding my feelings around Johnny, but found I couldn't do that any longer. My shell had shattered and no one could put me back together again.

"I don't know the city and I've only got ten dollars. Sorry to be such a complaining fool tonight, but I don't want to be dependent on anyone, and you've already been too kind. More than I deserve."

"You don't have to apologize. Who else are you gonna talk to?" He heated a pot of water on the stove. "I know you're anxious about money, but you'll get on your feet. Until then, I'm enjoying your company."

His words splashed another coat of guilt on me. "You're going to make me cry."

"No crying allowed." He reached for the jar of instant, but I stopped him.

"I'll make the coffee," I said. "You sit and relax."

"Girl, I'm not a helpless old man. I've been doing for myself the last fifty years and I ain't gonna change now."

Despite his protests, he sat on the couch. He watched me as he pulled off one shoe, rested from the effort before he eased off the other one. He wiggled his toes and let out a breath. When the water boiled I fixed two cups and brought them to the end table.

Carl picked up his cup and took a tentative sip before setting it down. "I brought home a bus schedule. There're several restaurants in Center City and you can get there by bus."

Waitressing again. I'd hoped to do something better, a typing job in an office. Before Johnny, I worked in a bank. My first job out of high school. Just a phone operator, but I could have advanced. Who knows? I might have been a bank manager by now if I hadn't stopped in that bar and became blinded by the silver-haired god in a wheelchair and thought my destiny was to save and heal my favorite Frank Yerby character.

I thanked Carl and let him relax while I fixed us a simple meal of tomato soup and crackers. Afterward, I washed the dishes and put them away. I wished I had money for food. Carl's tiny refrigerator barely stocked enough for him. I had to find a job and soon.

Early the next morning, I showered while Carl made coffee and oatmeal. I applied makeup quickly and brushed my hair in a ponytail. Some days I hated looking in the mirror, afraid of what I might see behind the mask. Not on this day, though. I bared my white teeth, straightened my shoulders, and flipped a finger to the image. *Take that!*

"All yours," I told Carl as I came out of the bathroom.

He glanced up, then pointed out an unruly blond swirl among the tame brown that fell across my forehead. "You got a rebel streak there, girl." His words made me smile.

He took over the bathroom while I dressed in my black pencil skirt. The hem fell just above the knee, modest and professional. I matched it with a tailored white blouse. I had two pairs of shoes, the black lace-up waitress shoes and my white plastic go-go boots. With the weather getting colder, I decided on the boots. Those and my lightweight jacket would have to do.

Carl came out of the bathroom with a bath towel wrapped around him and went into the closet to dress. When he reappeared, he held his wool overcoat over one arm. He stopped and looked me over with a critical eye.

"It'll snow soon," he warned. "You have warmer clothes?"

"This is it," I said. "That's another reason I need a job."

He glanced out the window. "We might have a white Christmas."

"Really? I've never seen snow before."

He looked surprised. "Even in Jersey?"

"Moved there in the spring when we left Florida. Johnny and I moved around a lot after we left California."

Like the time Johnny and I sneaked out of our hotel room in LA, caught a cab in the middle of the night with our sparse belongings, rushed to the airport, and boarded a plane bound for New York City. Johnny's paranoia that he was being chased had become worse. He even changed our name. There were several name changes after that. I shook off the memory and assumed a brighter tone. "Seems like I've managed to avoid snow my whole life."

"Some say that's lucky." He put on his overcoat. "You'll do fine today. But take my word, cold weather is right around the corner."

I nodded. "I'll find something today. Don't worry."

"Don't forget to lock the door when you leave." He opened a drawer under the counter and fished out a key. "Here's a spare."

After he left, I stood at the window and watched him walk to the bus stop. Relief and anticipation filled me, knowing I was finally on my own. I stepped out into the hall, locked the door behind me, and pocketed the key.

Out on the sidewalk I inhaled the brisk fall air and felt the wind slap my face. Carl had told me to take the bus to Center City, but it felt good to walk after days in that tiny apartment. I passed row houses identical to Carl's, all shades of reddish-brown brick. Tree branches stretched their crooked black arms. Dead fingers clawed against a sky bleached of color. The song of loneliness and cruel beauty sang its familiar tune and I walked to its rhythm.

Surprisingly, only a small number of people were on the sidewalk. A few dark faces with bold eyes glanced my way. They didn't scare me, despite the racially charged articles I read in the paper. Working with Jesse at the restaurant, now living with Carl, made me feel no different from them. Those men did more for me than most white men I'd known.

I gripped my jacket tighter as a blast of cold wind hit me. I passed cigar shops, liquor stores, even a pool hall where the sound of billiard balls cracking together reached the sidewalk and carried with the wind. No restaurants. The neighborhood of two-story brick houses, the smell of fried bacon, old cigars, and exhaust fumes from a passing bus made me feel at home in a way I couldn't explain. Maybe I'd lived here in a past life. I giggled at the thought. After an hour or so, I stopped thinking. My face felt icy, tears born of the chill wet my cheeks. My fingers and toes felt numb.

I had no idea where I was or what kind of job I wanted. I must have gone in the opposite direction from Center City. Discouraged, feeling like a failure, I was ready to go back the way I came. My feet ached. I was cold and thirsty. Carl's cozy apartment sounded real good.

A flurry of movement in the quiet street caught my attention. A man appeared at the corner, walking fast in my direction. *Johnny?* My chest contracted. My mouth went dry. A sharp pain knifed my gut. *No! Couldn't be!* The hat he wore, tucked down over his forehead, fur flaps covering his ears, concealed his hair. I froze, my legs turned to water. I tried to blank out the memory that wouldn't let me go, the unspeakable horror of what I'd done, the knowledge of what I was capable of doing. Panic rose in my throat.

The street blurred and I felt the air rush out of me. I reached out to the building next to me and clung to the bricks to keep from falling. My stomach roiled. I was going to be sick.

A wooden sign swayed on a black chain above a

door next to me. I dashed inside without reading the painted words. The familiar smells of beer and whiskey, mingled with cigarette smoke, assaulted my senses. I took a seat at the end of the bar where I could scrunch down and still keep an eye on the door. My heart raced, my cheeks burned. I took deep breaths and when I felt calm enough, I dared to look at my surroundings.

I faced a mirrored wall lined with a variety of bottles. Lighted beer signs hung from the ceiling. The bar's rich mahogany felt smooth and warm to my touch. The round tables and leather-covered booths could be in any of the many bars where Johnny and I drank the days away. I made furtive glances at the door, expecting to see him standing in the doorway.

He didn't appear. A handful of men on barstools cast lewd glances my way. A shiver ran down my back. *Ghosts.*

"Just water," I said when the bartender appeared in front of me.

"You gotta order a drink, girlie. So what'll it be?"

I fingered the ten in my pocket and hesitated, torn between leaving and facing whatever was out there, or spending what little money I had. I desperately craved a drink. I felt eyes staring at me and turned to see a man approach from the restroom. A dark business suit dressed a trim build. He had olive skin and black hair slicked back from a high forehead. Good looking in the only way an Italian can pull it off.

He winked at me. I ignored him and faced the bar again. I crossed my legs, uncrossed them and tugged at the hem, which had cruised up my thigh. The bartender drummed the bar with his fingers, impatient, waiting for my answer.

"What do you drink when you have a choice?" said a deep voice behind me.

The Italian slipped onto the stool next to me. Smooth.

"I usually order scotch and water," I replied.

My breathing returned to normal. The man on the street hadn't been Johnny. That was *my* paranoia. I let him get to me again. I was safe now. Safe in this bar.

The guy snapped his fingers and five seconds later two drinks appeared in front of us. Who was this man? He looked like a wiseguy, a mob guy. Wouldn't that be ironic? I'd become convinced after running from city to city with Johnny that he was being chased by mob guys. He never said, but he wouldn't tell me anything. Didn't trust me. Usually tight-lipped, Johnny once let it slip how he had almost killed his Sicilian ex-brother-in-law. I made the connection in my head. The Mafia was from Italy. The movies taught me that much.

I sipped my drink and met the Italian's eye. "Thanks."

"Haven't seen you in here before," he said.

"No reason you should. I'm new in town, looking for work. Only I think I made the wrong turn."

"The way you ran in here, I thought someone was chasing you."

"No," I said quickly. "I was cold, that's all. Looking for a warm place to sit awhile."

"Name's Tony Corelli," he said and raised his drink.

I picked up mine. "Erin Matthews."

His gaze traveled downward and finally met my eyes. "So, Erin, what kind of work you looking for?"

"Anything." That didn't sound right. "I have waitress experience."

"Where?"

"Florida, mostly. Key West, Fort Lauderdale, and Miami." Not mentioning the town I'd just left in New Jersey. "Hotels and high-end restaurants." The only work

I could get since Johnny and I moved so often, and I had to support him.

His eyes were dark and unreadable. "I might be able to help you. I have connections to a few bars downtown, if you think you'd be interested."

Bars? I wasn't sure about that, but I couldn't afford to turn away an offer. "I'm interested in making money."

"Good." He nodded in approval. "I think you could make a lot of money. Hope you like to dance."

Now I was curious. What did dancing have to do with being a waitress? "Sure. Why?"

"These particular clubs use dancers. That's where the money is." He reached in his pocket, but his hand came up empty. "Looks like I don't have the names or addresses on me. I have them at my apartment, if you wouldn't mind coming with me."

I admit I didn't know much about men. Johnny had been my world since I was seventeen. Since he never let me out of his sight, except when I was working, my experience was the equivalent of a narrow strip of light coming from a chained door. The voice in my head— *Johnny's*?—said I should walk out now. I knew what this guy wanted. No different from any other. But Johnny hadn't touched me in over a year. I no longer pleased him, but he wouldn't let me leave him either.

But Tony Corelli looked at me as if he liked what he saw. He did mention a job. What if he was legit? He sure looked like a mob guy. The dangerous type. Not as dangerous, though, as the thought that Johnny could be waiting outside for me. Rationally, I knew he wasn't. But he was in my head.

I left the bar with Tony Corelli. He said I moved like a dancer. I'd been told that before. After years of ballet and jazz lessons paid for by my father, I felt like I deserved the compliment. Did I like to dance? Oh, yes. The one time I danced for Johnny, trying to turn him on, his disgust made me feel like a whore.

Wouldn't it be a strange coincidence if Tony had heard of Johnny? Very strange indeed. Johnny lived in California when he was married to the beautiful, rich, Italian would-be actress. I didn't think he'd ever been to Philadelphia. To my horror, my thoughts translated into words. "You don't happen to know a Johnny Champion, do you?" I asked. "Or heard of him?"

Corelli's eyes hooded. He didn't break stride, but I sensed a difference in him. Was I crazy? Did the name mean anything to him? My breath caught as I waited for his answer.

"No," he said after a moment passed. "Why? Is he Italian?"

I almost laughed. "No. Half Apache."

"Is he your boyfriend?"

"No," I said, too quickly. Then, to change the subject, I said, "Is your apartment close by?"

He glanced at me, and let my question hang in the air for a long moment before answering. "Very close, only a couple of blocks."

I kept my mouth shut the rest of the way.

Tony's apartment differed from Carl's simple efficiency as Beverly Hills differed from Watts. The heavy furniture and chandeliers dominated the living room with old world touches.

Dark paintings decorated his walls. We didn't linger there. He led me across thick carpeting into the bedroom. I didn't run out of the door, but my breath quickened.

Tony's decor must have mirrored his personal taste, bold and masculine. Red silk sheets and a brocade spread covered a circular bed. The lacquered Chinese headboard matched the dresser. He strode to an expensive-looking entertainment center opposite the bed and put on a jazz album. With a wave of his hand, he indicated the space between the record player and the bed. While I planted myself there, he asked casually, "Where did you work last?"

I was still staring at the bed. "Smithville Inn," I said without thinking.

"In Jersey?"

Crap! Why did I tell him that? "Yeah, but not very long. What do you want me to do?"

He smiled. "Show me how you dance."

"Here? Now?" His meaning slowly registered. "This is an audition?"

"Why did you think you were here? Everyone auditions who wants to work for me. If you're good enough, I'll give you a job." He sprawled on the bed, raised up on one elbow.

Yesterday's dreams of becoming a professional ballerina had flown away in my teens due to faulty toes. Now I've been degraded to a bump and grind to turn on a prospective employer. What would Johnny do if he saw me now? Pour whiskey down my throat and screw me in the ass? That was what happened the last time he got angry and accused me of cheating on him. He had the nerve to accuse *me* of being full of hate. He didn't know the meaning of the word until I finally turned on him.

The hell with it. I needed this job. *I'm not seventeen anymore, Johnny. I've grown up. You've taught me well. There's nothing I can't do.*

I braced myself. Corelli wanted a show? I'd give him one.

I knew I could dance. After years of ballet training, maybe it was the only thing I did well. My body moved to music. Always had.

I'd never feared an audience either. Not even when I was thirteen and practicing in the garage in front of a captive audience, a boy who liked me. I lost myself on stage and in the music.

This was different, of course.

As I moved to the music and saw what I was doing to him, something inside me changed. What was it about older men? They all wanted young girls. Tony looked the same age as Johnny. Like Daddy's friends who came with their wives to play bridge and found excuses to seek me out alone.

But this wasn't a game. I could become that bad girl Johnny always knew lurked within me. Quiet on the outside. A flame bursting on the inside. I was a bad girl, and I was already capable of so much more.

My body picked up the rhythm of the music. I watched Tony as I moved, wanting, *seeking* his approval. I was superior to any of his dancers. *Look at me, I'm different.* But, *damn him,* his expression never changed.

After a few minutes he said, "Take off your clothes. I want to see your body."

So this was the answer. As I started to unbutton my blouse, I wasn't seeing Tony, but Johnny on that bed, wanting me. I felt the wetness in my crotch. It had been a long time. I wanted the touch of a man.

My face felt hot as I slipped off my blouse, taking my time. Unzipped my skirt and wiggled it over my hips, giving him the whole show. Finally, only the bra and panties were left. He pointed and waved his hand, motioning me to take off my bra. I kept on the French-cut panties. Every man wanted to be teased with a little mystery. It was the unwritten art of seduction. I'd read that somewhere.

I gyrated and let my hands run over my breasts and down to my navel. My breath quickened. The warmth in my abdomen spread and my knees felt weak. My mind went blank. I let the music take over. I was turning myself on by watching a stranger getting turned on. This man wanted me.

I knew I had him when his eyes glazed over and he licked his lips. Even if I left at that moment, I was sure the job would be mine. I wasn't going anywhere. When I crawled onto his bed, I was in control.

Until I wasn't.

CHAPTER 3

A deep funk took hold of me while walking back to Carl's apartment. I made up my mind I wouldn't see Tony again. When it was over, I felt only shame and disgust with myself. No job was worth the degradation he put me through, that I put myself through. The game was over.

The sky darkened and the wind swirled leaves in my path. As the shadows deepened, a growing anxiety led to panic. I quickened my steps. Carl would be home by now, worried and probably wondering if I'd run off.

When I reached the second floor of the row house, a light shone under the door. I knocked rather than used the key he'd given me. When the door opened, Carl's strained face softened to relief. He turned to the stove where he had been stirring something in a pot. "Did you have a good day?"

I tried to sound upbeat. "I got a job offer."

He gave me a warm smile. "Didn't I tell you? Don't leave an old man in suspense. What's the job and where?"

"Waitressing at a bar on Locust Street. I'll be dancing, too."

Carl dropped the spoon he had been stirring with,

turned off the burner, and faced me. "Please, sit down, Erin."

"What's the matter?" His expression scared me.

Did he know what had happened at Tony Corelli's apartment? Johnny would have guessed at once if I'd been with a man. He would have pronounced me guilty without proof. Punishment would follow without listening to my defense. Back then, I was mostly innocent, but he always caught me when I wasn't. When I wasn't, I confess, it was all about defiance. If you're accused of a deed enough times, why not be guilty once?

But Carl wasn't Johnny.

"Locust Street." Carl pronounced "Locust Street" as if it crawled and hissed. "Who offered you that job?"

"A guy I met in a bar. He let me audition. Carl, I need a job, but—"

He didn't let me finish. "He have a name?"

"Tony Corelli. He owns the bar. What's wrong?" Dread made my heart race.

He breathed a deep sigh. "Let me tell you about Locust Street. Clip joints and prostitutes run by the mob do business there. Your man, Tony Corelli, I never met, but I know of him. He's a wiseguy. Know what I'm talking about? The syndicate. The Mafia. Whatever you want to call it. Once you go to work for those people, they own you. I know what I'm talking about."

A lump formed in my throat. "I thought the mob was in Florida and New York."

"Don't kid yourself. They're everywhere."

I was seeing Tony Corelli in my mind. Slick Italian guy, dripping with style, with money to spare. That apartment…

But I had to make my case. "How do you know about Locust Street? You don't go into bars."

He shot me a fierce look. "Don't be telling me what I don't know."

The sharpness of his tone made me withdraw. I didn't know how to react to this side of Carl. He'd been so sweet and kind. *You've only known him for three days.* So much for reading people.

His eyes burned into mine. "Did you tell this guy where you lived?"

"Of course not. I'm not *that* stupid."

He rubbed his eyes and paced back and forth. Had I blown our living arrangement? What would I do if he kicked me out?

"Carl, really I'm sorry. You don't know me very well, but I swear I'd never do anything to hurt you. Do you want me to leave? I will, but I don't know where to go."

He cut me off. "It's not your fault."

"What's not my fault?" I could barely breathe.

He stopped pacing and wiped his brow. "Jesse didn't tell you about me, did he?"

My mind went blank for a second. "Just that you lived alone. What is it, Carl? Tell me."

Carl took a cup and filled it with water from the faucet. He raised the cup to his lips and drank. When he was finished, he set the cup in the sink and wiped his mouth with his hand.

He finally spoke. "He didn't tell you I used to be a musician?"

That was it? The big secret? So he was a musician. Big deal. "No, he never mentioned that. What did you play?"

He licked his lips. "The prettiest sax you ever heard. Had a fair voice, too."

"You played professionally?"

"For many years." He looked out the window as if

seeing the past in the smudged pane. "I made a fine living from it. The bosses sent me to play in the best clubs, the hottest joints, accompanying some of the biggest names in show business. I was *cookin'*." His eyes hardened and he turned his gaze to me. "Until one day I saw something I shouldn't have. Something I couldn't live with. I told them I wanted out."

I looked at Carl in disbelief. He worked for the mob? This wasn't the same man I'd known for three days. The irony of my thoughts escaped me for the moment. "What did you see?" *Stupid question. Like he's going to tell me?*

He shook his head slowly.

"So they let you quit. I'm mean, you're here." The evidence was right before me. What was so bad?

He gave a bitter laugh. "You don't quit. The boss wasn't Lucky Luciano, but he was big enough. Like this Corelli fella. I was nothing, just another musician. But I knew stuff. You can't help but see what goes on. Guys there one day and gone the next. I played where and when they sent me and kept my mouth shut."

"So you proved your loyalty."

"Didn't matter. One night they took me in a little room, worked me over. I got the message. They offered me a deal. I could stay alive on one condition. Get out of Jersey and never go back. Never play again. I show up for a gig, they'd break every finger. If they let me live."

I closed my eyes, but the pictures didn't go away.

"I'm happy living a quiet life," he said in a calmer tone. "I got used to it a long time ago." He pointed a finger at me. "It's best you never mention me to anyone you meet on the street, especially to wiseguys like Tony Corelli."

Don't talk about me. That's what Johnny always told me. Someone was after him. Why we always had to run. How did I manage to end up in the same old shit?

I said, "I didn't take the job."

Carl eyes narrowed. "What?"

"I turned him down."

He mulled this over. "Why?"

I swallowed hard. "I should tell you about Johnny. We were never married. I'm not sure if I knew his real name. Ever since we met in California, I've known he's been on the run. Every town, every state, he'd pick out a new name for us. He was paranoid. We couldn't have friends. At first, I thought he was running from the cops. Later, I guessed someone in the mob wanted him dead. He never told me anything. Guess he didn't trust me enough."

Carl's eyes darkened and he turned away. *Now he'll tell me to leave.* My hand slipped into my pocket and I felt the crisp fifty Tony had given me. An advance, he'd said. In case I changed my mind. I'd intended to share it with Carl. Now it was too late.

CHAPTER 4

Carl didn't kick me out as I'd feared. Turns out he thought I would be safest with him. I allowed myself to relax. Believing, hoping, I'd left the past behind.

The next morning, I walked to the corner and caught the bus to Center City. I asked the driver to let me off where I'd find the most restaurants. Twenty minutes later, the row houses disappeared and commercial buildings squeezed into city blocks and scratched the sky. I almost missed the driver's shout because my face was pressed against the window as I tried to familiarize myself with my new surroundings. I thanked him and stood mesmerized on the busy sidewalk as the bus lumbered off. I was surrounded by more activity and noise than I'd seen since leaving New York almost three years ago.

There were restaurants on every corner, more dwarfed by retail stores and office buildings. I decided it would take me most of the day to talk my way through all the restaurants. I needed a short cut.

Foot traffic pushed me aside. Buses, cabs, and cars clogged the streets. I soaked up the sound of voices and horns honking, the smells of people brushing up next to me, car fumes, and strange spices in the air. Someone ran past me, shouting for a cab. I saw the answer to my dilemma in the middle of the busy intersection. A traffic cop blew his whistle and used hand signals to direct vehicles and pedestrians. Who better to know this part of town? I made a dash between traffic to his side.

"Excuse me," I shouted. Cars swooshed past us and a cab barely missed me. "Excuse me, can you help me?"

"Beggin' ya pardon, miss?" A thick Irish brogue rolled off his tongue. "And just where do ya think ya are? Trying to get yourself killed?"

Unfazed, I gave him an apologetic grin and plunged on with my question. "I'm a waitress looking for work. Can you recommend a good place to make tips?"

He looked at me as if I were daft. I put on my eager face and he responded with a laugh.

"Yar there, girlie." He pointed across the street. "Monahan's. Always got a crowd."

Beer signs in neon. Windows facing the street showed silhouettes of men and women at tables covered with food. A sign above the door advertised world-class steaks, Philadelphia steak sandwiches, hamburgers, and seafood. My stomach rumbled. I smelled the grill.

"Food's not bad either. Good luck to ya." The cop turned and blew his whistle, stopping traffic for me while I raced across to the sidewalk. I smoothed my skirt, fluffed my hair, and opened the door to Monahan's.

A perky hostess about my age, wearing a red miniskirt and blue blouse, greeted me. When I asked to talk to the manager, she told me I'd have to wait while she seated the customers crowded around me. When I told her I was here for a job, she shrugged. The manager was tied up. Would I mind waiting? No problem.

I moved to where I could observe the dining area. I realized I'd come at the lunch hour and most of the tables were already filled. Waitresses in blue and red striped mini-skirts with matching shirts hustled from the kitchen to the tables, balancing food trays. Many diners looked college-aged or young professionals on their break from the office. Wooden tables and benches were arranged for optimal capacity. Booths lined the wall next to the windows and all of them were filled. I knew I could make money here.

After an hour spent sitting and pacing, the manager finally found me. I'd watched most of the customers pay their tab and leave. I didn't want to go through this again at another restaurant. I wanted this job. The pace and the clientele would be no problem.

"Sorry to keep you waiting." The manager appeared to be in his mid or late thirties. I looked for something in his manner that would be encouraging. His expression gave nothing away. "Your timing is fortunate. I had a girl quit last night and I need someone with experience to fill in."

"I have lots of experience." I said. "There's nothing I can't handle."

"Come with me to my office. You can fill out an application," he said.

I started to panic. How many applicants did he have already? I couldn't wait. "You said you were short a girl. I can start tomorrow. Or tonight, even, if you need someone right away."

He sized me up like I was prime beef. I didn't say another word, but held my breath. Either he would take a chance on me or not.

"You'll need to buy a uniform," he said flatly. "We supply them, and I think one might fit you."

"Perfect." I made my voice as cheery and positive as possible. At the same time, I wondered if I was supposed to pay for the uniform before I started work. What would I do if he wanted the money now?

He must have read my mind, because he said, "We can take it out of your first paycheck if you don't have the money. Now, come with me. You still need to fill out an application and we'll check on the size of that uniform."

Half an hour later, I left the restaurant with instructions to return at three o'clock the next day. I waved at the cop and, when he waved back, I did a little tap routine, ending with a flourish and a wide smile. He grinned back and saluted.

The bus was half empty on the return trip, but I could hardly sit still as it rumbled up the street. I flew up to Carl's apartment, rocketed through the door, and found Carl sitting next to a woman with a smooth face and gray hair artfully styled. A little too late, I realized why the door was unlocked.

Carl didn't seem disturbed by my appearance, but the woman's raised eyebrows gave a different impression. Disapproval furrowed her brow and thinned her lips.

Carl said, in his disarming way, "Nettie, this is Erin, the girl I was telling you about who will be staying with me a few days."

I smiled. "Nice meeting you, Nettie."

Nettie pursed her lips and didn't respond. Carl's and my living arrangements were probably against everything her church preached. They must have been discussing me before I burst in.

Too excited to contend with Nettie's attitude, I turned my attention to Carl. "I got a job, starting tomorrow. Waitressing, not dancing, Carl. At Monahan's. What do you think? Exciting news, huh?"

"Very nice." Carl's face split into a wide grin. "I know Monahan's, and the chef there is a friend. They do good business. With Christmas around the corner, the tips be generous."

Christmas. I'd almost forgotten. I would have to get Carl a nice gift. I had no one else to spend my money on.

Nettie grunted and stood.

"You don't have to leave on my account," I said.

She walked stiffly to the door and opened it, then turned and faced me. "Young lady, Carl is a gentleman. I wouldn't want to see him hurt in any way."

I was taken aback. You'd think I was out to seduce the man and steal everything he had. I went over to her, stepped into her space, and looked her in the eye. "Ma'am, I respect you and your warning, and you can rest your mind that I have no intention of causing Carl any harm."

She stood her ground and stared back. "If you were a decent sort, you would find a respectable job and get your own place."

"Ma'am, didn't you hear what I said? I've got a job, and I plan to move as soon as possible."

"Very well, see that you do," she said crisply. Keeping her dignity and her head high, she marched out of the apartment.

When the door closed behind her, I heard Carl laughing. Not loud so Nettie could hear.

I turned and raised my hands in a helpless gesture. "I'm sorry. She's your friend. I hope I didn't do any damage to your relationship. Is she your lady?"

He chuckled good-naturedly. "She's just a friend. Nettie has her ways, but she'll get over this." He beckoned to me. "Tell me about the interview."

I sat beside him and gave the short version.

"What do they wear?"

"They have their own uniforms and luckily they have one in my size."

"They charge you for it?" Carl knew the business all right.

"They'll take it out of my pay, but all the tips are mine."

"What about shoes?" Carl said.

"I have shoes."

He nodded. "Good."

The light dinner fare that evening was served with a celebratory air. I felt in turn giddy, scared, and impatient for tomorrow to arrive.

"Waitressing is not my life's ambition." I pushed my empty plate away. "I just want you to know that."

Carl gave me a quizzical look and waited.

"I've worked other jobs before I met Johnny. My first job was at a bank working the switchboard. And I once kept the books for some friends of my dad's."

"You don't have to try and impress me, girl. Nothing wrong with being a waitress."

"I didn't say that," I said impatiently. "I mean, it was the only job I could get, moving around the country with Johnny. I could get a waitress job the day we hit a new town. But what I want is an office job, with a regular salary and a chance to move up. Maybe have my own business someday." I pulled a pack of cigarettes from my pocket and offered one to Carl. He shook his head. I lit up and inhaled.

"What's stopping you?" Carl asked.

"Money. Opportunity. The usual."

"Those just excuses, girl. You gotta go after what you want and you don't stop till you get it. Don't let nothing or no one get in your way."

I thought about Johnny. He once had me on a leash, but no more. I cut free of him, once and for all. If only the nightmares would go away. There was always a price to pay.

CHAPTER 5

The first night of work in a busy restaurant always played havoc on my nerves. Most places wanted the new hire to train the first week or two, which meant following an experienced waiter or waitress until you learn where to find everything. During that time, the new person only earns the two dollars and fifty cent an hour pay. No tips.

At Monahan's there was no time for training and no experienced waitress who wanted to show a new girl around. They didn't have time. In my experience, the best trainer worked in the kitchen. Befriend the chef first, but don't leave out the cooks and helpers.

Both the chef and cooks were black. Not unusual. It didn't take me long to discover which girls they favored. The girls they didn't like had to wait longer for their orders and there was no guarantee the food would be cooked to order.

The head chef went by the name Big. He towered over the other cooks, but he carried his weight well. Didn't take me long to get on his good side. Show some appreciation, pick up orders on time, don't be afraid to flirt a little and, by the end of the night, Big answered all my questions.

Even felt free to tease me when I forgot a salad or misnamed a menu item.

The assistant chef, Crater, had a lean body with fluid movements and molded muscles. Unlike Big, Crater was soft spoken and gave out compliments. It didn't take long before we were communicating with eye contact and body language that had nothing to do with food. Big noticed as well as a few other cooks whose appreciation for my body was not as subtle as Crater's.

Izzy assisted Crater and looked more like a teenager than a man. He was short and thin with hair close to his scalp. He always had a smile for me and sometimes uttered a barbed sexual innuendo that made me uncomfortable and worried that someone would overhear him. He seemed to think he was being funny.

Living in a black man's world didn't bother me. I grew up in California with a family that taught equality and lived their values. Carl and I were comfortable with each other. Living with him in his neighborhood was no different to me than if I lived in a white neighborhood. Almost no one took notice of me anymore. That's the way I saw it. Johnny would never understand, but he wasn't here to stop me.

After a week had gone by, one of the other waitresses caught up with me in the ladies restroom.

"Look, it's none of my business what you do on your own time, but others around here are starting to notice how you act with the kitchen help."

"I can't be friendly?" My back stiffened. "They've been more helpful than most of you."

"I'm just warning you," she said. "Other people are talking, saying you're getting too friendly with the coloreds and it may be taken the wrong way. You could lose your job."

"If those men weren't in there cooking all the meals,

we would have nothing to serve. There wouldn't be a restaurant," I said.

The girl drew back. "I'm not arguing that with you.
We need them, I agree, but that doesn't mean you have to
sleep with them."

I felt my face go hot. "I am not sleeping with them,"
I said, measuring each word while trying to tamp down
my anger.

I watched her leave the room and when the door
shut, I threw a bottle of hand lotion against the wall. The
top came off and white cream splattered against the paint
and dripped on the floor. I started to leave the mess there,
but changed my mind once I thought about it. I cleaned
up the best I could before a customer or another waitress
came in.

My cheeks burned. I didn't want to face another
waitress. Were they all talking about me behind my back?
They weren't my friends. Those black men in the kitchen
were the only people who accepted me.

I managed to get through the rest of my shift by
keeping to myself and working my tables. I was in no
mood for small talk.

I stayed to wipe down tables after most of the waitresses had left. Finally I wandered back to the kitchen.
Big was writing a report in his corner. Crater looked up at
me.

"You lookin' a bit sad there, little miss. You needin'
some cheerin'?"

I shrugged. "I'm all right."

Crater sent a furtive glance around the room.
"There's a party after we done here," he whispered. "I'm
going and so is Izzy. We can take you if you want to go.
Have some drinks, get down and dirty, listen to jazz, and
shake off those blues."

Sounded good to me. I needed to get that bitch's

voice out of my head and I was too restless to go home to Carl. "Cool," I said.

Izzy was waiting outside for us when I left with Crater. Big followed us out and locked up. He gave me a funny look. "You going with them?"

I shrugged. "Why not?"

He hesitated for a moment, looking uncertain. Then he shrugged. "Hell, maybe I'll meet you there."

I got into the car with my new friends. Crater sat beside me and put his arm around me. The car reeked with the smell of fish and garlic and a mixture of other meat and garnishes that clung to their clothes. I didn't mind. I was ready for that drink and some jazz.

The party was in full swing when we arrived somewhere in the north side of town. Hoots of laughter boomed out of the small house as we tumbled out of the car. A trumpet blared and a deep voice sang in the distance.

As the only white girl in the party, I became the center of attention from the moment I walked in. Crater disappeared after the first ten minutes, but Izzy brought me a drink that looked like undiluted whiskey. I drank half without thinking.

He ran his hand down my back. "You are sooo sweet," he said in a sing-song voice. "Like vanilla ice cream. Be right back. Don't run away now."

After five minutes I felt surrounded. The faces weren't as friendly as I expected. Their interest in me sharpened like a pack of wolves ready to spring on a rabbit.

Where the fuck was Crater or Izzy? They were supposed to be with me. Everyone had a drink in their hands. The smell of marijuana was strong and I noticed a few men at a table snorting lines of what appeared to be cocaine.

When I felt a strange hand slip under my blouse and another blowing air in my ear, I panicked. Where the hell was I? I hadn't paid any attention to street signs or landmarks on the drive over.

I shook free of the hands. "Get off me. Where's Crater? Someone get him for me."

Laughter answered me. "Crater took off. His wife made him come home. She's one mean bitch. You don't want to mess with her man."

"I'm not messing with him." *Damn.* I was defending myself for the second time that night. "I want to find the guys who brought me so they can take me home."

"Aw, stick around, babe. I'll show you a fine time. What you need is somethin' to relax you. Know what I'm sayin'?"

The men closed in on me. Some were already half undressed and sweaty. Their eyes glazed. I thought of the stories I'd heard of girls being gang raped. My throat closed. I scoured the room for an exit.

Voices rose from the front of the house. There were shouts, and a door slammed. A huge dark form towered over the others. I gaped. Big carved a path through the crowd. He reached me in seconds and grabbed my hand. Without a word to the others, he pulled me toward the front door. I almost cried in relief. Then, to my shock and embarrassment, I saw Carl standing outside. His face contorted in rage.

Big finally spoke, not to me but to Carl. "Old man, no need to cause no shit at this house. Your girl ain't harmed. Now let me drive you both home."

Carl nodded. His face had turned almost purple. He took my hand and squeezed hard.

We didn't speak all the way to Carl's apartment, but I couldn't stop shaking even after we were safely inside.

"Carl," I began when the door was locked.

He held up his hand to stop me. He took off his coat and hung it up before easing into a chair. Slowly his color returned to normal.

"How did you find me?" I said.

"When you don't come home, I call the restaurant. No one answers 'cause they closed. I know Big 'cause we done worked together. I'd told him to keep an eye on you."

Little by little, the story came out. Big apparently got worried when I went to the party, and called Carl to see if I'd made it home okay.

"Good thing, too," Carl said gruffly. "When he tells me 'bout the party, I says to myself, she gettin' into some trouble, she just don't know it yet. Big tell me he know the address and the peoples, and he can take me there."

I covered my face with my hands. "I'm so ashamed. I thought it would be a fun party. But then I got scared. I was never so glad to see anyone in my life when I saw you and Big."

Carl seemed to struggle getting the next words out. "Girl, listen to me. You are with friends here. Them black men, they don't know you. You just white trash to them, an easy target for their anger that go way back. They not like Jesse and me, people who know and care about you. Yes, Jesse care 'bout you or you wouldn't be here now. They be good black folks and bad, same as white folks. Treat everyone like they their own person."

I swiped at my wet cheeks. "I don't know how I can show myself at work tomorrow."

Carl straightened like I'd thrown cold water in his face. "Girl, don't let me hear talk like that. You goin' right back and face those white girls you work with. They don't know what happened to you. Big and the others in the kitchen, they ain't your worry. They treat you no different than they treat you yesterday or the day before.

You learn, then you forget what happened tonight."

Carl made it all sound so simple. All I wanted was to find another job, but I knew that wouldn't happen right off. I had to stick with this one until something better came along. Just a matter of time.

CHAPTER 6

The weather got colder as the weeks passed. Christmas sneaked up on me when I wasn't looking. I awoke to the first snowfall of the year on Christmas Eve. I climbed out of the bed I still shared with Carl and went to the window. Everything looked clean and white. I shook Carl awake, feeling like a kid.

Carl sat up and blinked, bemused at my reaction until he realized what had me so excited. "I remember. You never seen snow."

"It's so beautiful."

Carl chuckled. "Enjoy while it's new. Won't be looking that way in a day or two when you be skidding and sliding at the bus stop, and sloshing around in dirty snow."

"I don't care. Right now it's perfect, I want to get dressed and take a long walk."

I had Christmas Eve off and Monahan's was closed for Christmas. I had been putting aside most of my paychecks and tips toward my own apartment while helping Carl with food. I was afraid to spend anything on myself except for a few skirts and sweaters, but I knew I would soon need a winter coat and fur-lined boots. Still, I didn't expect to see snow that morning.

Late that afternoon, Carl took me Christmas shopping in Center City. I put on a long skirt and sweater under my tweed jacket, pulled on my white plastic boots and tugged a knit hat close to my ears. We rode the bus until we came to the shops lit-up with Christmas decorations. The trees lining the streets twinkled with colored lights.

I caught furtive glances, and some outright glares, shooting our way. Did people think we were a couple? But it was Christmas Eve and they should be thinking Christian thoughts, or what to buy for Aunt Edna or Uncle Ben, or whoever, so to hell with them. So what if Carl had darker skin than mine? I remembered a diner I worked in Florida where the owner sang "The Lord's Prayer" on Sunday mornings then cussed out his black kitchen help a minute later. I knew the same thing happened here in Philly. Probably everywhere. Why couldn't people get along?

We went into a Woolworths and when Carl disappeared elsewhere in the store, I bought him a pair of warm slippers and some makeup for me. This wasn't the time to shop for clothes, but I eyed the fur-lined coats and boots with longing and wondered when I'd ever have enough to afford such things.

"It's still early," Carl said after we left the store. "How about a movie? They're playing *Doctor Zhivago* at the movie house a block over."

Getting lost in someone else's adventure sounded swell. I tried to think when I'd last seen a movie. New York, maybe, but I couldn't remember the name of the film.

Carl and I found seats in the middle section next to the aisle. Omar Sharif came on the screen, and I fell in love.

Hours later, seeing myself as Lara, adrift in Russia, I

became aware that the chill I was feeling was not on the screen, but in the theater.

"We'd better hurry home," Carl said, standing as the credits rolled.

"Why is it so cold in here?" I said, grabbing my shopping bag. "I can hardly feel my toes."

We stamped our feet, trying to get the circulation going as we hurried down the aisle to the lobby. Outside we found a different Center City than we left. Snowflakes swirled around us and our feet sank in a foot of the white stuff. I could barely see the traffic. Took a moment to realize there was no traffic.

"The worst blizzard in years," I heard someone say.

"The first storm of winter," Carl muttered. "I hope the buses are running. It will get worse before the night is over."

The wind whipped snow around us as we stood shivering at the bus stop. My white face was in the minority, but everyone looked as miserable as I felt, and no one seemed to care about color. A few people managed to grab the remaining cabs braving the slick icy roads. Most of an hour passed. By then we realized the buses weren't running and we followed others down the subway stairs.

"Don't worry, we'll be home soon," Carl kept assuring me.

If my toes don't get frostbite first. I pulled my ineffective coat around me and despised my thin plastic boots. My nose dripped and my eyes stung. At least we didn't have the driving wind down under the street. I thought the train would never come. My teeth chattered and I couldn't feel my fingers. Carl offered me his aged, fur-lined winter coat, but I shook my head.

"I'm going to buy you a coat, warm boots, and hat with my next check," he said.

"I'm working now so you don't have to. You can bet

that's next on my list, though, if this is what winter is like." My laugh sounded shaky, even to me.

At last, the train arrived and screeched to a stop. By that time a crowd had joined us. We were pushed and pulled inside where we huddled against strangers for warmth. The train lurched forward. At one point, my shopping bag dropped and Carl picked it up. I rubbed my glove-encased hands together and stamped my feet, hoping to get some feeling in them. I yearned to sit down and close my eyes, so sleepy, but there were no available seats. Carl made me move to keep the blood circulating. When we finally reached our stop and got out, the streets were empty.

"We are about four blocks away," Carl said. "Can you make it?"

I nodded, but my throat tightened. I was determined not to complain, not to cry, not to scream. My toes must be frostbitten.

Suddenly Carl moved forward, raised his hand, and waved like crazy. I saw the cab a second later and waved my arms as well. When he stopped to let us in, I almost cried. I wanted to kiss the driver. But I didn't do either. Instead, I leaned into Carl who put his arm around me. A few minutes later, we pulled up at the curb in front of Carl's apartment.

The apartment was heated, but it still took too long to get warm. I dropped my package in the closet and pulled a blanket around my shoulders. Carl fixed us hot chocolate while I pulled on two sets of Carl's thick socks. We sat in bed and drank the warm liquid before burrowing under the blanket with our backs to each other. If Johnny visited me in my dreams, as he had every night so far, I wasn't aware.

The warm apartment felt good the next morning. Christmas Day. Carl fixed pancakes while I took a hot shower. I crawled back to bed after eating, and tried not to think of Johnny and what my life had been with him. If only I'd been stronger. If only I'd been what he wanted me to be. If I hadn't been so young.

"You're feeling guilty?" Carl asked when I spilled self-pitying tears. "Are you forgetting you ran away from him? You don't do that unless you've been mistreated and you're scared."

Wonder what he would think if he knew what I had done? I could never tell him, couldn't tell anyone.

"Crazy, isn't it?" I sat up and tucked my legs under me. "I wish I knew why he chose me the night we met. Why did he pick me over anyone else at that bar?"

"I'd say your youth and beauty," Carl suggested. "Why did you stay with him when things got bad?"

I shrugged. "We met in Santa Monica after he'd fallen or jumped from a third story roof and fractured both feet. He'd left the hospital in a wheelchair with both legs in casts. He was living at a pink hotel on Ocean Avenue and I was getting over someone, living alone, and lonely. He invited me to move in with him. The next day, he soaked the casts off. His feet and legs were black up to his knees. But he wouldn't have anything more to do with hospital or doctors, probably because they might call the cops. They'd accused him of attempting suicide when they found him."

"Is that what happened?" Carl asked.

I shook my head. "He gave me different stories."

"So you took care of him."

"I tried. We found a Mineral Springs in Mexico between Tijuana and Ensenada where he soaked his feet. We always stayed close to the beach. He said the salt water was healing and walking on the sand would strengthen his legs. He had me rub his feet every night to get the circulation back. He was finally able to walk again without a limp."

"You feel a need to take care of men?" He smiled to soften the words.

"I guess." *Was that true?*

Carl regarded me thoughtfully. "That's quite a sacrifice you made for him. You could have been out dancing and having fun with someone your own age if you hadn't met him."

I could feel my cheeks redden and I slipped off the sofa bed. This conversation was getting too close to the bone. I'd revealed too much. "I say we open presents." I brought the box of slippers from the closet and dropped it in his lap. "I didn't have time to wrap it."

Carl's look of surprise was enough for me.

"You shouldn't have spent your last money on me." His tone was disapproving, but his eyes shone with delight. He opened the box, rubbed his fingers over the fur, and slipped them on. "How did you know the size?"

"I checked before we left," I said, pleased at his reaction.

"Well, now, very nice." He smiled and padded off to the closet and brought back a gift-wrapped package and handed it to me.

"Carl, you devil. You shouldn't have."

I tore apart the wrapping, lifted the woolen scarf to my face, and rubbed the softness against my cheek.

Later that afternoon, after I checked on the chicken roasting in the oven, I stretched out on the bed. Carl had Louis Armstrong playing on his worn record player. He lay next to me and we watched the snowflakes fall outside the window.

"Peace and quiet," I sighed. "This is the best Christmas."

I thought about the Christmas spent with Johnny during our stay in Ensenada. He'd been depressed and didn't want to be in a bar or around anyone else. We spent the day standing on a cliff overlooking the ocean, watching waves crash against the rocks. Later, we climbed down the hill and he surf fished alone while I watched.

The loneliness of that day came back to me. Even Carl's company wasn't enough to beat the Christmas blues. Sensing my mood, Carl caressed my arm in an effort to console me. Rather than give in to the tears that were threatening to choke me, I turned to him and moved into the comfort of his arms. Carl closed his eyes and caught his breath. I snuggled closer.

A nagging voice in my head warned me to pull away. I was inviting trouble and treading on quicksand. I could sink and not be able to crawl out. My heart thumped against my chest, but I didn't move. My mind stayed in limbo. I listened to Carl's heartbeat, felt his breath quicken. Slowly he turned on his side to face me. "I want to make love to you," he whispered. His hand moved to my thigh. "I've wanted to since the moment you stepped through my door."

My body reacted to his touch like being zapped with an electrical charge. His words were enough to send heat between my legs. I didn't move. Did I ask for this? Did I want this?

"Let me love you," Carl said huskily. "You don't have to do anything."

"Carl," I whispered, hesitant, feeling the need for his touch, but afraid of how this would change our relationship.

"Shhh," he said. He slowly removed the covers and let his gaze roam over my body. I held my breath as he scooted down to the end of the bed and crawled between my legs. He eased off my new silk panties and looked up at me. I swallowed and tensed, waiting for him. He lowered his head between my legs. No one had ever touched me that way. I inhaled sharply and tried to push him away, but he grasped my hands and held them.

Carl was more knowledgeable of a woman's body than any man I'd known. With an abandon I didn't know was in me, I released the guilt and embarrassment that had frozen me earlier. Waves of pleasure took over. I cried out with the intensity of my climax. He didn't stop, but brought me to the next plateau until I throbbed and bucked and cried out again. Still, he kept on until exquisite spasms left me breathless and dripping in sweat.

For a long time I couldn't move. My legs felt shaky. I closed my eyes and panted while I held his head against my chest.

I wanted only to close my eyes and sleep now with him next to me. But I couldn't be selfish. I rolled him over to reciprocate, but he stopped me.

"No, don't." He gently pushed me away. "I'm only sorry I can't do more for you."

"You've done so much. Let me do something for you."

He smiled sadly as he pulled the sheet to cover me. "No, sweetheart."

I propped my elbow on the bed and looked at his smooth brown face and watery brown eyes. "Can't or won't? Is it me?"

"No, it's me. I had a heart attack last year, during sex." He looked at me and smiled. "But I can give you what you want and need. That's what brings me pleasure."

I fell back and laughed softly. *How did I get so lucky?*

While Carl slept, I stared at the ceiling. What the hell did I just let happen?

I had to find my own place before Carl became another casualty.

CHAPTER 7

I met Melanie Farber early February when she came to work at Monahan's. High energy, about my age, and single. How could we not be friends?

"Monahan's just a temporary stop until my piggy bank's full," she told me after our lunch shift one day. We were sitting at a table in the bar area counting our tips.

"I'm going to look for a steady nine-to-five job when I get enough saved," I said.

"Where are you living?"

The inevitable question. "With a friend until I find my own apartment."

She looked at me with new interest. "Why don't you come by my place? I've been looking for a roommate. Two bedrooms and lots of space."

I was so ready. I would go tonight if we both weren't working the night shift. "When's a good time?"

She grinned. "We've got two hours before we're back to work."

"How far is your place?" I said doubtfully. I couldn't afford to be late.

"A quick bus ride. We got plenty of time if we leave now."

I grabbed my purse. We hurried out the door and crossed the street to the corner.

The bus let us off on a tree-lined street. Melanie led the way toward a three-story brick row house that looked like every other brick row house on the block. Steps led from a square patch of lawn up to a wide porch with a bench swing and a couple of chairs.

"Mine's the second floor," Melanie said as she keyed the front door. "The managers have the first floor, nosy old couple, always checking on who I bring up. Haven't seen much of my neighbors above me. I think they're newlyweds."

We raced up the stairs. My heart beat with anticipation as she unlocked the door to the apartment. We stepped inside and turned right into a large open kitchen. I stared at a full size refrigerator and stove. There was room to move around, space even for a kitchen table with four chairs. The window over the sink overlooked a garden and the house next door. I glanced at the counter and the stack of dirty dishes that Melanie probably didn't have time to take care of before work. The rest of the kitchen looked clean enough. I wasn't much for cooking, but I thought of the parties we could hold there.

"Come on, I'll show you the rest of the place. Don't mind the dishes. I was running late this morning."

"Forget it, I understand."

We walked through the kitchen to a second door which opened to the master bedroom.

"This is my room. Ignore the mess. I do." She laughed. The bedroom held a full size bed, a dresser, and end tables. She even had her own bathroom.

I followed her back through the kitchen to the hallway again. She pointed out the bathroom then stopped at the second bedroom, much smaller than hers, but bigger than Carl's apartment.

"This would be yours," she said.

It had a twin bed already made up and a small dresser. How wonderful it would be to have privacy and a bed of my own.

I lingered at the doorway, imagining how I might rearrange the room and decorate to my liking. Melanie called me from the front room and I shut the bedroom door and went to join her.

I gaped at the bay windows overlooking the street. There was even a window bench, perfect for curling up with a good book or just daydreaming. The few pieces of furniture looked worn, but I didn't see any tears or blemishes on the comfortable brown sofa. The maple coffee table matched the two end tables, which held nondescript table lamps. An imitation Persian rug covered the center of the hardwood floor. Four beanbag cushions were scattered randomly.

There were two built-in bookcases in the wall to my left. The bottom shelf held a record player and a row of albums filled the shelf above it. The rest were empty and just begging for books.

"What do you think?"

"It's nice." *What an understatement. Feels like home*, I thought, but didn't say the words aloud. I didn't want to get my hopes up. This place must cost her a small fortune.

Melanie plopped on one of the beanbags. "Like I said before, I need a roommate, and you're in the market. So what do you think? Does it suit?"

"How much is the rent?"

She told me. I did the math. I had been saving every bit I could from my tips, but I still wasn't there yet.

"You don't have to pay anything until the first of the month," she said.

That might work. Hell, I'd make it work. "I don't

have any furniture or much of anything of my own."

She waved her hand to encompass the room. "What's wrong with mine? And don't worry about stuff like dishes and pots and pans. I got plenty of those."

"I need to buy some bedding and towels."

"Later. I got enough." She waved her hand dismissively. "How do you like the place so far?"

"I like it." *I loved it.*

"Got a boyfriend?"

I shook my head. I wouldn't call Carl a boyfriend just because we had our version of sex now and then. He probably wouldn't be coming over to my apartment.

Melanie said, "I do. His name is Link. Don't get freaked out if he spends the night sometimes. He'll stay out of your way. So, what do you say? Do we have a deal?"

I put out my hand to shake. "Deal."

I could hardly contain my excitement as I served my tables that evening. All I could think about was my new home. A group of college students at one of my tables were rowdier than usual, but I kept the smile on my face until I saw the penny tip they left. The responsibility of rent struck me with sudden panic. I felt like throwing it back at them, even started toward the door, but Melanie restrained me.

"Forget those clods. You'll make it on the next table."

She was right, but the pressure was on. To add to my stress, I had to think about how to tell Carl my new plans.

I arrived home late after stopping for a celebratory drink with Melanie.

I dreaded confrontations. Carl and I had more or less settled into a routine since Christmas. We both knew that our arrangement would be temporary, but the inevitable change had transpired over time. He wanted more of me than I could give. In my mind, I had already moved on.

I opened the door quietly in case he was asleep. No such luck. He had waited up.

"You've been drinking," he said.

"Bring out the bottle. There's something we need to talk about."

He nodded somberly. "You've met someone."

I started to protest, but thought better of it. "Yes, in a way I have. I found a roommate. I'd call her a hippie and a little crazy, and I don't know her very well, but I think we'll get along. I fell in love with the apartment, Carl." I sat beside him. "You should be glad you're finally getting rid of me. It's been much longer than either of us planned."

He took my hand and placed it on his knee. "I been in no hurry to see you go."

I couldn't bear to look at his clouded eyes. "If I stay in one place too long, Johnny will be sure to find me. We're lucky Jesse didn't tell him before now. We gambled, but no sense in pushing our luck. I do want us always to be friends."

His lower lip trembled, but he forced a sad smile. "Of course, you must fly away. Your wings are stronger already. I know they'll soar high." Sounded like music he might have written.

I kissed his cheek. "We'll stay friends, won't we?"

He gave me a long look. "Of course we will."

My throat felt like I'd swallowed a peach pit. Why did I feel like crying all of a sudden?

಄಄಄

I moved a week later. I'd finished packing before Carl made it home after work, hoping to avoid the emotional goodbyes. At the last minute, I realized I couldn't leave without seeing him. It would be too much like running away again.

He walked in, holding his overcoat. He froze when he saw my bags. I almost wished I hadn't waited for him, but that would have been selfish.

Seeing my expression, he tried to hide his discomfort. "I'm glad I caught you before you left. I have something for you, a housewarming gift."

"Carl, you shouldn't have," I protested.

He went to the closet and when he reappeared he was holding a small gift-wrapped package, which he handed to me.

"I didn't get anything for you," I said as I tore the paper off. I caught my breath and let the wrappings fall to the floor. I held up a Christmas snow globe and blinked back tears.

"I wanted you to have something to remember me by," Carl said.

My voice caught. "Don't be silly. We'll be seeing each other."

But we both knew what would happen after I left. There would be no turning back.

CHAPTER 8

On the first Saturday in April, Melanie invited a few friends over for what she called a housewarming to "get to know the roommate." I was ready to let loose, drink a few beers, and meet some guys.

The weather promised sunshine. I put on shorts and a tie-dyed shirt and, after a quick breakfast, swept the floors and dusted.

Melanie staggered out of her bedroom. I got the impression she'd rolled out of bed late so she wouldn't have to help clean.

She wore a multi-colored peasant skirt and blouse and wrapped a cloth band around her forehead. A single blond braid draped over her left shoulder.

She laughed when she saw me sweating over the sink. "Why bother? It'll be a mess again within the hour. These guys won't notice." She walked straight to the coffee pot I'd prepared earlier and poured a cup.

"I'll notice," I said. Growing up with my grandmother, and later my step-mother, thorough cleanings were a Saturday ritual. Not a speck of dust was allowed, and the floors had to shine.

"Where's Link?"

They'd been together all night from what I could hear. While I was eating breakfast, I caught him slipping out the door.

She stirred milk in her coffee. "Went to get the drinks. Should be back any minute. What time is it? Shit, it's almost noon. We got to get the food ready."

She toasted two slices of bread and ate them while she made fondue.

"I thought we had enough drinks," I said, thinking of the cartons of beer in the fridge.

She rolled her eyes. "I'm talking real booze. You haven't met my friends yet."

"What do you want me to do?" I didn't have the slightest idea what folks served at parties. Johnny and I always kept to ourselves. No one was ever invited over for a meal, not even for a casual visit.

Melanie had planned the snacks and accordingly had done most of the shopping. She told me to take out the meatballs and sausages she had prepared the night before and put them in a skillet. "Can you make a cheese dip?"

"I think I can handle that much."

Link pounded on the door and I let him in. He set a box filled with bottles and a bag of ice. Link was tall and lanky with zits. I didn't consider him good-looking, nor did he have much going for him that I could see, outside of playing a mean guitar. Maybe it was the music that attracted Melanie. Who cared? As long as he stayed away from me, they could do as they pleased.

Link lined the counter with whiskey, scotch, vodka, and gin. He added club soda and ginger ale and poured the ice into a bucket.

"That must have cost a week's salary, at least," I said.

"Link works at the liquor store," Melanie pointed out. "He gets a discount."

"How many people are coming?"

Melanie glanced at Link, who shrugged. "Who knows?" she said.

Link reached into the fridge, grabbed two beers, and handed me one. "Have a brewski and hang loose, babe."

"Thanks." Since I didn't know anyone except the people at Monahan's, who I knew wouldn't show, and Carl, who said he wouldn't come, I relaxed. I couldn't remember when I had last spent time with people my own age.

I took my beer into the living room and sat cross-legged by the bookcase. There was a variety of records to choose from. I started with Dylan, Baez, Hendrix, Cream, and The Yardbirds, stacking them carefully on the record player. Soon I heard footsteps on the landing, followed by voices in the kitchen.

A few minutes later, I heard a male voice behind me. "Hey, that's some badass tunes." He knelt beside me and pointed to the album covers I'd put against the bookcase. He was kind of cute with his tight jeans and psychedelic shirt. I liked his hair. Wished mine would curl like his. "I feel some righteous vibes in here. You're the roommate, huh?"

"Good guess. Erin Matthews."

"I'm Steve."

"Have you known Melanie and Link very long?"

"Link was my roommate in college and when Mel came along we all started hanging out with these guys."

His attention drifted as more of his friends joined us. Girls with long straight hair, some wearing vinyl hot pants, others in peasant skirts or shorts. The guys showed off what muscles they had, if any, in torn T-shirts. Some had straggly beards or goatees, others had bushy side-burns.

"Wicked," one girl exclaimed as she knelt on the

window seat and looked down on the street. "What have you done to this place? I don't remember it being this nice."

Melanie wasn't much for decorating, but I'd found some pictures and other knick-knacks at curb sales. Making little improvements made the apartment feel more like my own.

"Hey, Erin," Melanie called from the kitchen. "Could use the assist here."

"Coming." I crossed one leg against the other so the heel pressed against my knee and pushed to a standing position.

A girl sitting cross-legged on a beanbag called out, "Erin? Are you a dancer?"

I looked at her in surprise. "I wish. Why do you ask?"

She tilted her head. "You move like one."

Tony Corelli had said the same thing. "I took ballet and jazz in high school. Do you dance?"

The guy with her laughed. "Does she dance? Man, she's cherry. The top go-go dancer in Center City. You might call her the Peggy Fleming of dance."

"Oh, Marty, you'll embarrass me." She blushed and slapped him lightly on the arm. "Name's Dani and this is my friend, Marty. I dance at Foxy Lady, one of the clubs downtown."

"Makes a ton," the guy added. He rubbed his thumb and forefinger together. "I know. I'm the bouncer there. I see everything that goes on."

"Used to have an agent until I got hired on my own," Dani said. "If you're interested, I can give you his name."

Yes! But before I could respond, Melanie shrieked an SOS. I sprinted to the kitchen. After tossing a pan of burnt sausages in the garbage and calming a hysterical Melanie, I made another plate and took them to the living room, now crowded with bodies. The sausages were gone before I could set them down. I got another beer from the fridge and noticed the door to the apartment propped open with a painted sign that read, "Don't complain. Join the fun."

"Did someone complain?" I asked Melanie, who was lighting a flame under the fondue pot.

"That's a precaution," she said. "I told the managers they were welcome, but I guess they're too old. The couple upstairs came. They're here somewhere."

An arm wrapped around my shoulders, and I turned to find a friendly face. Steve. He kept the proprietary arm around me and addressed the rest of the gang in the kitchen. "We got some badass stash in the other room if anyone wants to partake."

Melanie picked up a half-full glass of amber liquid and gave him a crooked smile. "I'm so ready to get high with my friends." She giggled and slapped Link on the arm. "Come on, baby."

"I'll bring the fondue pot," I said to her retreating back. I leaned into Steve as we went down the hall.

Reefer smoke overpowered the cigarette smoke. All the beanbags were occupied as were the sofa and chairs. Some people stretched out on the rug, heads on a friend's lap. I didn't see Dani or Marty. Someone offered me a joint. I took a few tokes and closed my eyes.

"We're doing a sit-in tomorrow," Steve was saying. "Making the scene all over Center City."

"Sit-in for what?" I asked. I knew the term, attended a rally once with Melanie, but the war seemed so distance and far from my everyday life.

"Protesting 'Nam. We got to make our voices heard. We plan to sit in front of City Hall with signs and banners. Who's in?"

Several voices affirmed.

"I have to work that day," I said.

"So take the day off," Steve said.

I peered up at him. "You're going to pay me for the day?"

"Where's your conscience, woman? You know we're in an amoral war that must be stopped."

"I sat in a protest once." My eyelids wanted to close. I half listened to the discussion that followed. I didn't know anyone who fought in Vietnam, but I did my part by playing Bob Dylan and Joan Baez songs on my days off.

The subject of war continued, but I lost interest. The college kids talked of rebellion and how they would rather flee to Canada than fight the unpopular war. If I were a man, I decided, I would fight.

Feeling left out and depressed, I returned to the kitchen for another beer. I heard a couple arguing in the bathroom about how much he had to drink. I had more in common with them.

Instead of returning to the party, I lit a cigarette and took my beer out the door, down the stairs, and sat on the porch steps. The weatherman got it wrong again. The sun disappeared. The air smelled like approaching rain and pewter-gray clouds were already rolling across the sky. I didn't know how long the party would last. Most were pretty mellow by now and no one seemed to have the slightest inclination to leave.

It might have been a good party if I had anything in common with Melanie's friends. Steve seemed interested at first, but he drifted off to someone else. I thought of the go-go dancer, Dani, and decided to ask for her agent's name before she left.

I looked up to see a dark ominous cloud relieve itself on my street. Large wet drops fell on my face and I caught a few on my tongue.

Maybe I'll smoke a few joints, drink a few beers, and maybe I won't think about Johnny today.

CHAPTER 9

Moe's Tavern was a short two blocks from my apartment and across the street from the bus stop. I saw the blinking neon sign every night as the bus slowed, but I'd never been tempted until now. I was sick to death of listening to Link and Melanie screw in her bedroom, waking up to the mess they left behind in the kitchen, and hearing the furtive whispers when I was around. Moe's sign over the tavern door drew me like a pigeon to a chunk of bread.

Open the door to Moe's Tavern and you might think you're in Ireland. Rows of old fashioned mugs filled the dark wood shelves. The proverbial pot of gold sat in the unused fireplace. While I waited for the bartender, I read the Irish names off beer bottles and draft handles. I was fascinated because Johnny was not a beer drinker. Scotch, brandy stinger with a Galliano float, or vodka, straight or with a mix, were his personal "flavorites" as I liked to call them.

The bartender strolled my way. He reminded me of the guy who played Rockford in the Rockford files. He picked up on my interest and grinned at me. "You're looking at what we call the Blessed Trinity of Irish beers. Guinness, Murphy's, and Beamish. Which shall it be?"

I smiled. "What if I don't like any of them?"

"We have American, too." He filled a shot glass with Guinness draft. "First taste, then judge."

I sipped the Guinness. The taste was rich-bodied and robust, like no beer I'd tasted before. "Different, but good. I like it."

"Thadda girl. The Irish tops the American any day."

I pursed my lips. "Always?"

He leaned toward me, smoky blue eyes at half-mast. "You have to savor the entire experience to know for sure. Shall I pour you a mug?"

I lifted my shot glass in a salute. "Coming from an Irishman, I presume. Why the hell not?"

He poured the draft and set the mug in front of me. "Brady Case, at your service. You can't get more Irish than a Black Irish."

"You're very white for a Black Irish."

He laughed. "The term refers to my blue eyes and black hair."

"That's the dumbest thing I've ever heard." I said, laughing with him. "As long as we're talking about the Irish, I work at Monahan's. Know of it?"

He made a sour face and straightened. "Monahan's. Irish, in name only."

"But the food's tasty."

He shrugged like he wasn't entirely convinced. "You always get off the bus this late?"

"How did you—"

He glanced up at the window with a view of the street. "I saw you. It's an observant fellow I am."

I regarded him with increasing interest.

"I'm here until two-thirty every night." He offered the information in a casual manner, leaving me to decide what to do with this tidbit.

"No days off?"

"One or two, depending. You live around here?"

"Nosy, aren't you?" I sipped the Guinness, covering my smile.

"I'm a concerned citizen. You must live within walking distance."

Before I could think how to answer, a customer at the other end called for a refill.

Brady's blue eyes captured me. "Don't go away, Miss Independent. I'll be right back."

He tended his customer before sauntering back to me, his manner casual. "How's your drink?" he said.

"Not bad. Where's yours?"

"Never drink on the job. You ever go to after-hours clubs?"

"There are such places?"

His eyes widened in disbelief. "Where are you from, honey? Never mind. Takes all kinds, I always say. Anyway, you should check out the clubs some time. But don't go alone. It's more fun to go with someone." He winked.

"I don't go to bars alone."

"Except safe neighborhood establishments, like this one."

"That's right. And now I know you."

He leaned his elbows on the bar. "But you still haven't told me your name."

"Erin."

"Erin, begorrah," he said with a grin. "I can't believe I'm meeting an Irish gal."

I finished the Guinness and slid off the bar stool. "Nice meeting you, Brady."

"Come back again sometime." He took my empty glass. "You keep safe now."

"Always." I put enough cash on the bar to cover my beer plus a dollar tip, made a restroom stop, and headed for the door without looking back.

I stood outside a moment, breathing in the night air, hearing engine noise from a passing car. Lingering cooking smells from the row houses down the street mingled with the odors of wet grass and distant fireplaces.

I hadn't felt a physical attraction to a man in a long time. Brady triggered a response I hadn't expected. I sensed the feeling was mutual. But the idea of introducing a new man into my life was scary as shit.

I returned to Moe's the next night. And the night after that. I think I saw more of Moe's Tavern in the following weeks than I did my apartment. With each visit, I found Brady easier to be around. I learned that he used to participate in his hometown community theater. He particularly liked musicals. One night when there were only a few customers, he accompanied Frank Sinatra on the jukebox.

"I always wanted to be a professional dancer," I confided.

He rested his elbows on the bar. "What kind?"

"I don't know. I'm too old for ballet. No, really, I am. I'm more into freestyle. The music sends the steps to my feet. I don't have to think about it. My body hears the rhythm and responds. That's the only way I can explain it."

"I'd like to see that. Have you ever thought of dancing professionally?" He raised his hand when I laughed out loud. "No wait. I worked in a bar that hired go-go dancers once. They made good money."

Dani's words came back to me. "I met a go-go dancer once. She worked at Foxy Lady."

Brady frowned. "Isn't that on Locust Street? From what I heard, the girls there do more than dance."

Locust Street. Tony Corelli. Carl's angry words came back to me.

"What kind of things?" I said.

"Come on, you're not that naïve. I'm talking bar girls. Meaning, after they dance, they have to sit at the bar and get guys to buy them drinks. Only the drinks are watered down, or they order a shot with a water-back. The shot is usually tea. They pretend to drink, but spit it out in the water glass. They get commission on what the customer buys."

"I could never do that," I said.

"I've met lots of dancers. Seen them get hard and cynical toward men."

I decided to change the subject. "Do you live close by? It must be hard to find a cab or bus by the time you get off work."

He pointed his thumb upward. "My room's above the bar. How about you? Do you live alone?"

I told him about Melanie and her boyfriend.

"No wonder you don't like going straight home," he said.

I gave him my Mona Lisa smile. "That's one reason."

A few weeks later on a balmy June night, I stuck around until closing. Brady retrieved two beers from the cooler and tucked them into his pocket. He told me he wanted to walk me home. I didn't argue.

Because Melanie was upstairs, probably with Link, I didn't invite Brady inside. He seemed okay with that. The air was cool with a light breeze. We sat on the porch, watched the stars, and sipped our beer while we listened to the city's muted noises.

Brady put his arm around me and I stiffened. He frowned and withdrew his arm. "What's wrong?"

"Nothing." I tried to sound natural. "I don't know. No one's touched me in a long time. I wasn't expecting it." *What was wrong with me?*

"Hey, it's all right," he said. "You don't have to tell me all your secrets now."

I laughed uncomfortably. "What secrets?"

"Whatever it is you don't want to tell me." He moved closer and caressed my arm. I felt his breath on my neck.

I inhaled his masculine scent. His touch vibrated through me and I couldn't ignore the way my body responded. The words slipped out. "Want to come in?"

He looked surprised. He hesitated only a second. "Are you sure?"

"Do you always answer a question with a question?"

Before he could answer, I reached over and kissed him, slow and hard.

After a long moment, he pushed me away, but only far enough to search my eyes. Whatever he was looking for, he must have found. We rose to our feet. I dug in my purse for the key and opened the front door. In seconds, we bounded up the stairs. Inside the apartment, I listened for noises, but heard nothing. Still, I motioned for quiet and he followed me into my bedroom. I shut the door. He glanced at the twin bed, then turned to me.

The first object I saw was the snow globe Carl had given me the day I left his apartment. I pushed it behind my radio so I wouldn't have to look at it. I walked into Brady's waiting arms. My heart beat double time. He gently pushed my hair back from my face and tilted my chin up.

He kissed me like I was fragile and might break. I kissed him again, deeper, tongue darting tentatively then thrusting. We couldn't shed our clothes fast enough.

CHAPTER 10

After a busy Friday night in July, I made my regular stop at Moe's. I was tired and the tavern was crowded and hot. Brady worked the bar, had no time for talk. I had one drink and left. The weather was perfect for walking.

Half a block from my apartment, I saw a jeep barreling toward down the street. I wouldn't have paid it a second's notice except the top was down. Suitcases and liquor store boxes were piled high in the back seat.

The jeep slowed its approach. The driver looked familiar. It took a moment before I recognized Link and the woman next to him. Dumbstruck, I stared at Melanie. It was past midnight. Where could they be going with all that stuff? A bad feeling tightened my chest and my stomach clenched.

I waved at them to stop, but the jeep only slowed enough to allow me to catch up. I jogged alongside.

"Melanie? What's going on?"

Melanie shifted forward so I could see her behind Link. "Link and I've been talking about moving to Alaska. Didn't I tell you? Tonight we decided to just do it."

"Just do what? What are you talking about?"

"We're *moving,* Erin. I'm sorry I didn't give you notice. This was all spur of the moment. Don't worry. I'm sure you'll find another roommate. You'll make out okay."

Before I could respond, Link hit the gas. Feeling like an idiot, I watched the jeep disappear around the corner.

Alaska?

I stood in the middle of the street and felt my knees grow weak. Finally, I made myself look up at the darkened windows of the second floor apartment—all mine now. All that space. All the rent I would have to come up with each month instead of half. It hit me that Melanie must have planned to be gone by the time I got home. Would there be a note waiting for me upstairs? I doubted it. I bolted upstairs, angry tears stung my eyes. I unlocked the door with shaking hands and burst inside. The furniture was all there, of course. She couldn't fit that in a jeep.

I walked through the apartment, one room at a time. I opened cupboards and closet doors. All empty. I went through the kitchen, the bedrooms, the bathrooms. All bare except for my bedding. No towels, no dishes, glasses, or silverware.

No note. And nothing I could do about it.

Melanie and I had never bonded, but I didn't expect this. It would have hurt less if she had just told me she was leaving, but she did it behind my back. Worse yet, I didn't have the money to replace the things she had taken. I had given her all I had to pay my half of the rent and cover food and liquor bills. Did she even pay this month's rent? Or was that her moving money? I couldn't believe this.

I was numb, unable to think. I sat on the floor in the middle of the living room and stared unseeing out the window.

I finally looked at my watch. Two o'clock in the

morning. Brady would be closing up the bar. I rose on shaky legs, walked out of the apartment, and locked the door behind me. Ten minutes later I knocked on the door to Moe's Tavern. I could see Brady wiping down the bar through the frosted window. I kept knocking until he looked up. The smiling face that greeted me turned into a puzzled frown as he reached the door and let me in.

"What's wrong?" he said.

His words broke the dam I'd been holding back. He led me to a table and brought two bottles of beer. I downed half of mine before I could find my voice and tell him what happened.

"How could she do that to you?" he said. "Can you call the police?"

"For what? All that stuff was hers. I paid half the rent, paid for food, but I didn't own anything in that apartment. I had complete use of her things, so I didn't buy any. All right, maybe that was stupid, but the stuff was there so I didn't feel I had to rush out and buy my own. What the hell am I going to do?"

We finished our beer and Brady walked me back to my apartment. "Do you want me to stay?" he said as I unlocked the door.

I considered this, but his pity and solicitude had started to grate on my nerves. I needed to be alone to figure out my next move. "I wouldn't be good company."

"More reason not to be by yourself." He stepped closer.

I moved away. "Come by tomorrow."

"Okay." He frowned in concern. "Let me see what I can come up with by then."

"What? You're going to buy me stuff? Is that your solution?"

Anger spiked my mood. I didn't need anyone rescuing me. I needed another job. Or a second one. Maybe a third after that. I'd be damned if I'd let anyone put me in this position again.

Brady looked puzzled. Finally, he said, "Calm down. I'll talk to you tomorrow."

After the door closed and I heard his footsteps recede, I almost called him back. A good round of sex could make this nightmare disappear for a short while. But it wouldn't turn back the clock. It wouldn't change anything. How did he expect to help me? He didn't have money to spare. He lived paycheck to paycheck, plus tips, same as me.

I stepped into my bedroom and looked around. For the first time since I'd moved in, I felt claustrophobic. Moonlight drifting in the window barely illuminated my things. I gathered up my blanket and pillow from my unmade bed to carry into the living room. At the last moment, I added the snow globe Carl had given me. Tomorrow I would air out Melanie's bedroom and get new sheets to fit the full-size bed. I didn't want Melanie and Link's scent mingled with mine. I made a mental list of everything I needed. I would find the money somehow. I would be okay. I'd survived worse. I stretched out on the sofa and watched the bright pinpoints of starlight until they dimmed.

Someone pounding on the door woke me. Bleary-eyed, I checked my watch. Almost noon. I'd slept through the night. More pounding. I sat up and swung my legs to the floor and finger-combed my hair. Melanie? No, she was in Alaska. *Alaska.*

I still wore my waitress uniform and wanted to change clothes, maybe catch a shower, but the asshole at the door was insistent. I detoured to the bathroom and splashed water on my face before I flung open the door to find Brady. He held out a bulging sack while balancing two paper cups of coffee.

"Donuts," he said.

My anger subsided and I stepped aside to let him in. The aroma of sugar, cinnamon, and chocolate swirled around me. "Coffee." I took one of the cups from his hand.

He followed me into the kitchen and set the bag on the table. We sat opposite each other and I picked out a powdered donut.

"Did you sleep?" he asked.

"Not much. Get any bright ideas since last night?" I didn't expect a miracle but his anxious expression hinted that he'd come up with a plan.

"Baby, you know I'd give you the money if I had it. But I've got an alternative. I have this friend who has a credit card you can borrow."

"Credit card," I repeated. "This is your idea? You want me to use some guy's credit card?" I never had a credit card. I never had credit, period. But I knew enough about them to be wary.

"He says you can use it to get a few essentials. Towels and some stuff for the kitchen. That will help you out, won't it?"

"Sure, but I don't get it. Why would a stranger let me use his credit card?"

"He knows me. I vouched for you."

I thought of my list. If I could get a few necessities, what harm could it do? I pushed away the warning signals going off in my head.

"Are you sure that's legal?" I said. "The card belongs to him?"

He shrugged. "Look, it's up to you. You can meet him. Talk to him. I told him it's an emergency. A one-time deal. He's good with that."

There's a saying, if something sounds too good to be true... I wiped the thought from my mind.

Maybe the guy owed Brady. That could explain it, and if so I'd be doing Brady a favor. It would certainly help me cover this ditch in my life. "Sure, tell him to come over."

He breathed through his mouth. "I'll call him when I get to Moe's."

I really had to get a telephone. He could have called his friend from my place and I could have listened in. Maybe talked to the guy myself.

"I'm working today," he added, "but if I can arrange it, I'll bring him over before my shift starts."

Two hours later, another knock on the door. I had used the time since Brady left to clean myself up a little, using what few toiletries and cosmetics I owned, so when I opened the door I looked at least respectable.

Brady introduced his friend, Scotty Weber, a short, stubby guy with a pockmarked face. His slicked-back brown hair was plastered to his skull with some kind of oily substance. He wore a brown plaid jacket over a yellow shirt and brown pants. A fox with fashion sense.

We went into the living room and I sat on the sofa. Brady and Scotty pulled their chairs next to each other and faced me. He had the credit card in his hand and kept turning it over.

"You really don't mind if I use your card?" I said to Scotty.

"Hey, sweetie, Brady says you're okay, you're okay. I trust you. He told me about your roommate. That's pretty crummy. Damn lousy cards you were dealt. So I'm here to help a friend's friend. Nothing wrong with that. I'm a generous guy."

He held out the card so I could see before he pulled it away.

"Now here's the thing, you don't want to charge more than fifty dollars. Are we clear?"

"Sure." I made a few calculations. A couple of towels, a toaster, couple of glasses, and plates. Fifty could get me started. Even if it wasn't legit, I could bluff my way through. It was only fifty. "Thanks. All right if I get this back to you tomorrow?"

Brady and Scotty exchanged looks.

"Sure, sure. No problem." Scotty handed me the card. "Remember, now. No more than fifty."

I fingered the plastic. "I can't pay you back until I get paid next week. Is that okay?"

Scotty flashed another look at Brady. "He says you're cool, I don't worry." He stood. "Well, then, you kids have a good night, hear?"

Brady walked him to the door. I couldn't wait until they left so I could go shopping.

When Brady came back into the living room, he looked somber.

"Erin, are you sure this is what you want to do?" he said.

He looked anxious and, for a moment, I had second thoughts. I reminded myself he was trying to help me the only way he could. No skin off his back if something went wrong. I'd take the heat. But nothing would go wrong.

I kept my voice light. "I know the score. Don't you have to go to work?"

His lips brushed against mine. "Yeah. Be careful. Call me."

"Don't worry. I won't overspend."

And if I do, I'll pay him back.

CHAPTER 11

I clutched the black pay phone to my ear and spoke over the noise. "Brady? I'm in jail."

I heard him groan. "What happened?"

"What the hell do you think? You knew that card was stolen."

"Shut up. Someone will hear you. Fuck. You overcharged, didn't you?"

"Well, dummy me, I guess I can't count. Anyway, I didn't know I would be arrested. I never had a credit card. Now I never will. Shit, Brady, you got to get me out of this."

Silence at the other end stretched forever. I gripped the receiver so tight I expected to see grooves in it when I let go. Damn, I couldn't believe how stupid I'd been. Anyway, it was all Brady's fault. He shouldn't have brought the guy to me in the first place.

"Brady?"

"I know a lawyer," he said finally. "I'll make the call. Don't worry. I'll get you out."

My hand shook as I disconnected. How was I supposed to pay for a damn lawyer? Did Brady really know one? Shit, I was going to jail.

I was with other women. Prostitutes mostly. Easy to

tell the regulars, bitches with cruel lips and hard eyes. I felt cold and alone.

The arresting officer had been nice. He believed me when I told him I'd never been arrested before. Guess he felt sorry for me, because he took the cuffs off my wrists after we got in the patrol car. They came back on before we entered the station. He brought me into a room where an armed guard stood watch. The cuffs came off again.

They searched my purse and gave it back to me. I hadn't been arrested yet, still waiting to be processed. My throat felt strangled. I had to do something to take my mind off what was happening. I moved to the far wall, took out my nail polish, and proceeded to paint my fingernails. I wanted to appear tough, like this meant nothing. I didn't want any of those bitches thinking I was green or weak. Funny how something as simple as polishing one's nails could be calming while you appeared not to give a shit. I almost believed my own act. At least my hands stopped shaking. I blew on the wet nails until they dried.

The guard took a call and motioned to me when he hung up. "Erin Matthews?"

I nodded. Did this mean my lawyer had arrived? No. He took my purse and brought me to another room to be fingerprinted. Next I had my photo taken holding a placard with a number. I tried not to blink when the flash went off in my face. I was turned sideways and another flash went off. Another guard led me to a nine-by-six room with a flat metal bench attached to the wall.

"Someone's called a lawyer for me," I told the guard.

"We'll come and get you when he arrives."

"Can I have my purse back?"

I swear he wanted to smile, but his lips only twitched. "When and if you're released." He left and the metal door clicked in place.

If I'm released? I realized then I could be there over-night, or longer. I sat. I paced. I cursed Brady Case and his oily friend, and the lawyer who hadn't shown up. Hours went by. I marked the time by going over and over the details of my crime. I'd tried to keep the purchases under fifty dollars. I didn't count on the damn sales tax.

I stared at the faint black stain on my fingers. The soot, or whatever it was, smeared on my freshly painted nails. Even the police wipes could not completely get them clean. *Out, out, damned spot!* Fuck, I was really los-ing it. The walls were closing in. No windows. No air. I would suffocate if they didn't open that door soon. I had to stay calm. I couldn't let this beat me.

I sat back on the metal bench and closed my eyes. If I could sleep, I wouldn't think. What if nobody came? I pushed that thought aside. No matter what, I would not cry.

The lock turned and the guard appeared in the door-way and said, "Follow me. Your lawyer's here."

I lifted my chin, straightened my shoulders and stumbled out of the cell. I stopped long enough for my soggy brain to send a message to my knees and tell them not to buckle. Brady and a stranger met me in an inter-view room.

"Erin, this is Andrew Kramer," Brady said. "The lawyer I mentioned. You're being released on an OR."

"What's that?"

"Own Recognizance. That means the court didn't set bail because this is a first offense and you are employed. You're not to leave town and you must appear before the judge when you're summoned."

"How much do you charge?"

"We'll discuss that later," Kramer said. "First let's get you out of here."

"Fine by me."

When we reached the sidewalk, I realized day had turned to night. My stomach rumbled.

"Do I have to go right home?" I asked. "There's no food in my fridge."

"You hungry?" Brady asked.

"Yeah." *What did he think?*

Brady looked at the lawyer as if he had to ask his permission. Kramer nodded.

They decided on Stoney's Bar and Grill on Pine. I ordered a grilled ham and cheese on rye and a Bud, since they didn't have anything stronger.

Brady joined me with the beer and Kramer ordered coffee.

While we waited for my food to appear, Kramer opened his briefcase and took out a legal-sized contract. I skimmed over the fine print and signed.

Kramer said, "Brady tells me you were not aware that the card had been stolen. Is that correct?"

"I just thought the guy was being generous by helping out a friend of a friend. I never would have used the card if I'd known." I glanced at Brady, who said nothing. "Are we asking for a jury trial?"

"No, we'll take it to the judge. It's better that way. With a first offense, there is a chance I can get you no-billed. It's my understanding that none of the items purchased with the card were taken out of the store."

"That's in my favor, right?" I said. When he didn't answer, I explained further. "The clerk took my card and went into the back room. The next thing I knew, the cops arrived and arrested me. I was shaking so hard they could barely get the cuffs on."

Kramer didn't look sympathetic. "So outside of attempting to use a stolen card that you didn't know was stolen, you haven't really committed a crime. That's your defense."

Sounded good to me.

"But she'll still have an arrest record, won't she?" Brady injected. "Isn't there something you can do about that?"

Christ, I hadn't thought about that. A public court record would follow me all my life. Might even make it easy for Johnny to find me, if he was able to look.

"Yeah, what *can* you do about that?" I said.

"It depends on whether or not you're cleared by the judge. If so, we can ask the court to expunge your record."

"That's what you have to do, counselor," Brady said.

Our drinks and my food arrived. My mouth salivated. Peering over my sandwich, I watched Brady down his beer like it was water and he was in the desert. He ordered another.

Kramer barely touched his coffee. Instead, he folded the signed contract and stuffed it back into his briefcase. He met my eyes. "Erin, sorry we had to meet under these circumstances, but you seem like a good kid. We can win this."

I put down my sandwich. "I'm getting another job. I don't know what your arrangement is with Brady, but I'll pay you. I can't do it all at once, but you'll get it eventually. I promise."

He smiled and stood. "That's my understanding." He looked at Brady and I could swear there was some communication between them I didn't get.

"What did he mean?" I said when the lawyer left.

Brady took the last sip of his beer. He waved to the waitress and pointed at his glass. "Just what he said."

"Something else is going on and I want to know what it is. I'm telling you right now, I meant it when I said I'll pay him. I don't care what you have going with him." I sat back so fast that my head hit the back of the booth. "Wait. He's yours and Scotty's lawyer, isn't he? That's why he agreed to represent me."

The waitress arrived and neither of us spoke until she put his beer in front of him and left.

Brady gritted his teeth. "That has nothing to do with you or how he handles your case."

"Bullshit." I felt the heat burn my cheeks. "I almost spent the night in that cell, while you and your friend walk away clean. No questions asked about where I got the card. Tell me, asshole, what's in this for you?"

"You can stop acting like you just got off the bus, sweetheart." His blue eyes were like glaciers. "Who the hell got the lawyer for you, and why are you suddenly acting like the victim? You knew the score when you took the card. If you'd listened to us, you wouldn't be in this spot."

"I could have told the cops who gave it to me."

Brady reached over the table and gripped my arm so hard it hurt. "You want to get us both killed?"

I jerked my arm away. "Why? Is he some sort of mafia guy?" *Is the world full of guys like Johnny? Shit!*

He looked around. "Shut up."

I picked up my beer and gulped down the rest. I slammed the bottle on the table. "I'll pay him if I have to get three jobs. I won't owe you a dime after this."

He threw up his hands. "Is this what I get for trying to help you?"

He waved for the waitress.

"No more drinks," I said.

"I'm getting the check."

"I'll pay it." I dug in my purse. My wallet was empty. "Shit."

He nodded, started to grin then apparently decided against it. He pulled a twenty out of his pocket and slapped it on the table. "Next time."

"I'll pay you back."

"Yeah, fine. Let's get the hell out of here."

When we reached the pavement, his voice lowered. "I'm sorry I got you into this. If you insist, I'll let you pay Kramer."

"Wow, that's really knightly of you," I said. "That's what I told you already."

He jerked to a stop and yanked me against him with such force I had no choice but to go limp. His eyes were as hard as stone. His mouth covered mine like a starving animal's and, despite what my brain was saying, my body responded. All my anger and frustration erupted like a volcano, molten fire between my legs, betraying all my good intentions. He tore away from me long enough to hail a taxi and we slammed into the back seat, groping like teenagers. I needed to fuck. I needed to take him home and fuck until I couldn't think, until I drove all the hurt away.

CHAPTER 12

I woke to rain slashing against the windows. I groaned as Kramer's words came back like a swarm of killer bees. He expected his fee before the trial, set in two months. If he didn't get paid, I'd be headed for jail. As if that wasn't enough, I owed rent.

Panic wrapped around my throat and tightened. I had to do something. My combined income from salary and tips at Monahan's wouldn't pay enough to cover lawyer's fees and rent. Not by a long shot.

I ate my meals at Monahan's and scrimped on everything else. The one expense I couldn't cut was the service for a blue Princess phone that never rang. I scoured the paper for want ads and applied at all the employment agencies. I knew how to type, though I hadn't held an office job since before I met Johnny. I even bluffed my way through the interviews for jobs I didn't qualify for. Still, no calls.

I sipped my third cup of coffee and remembered Dani's friend at our housewarming party, bragging how she made a ton of money dancing at clubs. I grabbed the Yellow Pages and looked under Agents. I ran my finger down a short list of names. I found the name she had mentioned—Rico—near the bottom, in one of the few ads looking for dancers. I called the number and was given an appointment for that afternoon.

The day didn't look any brighter than it had earlier. Rain came down in sheets when I went to catch the bus. I arrived for my interview with soaked clothes and hair as limp as cooked spaghetti. Some impression I'd make. I detoured to the bathroom and repaired what I could with makeup and swept my hair up into a French twist.

Rico's "office" was a dance studio on the fringes of Center City. White light filled the room, and I shielded my eyes against the glare. A camera man was waving directions at a bikini-clad girl, who looked to be in her teens, standing on a raised stage.

On the other side of the room, a man with the slim, firm body of a dancer waved his hand. He wore black slacks and a starched white shirt open to his navel, revealing black chest hairs. His fingers fluttered an invitation. My white go-go boots clicked across the hall and left wet prints on the floor.

The man scowled. "You're the girl who called this morning?"

I held out my hand. "Erin Matthews."

He ignored the gesture. Instead, he told me to stand still while he circled me, scrutinizing me like I was on the auctioning block. He stopped, folded his arms. "A little thin, and your tits are small. Can you dance?"

I tried to tell him about my ballet lessons, but he waved me off. "Never mind. If you can't, the other girls will teach you. You got a costume?"

I had to buy a costume? With what? I was here to make money, not spend what I didn't have. "What kind of costume?"

"You know. A costume, like all the girls wear." He gave an exasperated sigh.

"Of course," I said, bluffing. That was what I was good at.

He must have read my mind because he leaned toward me and winked like he was letting me in on his secret to fame and riches. "You don't have to spend a fortune at the costume shop. You got a bra and panties, don't you? Buy some cheap beads and sequins and sew them on. Add a little fringe and you've got a costume." He shrugged, like it was as easy as spreading butter on toast. He glanced at his calendar. "I got a spot to fill Thursday night. Can you make it?"

Two days to get ready. I felt the knot tighten my stomach. "Sure. Where and what time?"

ᗡᗡ

By Thursday I had one costume made. I stuffed it in a sack and caught a cab to the seedy part of Spanish town. A neon sign above the bar blinked the name, El Gato Negro. A nervous little man greeted me as I walked in and rushed me toward a narrow stairwell.

"You're late. Dressing room's up there. The other girls will show you what to do."

He rushed off again, no doubt to give orders to someone else. The stairwell was dark and barely wide enough for me, and I was pretty skinny. A tall black girl appeared through two dark curtains behind the stage.

"Erin? In here." She guided me into a small dressing room. "I'm Monique. You right on time."

An olive-skinned girl poked her head around Monique. "I'm Flora," she said. "I'm on next. You'll go on after me."

In this room, two was a crowd, three a sandwich. The smell of hair spray mixed with heavy cologne hit me and my eyes watered.

Street clothes and costume changes were jammed against one corner. I changed quickly.

"Did Ike show you how to play your music on the jukebox?" Monique asked.

That must have been the little man I'd met. "He showed me the stairs and that's it."

"Figures." Monique proceeded to pencil in her eyebrows in front of the foot-high mirror that ran along the wall above the narrow counter.

"He's an asshole." Flora adjusted her costume top. I noticed it was a bra covered with beads and fringe like mine. "But he pays, so who's bitching?"

A Spanish tune came on. Flora shook her hips in front of the mirror before brushing past me. "That's my cue. See ya bitches later, yo."

Monique motioned me back toward the stairs. "Come on, I'll show you where the jukebox is. Three songs to a set. The selections play in the order they're picked. You'll have time after Flora gets off the stage before your music starts."

I kept glancing at the stage as we went back downstairs. Monique guided me to the jukebox. Flora could shake hips and tits and had some moves I'd like to copy. The audience loved her. I turned to the selections and saw nothing but Spanish. I had no idea if the tunes were fast or slow.

There had to be some music I recognized. There was. "Granada." What flamenco I knew I'd picked up in Tijuana and Ensenada during a six-month stay in Baja with Johnny.

I picked two more. As long as they had a beat, and what Spanish music didn't, I could dance to them. I made my way up the stairs again. My heart thumped and my throat tightened. I could barely breathe. This was how I felt when I had to get up in front of my high school class or perform at a dance recital. But it was nothing like my audition in front of Tony Corelli.

Flora came off the stage and barged in the dressing room, sweating. "Fuck, it's hot out there. You're on, whatever your name is."

"Erin," I said, and stepped out of the dressing room.

The stage was accessible from the stairwell. Three steps down I came to a curtain on my left. I parted the thin material and walked to the middle of the stage. I felt awkward standing there, waiting for the music. I couldn't see the bartender beneath the stage, only the customers sitting behind the semi-circular bar. The seats were filled with brown-faced men who leered up at me, but I was high enough to be untouchable.

The first notes of "Granada" reached me and I moved into position. Flamenco wasn't as easy as it used to be, not on this stage.

It was hot and the smell of sweat, cigarettes, and beer enveloped me. I concentrated on my music and let the rhythm dictate my moves.

The crowd's reaction was less than I'd hoped for, but a few wolf whistles encouraged me. One asshole kept sticking out his tongue and wagging it. Did he really think he'd turn someone on with that action?

The rest of the set didn't go as well. I danced my heart out with all the rhythm and shake I could force my body to do. I even slipped some ballet moves into the act, trying to give my act more class, but my performance got a ho-hum response. Not even a tongue wag. The men went back to their drinking. What was wrong with them? I could dance. I felt the music. I gave it my all. What the hell?

"Can I give you some advice?" Monique said when I came off stage.

"Sure. I'll take anything right now." My skin glistened. Drops of sweat dripped from my hairline down my forehead and rolled to my chin.

"You can dance and you got rhythm. This your first gig?"

That obvious? "Yeah, so what am I doing wrong?"

"You're moving too fast. Slow it down. Roll your hips. Works better than a fast pump. Think and breathe sex. That's what the men want. If they stick their asses to the seats and drink fast because they're getting off on the girls, management will love you and you'll get called back."

My next set didn't win any standing ovations, but I got more attention by following Monique's advice. I let my hips undulate, put in some pelvic thrusts, bent over with my ass facing the audience, turned, and shook the fringe covering my bra. I saw the guy with the tongue get up and leave, but some others clapped. Over the music I heard shouts of "*conchita*" and "*puta*" and other words I didn't understand.

That gig lasted four weekends. Little by little I overcame stage fright as I worked on my routine. I watched the other dancers, and in my spare time bought more costume material with the money I earned. A couple of extra push-up padded bras covered with sequins and fringe with matching bikini bottoms varied my costumes. My white plastic go-go boots were getting plenty of *sole* time.

The Monday after the gig ended, Rico called to say he had an after-hours club that paid double the regular gigs. Would I be interested?

Damn right. I worked the lunch hours at Monahan's and danced weekends, and I still barely made the rent and payments to the lawyer.

∽∾

The club was small and intimate, the stage a raised platform in one corner by the bar.

"We're a 'members only' club," the manager told me as I prepared to go on stage. "You'll go topless."

I stared at him. "No way. I don't go topless."

The way he looked at me, I didn't think anyone ever told him no before. I immediately thought of Tony Corelli and Locust Street. But this wasn't Locust Street, and I didn't have to do anything I didn't want to do. What I did for Corelli was a whole different story. Come to think of it, he didn't mind my small tits at all.

"Look," the guy tried again. "Everyone dances topless here. The members expect it."

"Not from me they don't." I put my hands on my hips and didn't move.

"We're paying the big bucks, so I don't give a fuck about your standards. You're the only girl here tonight and these guys are waiting to see boobs."

How could I talk him out of this? "I'll do it for an extra hundred," I offered, figuring he would laugh at me.

He smirked. "You got to be kidding. Who's your fucking agent?"

"Rico didn't tell me I had to go topless," I said.

He tapped his foot and ground his teeth. He had a waiting audience. "I'll give you an extra twenty," he said at last.

"Eighty," I shot back.

He swore under his breath. "Fifty. That's my final offer."

I swallowed. My mouth felt dry. "You win."

There were scruples, and there were scruples with conditions. Like making that next payment to the lawyer. I still hesitated. I mean, when you had tits as small as mine, who'd want to see them, anyway? Maybe I should get the fifty up front.

I didn't hesitate too long. What the hell? I knew no one in the bar and I'd never be back. Who would pay attention to me? I slowly unhooked my bra and let it drop. I walked onto the stage and every man in the room cheered. Guess size didn't matter. As the music began, I raised my arms to shoulder height and undulated like a snake curling out of a basket. My face grew hot. Whistles accompanied shouts of "come on, baby" and "take it all off." I turned my back to the audience and worked my hips. I let myself zone out, be carried away to somewhere else—the beach in Florida, which, unfortunately, brought Johnny to mind. *If he could see me now, I'd be dead.* I blinked back to the present as the music came to a close.

I couldn't wait until the set was over. I could dance sexy without my boobs showing. I didn't need to feel this humiliated. I ran out the door when the bar closed at four in the morning. The cab the bartender called for me waited by the entrance with its back door open. I slid down in the seat, angry at myself for letting someone talk me into doing something I didn't want to do.

Brady was at the apartment when I arrived home. He hadn't moved in yet, but I'd given him a key and he often stayed the night. Too bad he picked that night. Beer bottles were strewn through the kitchen and living room. He was asleep, sprawled on the couch. I didn't bother to wake him, but went into the bedroom and shut the door. I lay there and stared up at the ceiling. Dancing topless, I decided, changed the dance. Wasn't fun anymore. Morality didn't have shit to do with it. I was a professional, damn it. I would make the rules from now on.

I should have walked out on the job. But I couldn't afford to. I needed the money. I turned on my side and clutched my pillow. My tears soaked the pillowcase and there was no one I could turn to for comfort.

CHAPTER 13

"Aren't there any respectable jobs out there?" Kramer said.

I sat in his office dressed in a sheer white blouse and a striped mini-skirt. My damp palms pressed against my thighs. I listened to him while he put down my line of work.

Waitressing and dancing was not *respectable* enough for the judge? I felt steam rise off my cheeks.

"I just paid half your fee from dancing," I retorted. "If that's tainted money, then give it back."

"Good enough for me," Kramer said, straight-faced. "Not for the judge." He scribbled something on a piece of paper and handed it to me. "Here's the address of the new Martin Luther King Hospital. You said you can type, and they need a girl in the secretarial pool. You will see a Mrs. Johnson in Human Resources. She knows you're coming."

"Now?" I glanced at my watch. "It's one in the afternoon."

"Your appointment's at four. Don't be late."

"I have to be at work at five." The Crystal Club liked their dancers to arrive on time.

Kramer scowled at me from his seat behind his

enormous mahogany desk. "What's more important, pleasing a bartender or a judge?"

"If I can't make a decent buck, I won't please either one."

"Don't get flip, Erin. Take my advice, that's what you're paying me for."

I didn't bother to answer. I didn't need this bastard to threaten me.

"Do you have a knee-length skirt to wear for the interview?" he said when I reached the door.

I glanced down at my bare thighs and legs. I thought about my spare wardrobe. "I don't have the money to shop for clothes."

"You have enough to make costumes."

How did he know that? Did Brady tell him? "I may have one skirt that'll work."

That meant I had to rush home to change and freshen up. The hot May weather didn't cool my spirits or my armpits.

I told Kramer I'd keep in touch and rushed out the door. I made it home in time to splash water and soap on my face, put on fresh makeup, and change into the black pencil skirt I'd packed to come to Philly, and worn the day I met Corelli. I added a white blouse I bought at a sidewalk sale for two dollars shortly after Melanie left town. It was three-thirty by the time I caught the bus to North Philly. Five to four when I reached the steps of the hospital.

The air inside the building raised goose bumps on my sweat-soaked skin. *Fucking Kramer, making me do this today.* Nurses in white uniforms brushed past me. Wheelchairs clogged the way to the information desk where a gray-haired woman peered at me over wire-framed glasses and pointed me in the direction of the elevators. I tapped my foot impatiently until the steel doors opened and, as they closed, I pressed the button for the third floor. A few minutes later, I opened the door to the Human Resources office. A receptionist took my name and lifted the phone to announce my arrival. She handed me a stack of papers to fill out while I waited.

"Miss Johnson will be with you shortly," she said.

I finished the questionnaire and gave the stack of papers to the receptionist. She took them to an interior office. I wandered to the wide window, looked out at the grounds below to a parking lot filled with cars. Finally, I heard the door open. A statuesque, dark-skinned woman appeared and waved me inside.

I took the chair facing Miss Johnson's desk. Silence followed as she scanned through the paperwork.

"So Andrew Kramer referred you," she said finally.

That's all she got from my written answers? Gee whiz, I could have told her that. I wondered if Kramer had spoken to her. I wasn't about to say I was his criminal client, so I just nodded.

"The last time you worked in an office was over four years ago. Is that correct?"

"Yes," I said. "But I catch up quick. I'm fast and accurate and a good organizer." All the words Kramer told me to use.

I held my breath while she scrutinized the application.

Finally, she rested her hands on top of the papers. "Kramer's picks are hits or misses. We'll see which category you fit into. I had a girl leave a couple of days ago, leaving me short. I need someone now. How soon can you start?"

I exhaled. "Tomorrow?"

On my way home, I stopped at Monahan's and told them I wouldn't be working there anymore. I hadn't made many friends there, so no tears, no regrets. I was moving on. But later that night, I couldn't sleep. I'd told Brady to stay at his place so I could wake up rested. I ended up staring at the ceiling for hours, picturing myself at the typewriter, making mistakes and having doctors yell at me for being too slow or too sloppy. I must have finally dozed off early in the morning, because when the alarm went off, I almost didn't hear it and felt groggy when I finally dragged myself to the bathroom.

A cold shower revived me somewhat and an hour later I arrived on time at the hospital. Another woman showed me to a large room filled with desks. Each desk had an electric typewriter and a Dictaphone with head-sets. The other secretaries breezed in and took their assigned places. Like high school typing class without a teacher.

I got the hang of the work in less time than I'd feared. I made mistakes, but that was what the white-out bottle was for. The worst part wasn't looking up complicated medical terms for their spelling, but the accents of some of the doctors from India or Iran, and there were many of those.

To save money, I brought my lunch and ate at my desk, but one day after I'd been working there for two weeks, the need to escape, to breathe fresh air and stretch my legs became irresistible. I ventured out alone in a shotgun neighborhood and realized this wasn't anything like my neighborhood or Carl's. I thought one angry-looking old man was going to throw tomatoes at me.

Hostile eyes glared. I smelled suspicion and outright hatred in the air.

One woman wore a colorful red and purple turban over her hair and a full length white apron covered her clothes. She stepped out onto her porch and screeched, "What you lookin' at, honky? You slummin'?"

In other words, what was this white girl doing

breathing with her snotty nose in her neighborhood?

I resisted the impulse to bow my head and hurry on past. Instead, I beamed a smile and waved at her. "I work at the hospital. Taking a break to enjoy this beautiful spring day. How about you?"

She harrumphed, shook her head, turned, and went back inside. I saw the curtains at her window twitch. I smiled to myself and kept walking.

I was still feeling good when I came back to work. Tamara, the girl who sat next to me, a striking black girl, looked up sharply.

I told her about the woman I'd met on my walk.

"She probably doesn't see many white faces," Tamara said, straightening in her chair, posed to return to work.

"I didn't mean to annoy her."

She gave me a curious look. "Why didn't you stay here and eat?"

I shrugged. "I get feeling closed in sometimes. Don't you ever feel that way?"

"No. I like to be inside. It's safer."

"I'm more the adventurous type."

She looked down. "I wish I could be more like you."

I was startled. I'd often caught her staring at me when she thought I was working. "What do you mean?"

"Act like you don't care about the work, like nothing bothers you, always smiling."

"Who wants to be serious all the time?" I said. "Next time go for a walk with me."

She surprised me by laughing. I'd never heard such a sweet sound. Low and throaty like her speaking voice, but cautious like she was afraid someone might hear.

"Maybe we can eat lunch together," she suggested, somewhat shyly.

After that, we met often during breaks and found we

had similar philosophies on life. We talked about everything and our conversations were all too brief. We discussed politics, civil rights, the war, and our career choices. But, for some reason, I hesitated telling her about my
second job. The way she held herself so wound up, I had
the feeling she would disapprove.

I came in one Friday morning after a particularly late
night. I'd wanted desperately to call in sick. After working until two in the morning for the third night in a row, I
still had to get up by seven. Tamara had to shake me
awake twice after I'd rested my head on my desk to close
my eyes, just for a minute.

"What do you do at night?" she asked after she had
poked me awake the second time. She let her hand rest on
my shoulder.

I looked around. "You can't tell anyone."

"So what's the big secret? You carrying on a forbid-
den affair with a married doctor?"

I laughed. "Nothing like that." I paused and leaned
closer to her. "I have a second job. Some nights are later
than others."

"A second job?" She looked askance. "What kind of
work can you do at night?"

When I told her she looked stunned. "My god. You
dance in front of strangers? In a bar?"

"You get used to it, so they tell me." I looked for
signs of disapproval, but couldn't read her expression.
"It's just temporary. But I make more in four hours at
night than I do working here all day." I didn't mention
that sometimes, like the night before, I worked a double
shift.

"I can't imagine doing that." The disapproval I'd
looked for appeared. Or did I imagine it?

"Sorry to disappoint you," I said, harsher than I mean
to. "I need the money."

Her eyes widened. "No, I didn't mean—I don't think it's wrong. I would never have your courage. I don't even know how to dance. It's me. I—I wouldn't like being on a stage stared at by men." She shivered as if the idea made her skin ripple.

"It's totally impersonal," I said, softening my tone. "It's just an act. Men are voyeurs. They don't get to touch. They come out without their wives, if they're married, and fantasize about the dancers. We're entertainment."

She hugged herself. "I think it's gross."

"What is? Dancing?"

"No, the men." She looked at me and there was something hauntingly beautiful about her almond eyes. She reached out her hand and caressed my arm. "You are so brave."

Brave? Me? "You must be thinking of someone else." I laughed nervously. "I'm not at all like that. In fact, I'm scared most of the time. I just refuse to let others see."

"You're lucky you can do that," she said softly.

I had a fleeting thought that she might be gay. She looked so fragile. I wanted to tell her she was the lucky one. I knew a lesbian couple back in California. Both were masculine and heavy. Not like Tamara, who reminded me of a black swan.

I thought of her that night while making love to Brady. When we finished, he slid off my sweat-soaked body. "Wow, baby, you were hot tonight. Whatever it was, remember it for next time." He grabbed his beer from the bedside table and finished it off. He lay back and stared dreamily up at the ceiling.

"Do you know what turns me on?" he said after a drawn out silence. "Man's most erotic dream."

"Oh? Tell me more."

"Two women making it." A slow grin widened. "With me watching."

The idea wasn't new to me. I'd met a few daring couples at the clubs where I danced. One girl told me about her adventures with another girl and her boyfriend. Johnny would have been shocked, if the idea was ever brought up. He would have looked at the suggestion the same way he looked at dancing. I found Brady's words stimulating. That night I dreamt about Tamara.

CHAPTER 14

The Zodiac Club with its live bands, crowded dance floor, and free-flowing drinks was what I needed to unwind after a five-to-nine shift at the Palace on a Friday night. Accepting the invitation from two of the other girls I worked with that night was better than sitting at Moe's waiting until Brady got off work. At the Zodiac, there was always a bunch of good-looking guys who wanted to dance. I envied the girls who didn't have to get up early for a day job.

I downed my second scotch, ordered a third, and sipped it while I threaded my way through the crowd looking for familiar faces. Almost everyone wore tight mini-skirts and revealing tops. I spotted one girl I hadn't expected to see. Dani, the go-go dancer at my housewarming party with Melanie. Tonight her pixie face looked exotic under stage makeup. Her dark curls were piled on her head like they had been sprayed on by an artist. I reached her side, but she was too busy chatting with another girl to notice. I tapped her shoulder.

She recognized me right away. "Erin? That's you, isn't it? Damn, can't believe I remembered your name." She burst into bubbling laughter. "Jeez, small world, isn't it? How's Melanie? Girl, haven't seen that bitch in ages."

"Splitsville to Alaska, can you believe?"

"No kidding? Alaska? Wow. Hey, girl, you take my advice and call that agent?"

"Yeah, I did. Thanks for the tip."

"Hope he didn't screw you like he did me. Where're you working now?"

"A few different places. Nothing regular yet."

"You know I can get you a sweet job. Real steady, too. I'll tell Tony to hire you. He's the big boss. He's always looking for girls."

"Tony?"

"Tony Corelli. You heard of him? Probably so, huh? Everybody knows ol' Tony." She giggled. "He runs the clubs on Locust Street."

Tony Corelli. Yeah, I remembered him all right. *Shit.* I remembered the calculating look in Corelli's eyes as he watched me dance in his bedroom, and then what happened afterward that I wished now hadn't happened. Carl's words came back to me, and the warning he gave. *The girls had to do whatever they were told or else.* Or else, what?

"I've heard of him," I said. "That's who you work for?"

"Yeah, I'm still at the Foxy Lady. My boyfriend, Bix, is the bartender." Her words came out too fast, and I noticed her eyes were dilated. She leaned into me. "Listen, I got to go, but if you want, I'll give your name to Tony or Bix."

"Thanks, but I'm fine on my own."

"Gee, I'm glad to see you. I never get around the old crowd anymore. It's really cool you're here. Hey, there's Bix now. Are you sure about a job? I could introduce you."

"No, really, but thanks."

She took off with an unsteady gait, turned, and gave

me a three-finger wave and a wide grin. She met the guy she called Bix halfway as he strode through the crowd, knocking against people like they were chess pieces blocking his way. His plastic smile melted into a frown when he glanced over her shoulder at me. He took Dani's arm with a vise-like grip, or that's what it looked like. His face darkened, and he whispered something in her ear.

I decided I didn't like Bix and wondered what happened to the guy she was with at the party. He seemed nice.

What was his name? Started with a M. Marty?

I realized with a start that Marty stood in my line of sight. Talk about coincidence. He was surrounded by women.

I'd forgotten how good looking he was, or maybe I hadn't paid that much attention to him at the party. With his black curly hair, sensuous mouth, and bedroom dark eyes, he stood out from the dancers.

As I approached, I heard him say. "If that bastard touches Dani one more time, I'll kill him."

"Next time, he might kill her," one girl said.

Another nodded in agreement.

I glanced back at Dani who was being led outside.

"Isn't that her boyfriend?" I asked.

He turned to me in surprise. "Yeah, Bix." He tilted his head. "You look familiar. Have we met before?" He grinned. "That's not a line. We really have met, haven't we?"

I laughed. "Yes, seems like years ago. I'd just moved in with Melanie."

His eyes brightened. "I remember now. How is Melanie?"

"Moved to Alaska with her boyfriend." I was more interested in talking about Dani. "It's good seeing you and Dani again. I thought…I mean, at the party the two of you looked close."

A shadow dimmed his eyes for a second. "Nah, we're just friends. She's hung up on Bix."

Did Marty think no one could see how he really felt about Dani? To me it looked obvious. I didn't pursue it. "I've been using the agent she told me about."

His smile was genuine. "So you're dancing, too?"

"I just finished at the Palace," I said.

"If you're looking for someplace steady, stay off Locust Street. That's my free advice for the night." He glanced over my shoulder then back at me. "Have you checked out Dreamscape in Center City? I hear they're looking for more dancers, and they treat their girls pretty fair. That's why most of them stay."

"So it's not like Locust Street?"

"Nah, that place is run by cops. Can't get more protected than that."

"Cops? Are you serious?"

"Actually, it works well. These guys used to work Vice. Now they can run the place however they want. Who's going to stop them?"

"You don't make it sound much different than Locust Street," I said.

"Didn't mean it that way. They protect their girls. Don't let them get into trouble. They get a good clientele. You wouldn't go wrong working for them."

"Is that where you work?"

"Uh-uh. That place don't need bouncers on account of the cop bartender. I work on Locust at the Foxy Lady, same as Dani and Bix."

"How do you know Dreamscape?" I asked.

He grinned. "I know most of the clubs around town. I party with the girls."

"Maybe I'll check it out."

He gave me an address and supplied directions.

❧❧❧

What Marty had told me about the cops running Dreamscape made me put off going there for a couple of weeks. Did they check criminal records before hiring dancers? I hadn't committed any crimes outside of using a stolen credit card, and I hadn't been convicted yet.

I did like the idea of having a regular gig instead of being sent to a new bar every few weeks. I ruled out Locust Street, though. I thought about Tony Corelli, who sounded like nothing more than a glorified pimp. I meant to keep my promise to Carl.

My pressing reason for working two jobs had to do with my up-coming court date. Kramer called more frequently. I hadn't finished paying him off. Weekend work helped, but it still wasn't enough.

"You don't want to go to jail," Kramer told me during our last appointment in his office. "That's what you could be facing."

"But you said you cut a deal with the prosecutor."

"That's right, but the judge has to approve it. We need to show that you are an upstanding citizen with verifiable employment. Getting the hospital job was smart, but it's only a beginning. Brady tells me you have a second job as well?"

I didn't want him to know I danced in a bar. I said, "I'm in show business."

He looked down at his notes and drummed his desk. Finally, he looked up. "Don't lose the hospital job."

I wondered how he thought I could pay rent, court fees, and his bill from a secretary's pay. But I kept my mouth shut.

"I would help," Brady said later that afternoon as he

dressed for work. "But I'm strapped for cash."

"It's okay," I said. "If I have to work two or three jobs, so be it."

☙☜☙

I took the bus early one Saturday evening to Dreamscape. The nightclub was in a two-story building in the middle of a narrow street in Center City. The bar was oval-shaped in the middle of the room with plenty of stools for customers. Small round tables lined the walls. Upstairs, the open stage faced the audience and the front door. I saw what looked to me like offices on both sides.

At five in the evening, the place was almost empty. The bartender wore black slacks and a white shirt with a slender red tie. He was tall, had a slender build, and wore his thinning amber hair combed straight back. He was washing glasses when I walked in.

"Are you Joe?" I said. "Marty from the Foxy Lady told me you'd be the one to talk to about a job."

He continued to wash and dry as he looked me over, taking his time to check out my attributes. "Foxy Lady? You worked there?"

"No. I met Marty through mutual friends." I named the clubs where I had danced.

He nodded. "Good places."

"I have a day job at a hospital," I said, "but I need a second job to supplement my income."

"What kind of hours are you looking for?"

"I get off at five during the week."

He grabbed a towel and wiped his hands. "I can use someone from five to nine. Can you do that?"

I wondered how the hell I would get here by five. The hospital's hours were rigid.

He must have seen my hesitation, because he added, "Are you sure that isn't a problem?"

"Maybe I could leave a little early from the hospital."

"Don't worry about that." His serious expression relaxed into a grin. "We don't punch clocks. We're pretty flexible as long as you put in the time. When do you want to start?"

"Soon as possible," I said. "I've got costumes, and I can dance to any kind of music."

He turned to an older man sitting at the bar. I thought he was a customer until that moment. "What do you think, Lewis? Up to you."

Lewis didn't bother standing, but from what I could see in the dim light, he had a barrel chest, thick arms, and an abundance of salt-and-pepper hair. He looked at least fifty. "What's your name, young lady?"

"Erin Matthews."

"Well, Erin, Joe and I own this place. I'm also a retired cop. Joe is still a cop. This is his second job, too. We don't get any trouble because people know who we are."

I gave a nervous laugh. "Sounds good to me. My kind of place."

"I'll let Joe explain how we run the business."

Joe smiled at me. "How did you work at the other places? You just danced?"

I shrugged. "Yes."

"You won't make very much that way. This is what we suggest. You dance a set of three. When you're done, come down to the bar. Have a drink with the customers. My rules are simple. You don't get drunk and you don't leave with a customer. I want to make that very clear. We don't run this place like Locust Street. Understand? The customer asks you what you drink, you say whiskey or scotch with a water back. What I give you is watered down whiskey that you spit back in the water. Keeps you sober."

Marty left out some details about Dreamscape. "What if I want a real drink?"

"I give you one, but you'll be drinking up your profits. If you get sloppy drunk, you're out."

I thought about this. "So basically I'll be on commission."

Joe and Lewis exchanged glances. Joe smiled. "You get salary for dancing, too."

Lewis said, "All perfectly legal. And we make sure you're safe."

"The hours you'll work are easy," Joe said. "You get paid by the hour and what you make extra is up to you."

"As long as you keep your activities inside the bar," Lewis said,

As if reading my mind, Joe said, "We don't make you do anything you don't want to do. If you don't want to get close to customers, you don't have to. Depends on whether you need the money."

I needed the money. "I'm in."

CHAPTER 15

Something happened when a seed was planted. Sometimes a flower grew—sometimes it was a weed. The idea of a ménage a trois grew in my mind like a weed, but Brady kept pouring on the water and fertilizer. I was intrigued with the thought, but Brady went further.

He tantalized me with visions that heated my overactive libido until I began to fantasize with him. The question remained to be asked. Who would be a willing partner? In my dreams, I only saw one, but I doubted she would be willing.

I couldn't fool Brady. He was good at reading my mind.

"You're thinking of someone, I can tell," he said as we lay in bed late one night. He had already aroused me, but held back, teasing me with ideas of what could happen if another joined us.

"Maybe," I said.

"Who? One of your dancer friends?"

"No. I was thinking of someone I work with at the hospital. Do you have anything against black girls?"

His breath quickened. His hand reached over and massaged my breast. "I know what I'd like to rub against dark skin with the two of you together. Black against white, I'm getting hard thinking about it."

He wasn't lying. Smiling he moved my hand away and whispered, "Not yet."

His turn to explore. I couldn't speak while his fingers found my erotic zones. Any thoughts flew out of my head. Feeling was all the sense I had left. I moaned and writhed under his manipulation, and when I thought I would explode, he stopped and took away his hand.

"Can you picture doing that to her?" he said softly.

"She would never go for the idea," I gasped.

He pulled back. "How do you know? Have you asked her?"

"Of course not. I can't just come out and ask her something like that."

His lips pressed against my ear. "Does she turn you on?"

I pictured Tamara, skin like caramel, slender body with soft curves, sensual lips and luminous eyes. My hips moved. I ached for release.

Brady continued with his hot breath on my neck. "Tell her you're attracted to her, but you've never been with a woman before. You want her to be the first. See how she reacts. You'll know if she feels the same way. If she does, you bring her here. I'll stay away until the moment is right, then I'll join you."

The picture was planted in my mind. Brady's fingers returned and I hitched a breath. "I don't think she likes men," I whispered.

Brady rose on one elbow so he could read my expression. "She's gay? You didn't tell me that."

"I'm telling you now. That's why this won't work. I'll find someone else."

"Wait now." Brady laid back, deflated, and left me throbbing and unsatisfied. "Maybe she's never had a good man. If you warmed her up, got her hot and ready, she might accept the idea of the three of us together. I know she'll enjoy the experience."

That's the male ego, I thought.

Then he began to describe what it would be like and, while I pictured the three of us together, I felt Brady lips traveling down my abdomen to the mound and, finally, to the throbbing center of my being, wet and open. Thinking of Tamara sent me over the edge faster than usual. Then he lifted his head and shifted. He plunged deep inside me. He rode me hard, punishing me with a fierce attack that only made me more excited and demanding. I met him with equal abandon, hips smacking against his, nails raking his back. He flipped me over and went deeper, harder, pumping against a sweet spot I didn't know existed, until finally I screamed with a climax so intense I didn't want to let go until our juices combined and overflowed.

When it was over and I lay spent and slick with sweat, waiting for my heart beat to slow back to normal, I glanced at his prone body next to mine. His chest heaved, his eyes were shut, a small smile quivered his lips. After a moment, he opened his eyes and turned his head toward me.

"Wow," he whispered. "I don't know what happened, but—wow. That was different." His smiled widened and his arm went around me. I snuggled against him.

Different. Yes. For a disquieting moment, I didn't think about Brady or Tamara. I could only think about Johnny. I knew how he would react to the mention of a threesome. Disgust. Anger. Anything bordering on homosexual behavior was abnormal to his way of thinking. He thought male ballerinas were sissies. He was the first, however, to discover how I responded to rough sex. It was the beginning of my own awareness of how my body reacted to stimulus. Apparently, I was still learning.

"What are you thinking?" Brady asked, interrupting my reverie.

I smiled. "How good that was. How much I love you." I snuggled closer.

"So you'll talk to your girlfriend?" he said quietly.

I stiffened slightly, then nodded and put one leg across his.

∾∾∾

The following Friday Tamara and I ate lunch at our desks, which had become our normal routine. We were alone in the secretarial pool room.

After small talk during which my mind wandered, I blurted, "I think you are the most beautiful woman I've ever known."

Her eyes widened in surprise. She stared at me for a long moment as if trying to decide how to respond. I didn't expect her answer to be, "I think you're lying."

I was quick to say, "No, I mean it. You are." I shifted my gaze to the floor. "Have you ever thought that way about another woman?"

Her voice turned cold. "What are you saying? You like women?"

I felt a chill run down my back. Had I been so completely wrong about her sexual orientation? "I've never been with a woman. Have you?"

She looked away. "Why are we talking about this?"

"I don't know." I swallowed. "I like men. I like sex. Sometimes I imagine being with you."

Her eyes widened.

I went on, "I don't want to hurt our friendship. But I don't see anything bad in feeling an attraction to another woman. Haven't you ever felt that way?"

No answer. She picked up her sandwich and I just knew that was the end of it. She'd probably never speak to me again. But before the bread reached her mouth, she stopped. The words came out so softly, I barely heard her. "What if I have?"

"Maybe we could see what it's like." My heart beat so hard she must have heard it. "Would you like to come to my apartment sometime?"

Without looking at me, she said, "When?"

I swallowed. "We can go this afternoon after work." *Before I lose my nerve, and before she changes her mind.*

Her eyes widened. "Today?"

"Why not?" I whispered.

She was breathing hard now. She looked at me straight in the eyes, and nodded.

I couldn't believe it. She'd actually agreed to come over. Wait until I told Brady.

Brady. She hadn't agreed to him. I hadn't even mentioned Brady. The pulse in my temple raced and drove heat to my cheeks. What would be Tamara's reaction? Maybe I could put him off until another time. For the first time, reality hit me. I wanted to see what it would be like to be with her. Not with Brady. Not at first.

Tamara and I couldn't look at each other the rest of the afternoon. Both of us acted like we were pouring our energy into work, but I doubt I even registered the words I transcribed.

I didn't call Brady. I thought about not calling him at all. But my telephone extension rang before we left the hospital. "Did you talk to her?"

I couldn't lie to him. "Yes."

"Well? Is she coming?"

I hesitated too long before answering. "We'll have a visitor."

"Oh, babe, that's fantastic."

"Brady, maybe you shouldn't come this time. You might scare her."

There was silence for a long moment. "What are you saying?"

"I want to make sure she's ready for this." My heart raced.

"Stop worrying. I promise not to do anything that would frighten her. Don't get cold feet on me now. If you recall, you brought it up first."

I didn't remember that part. He hung up before I could argue.

Tamara rode the bus home with me. We chatted about everything except sex, which we carefully avoided. I wanted to tell her about Brady. Warn her, at least. But there was never the right moment. I was afraid I'd spoil everything before we got started. She might pull the brake strap on the bus and run off. I'd tell her once we got there.

I played the conversation in my mind as we walked through my apartment. But somehow I still couldn't find the right words to mention my boyfriend would be joining us.

"You want a drink?" I offered. "I've got wine or beer. Scotch?"

She hugged herself, looking small and vulnerable, and shook her head.

"This is my bedroom. I put on clean sheets this morning." I was babbling. My hands shook.

Tamara smiled. "You're as nervous as I am."

"Yeah." I agreed.

She walked to the bed and we slowly took off our clothes. Her bronze body was even more beautiful than I'd imagined. She turned to me and, after hesitating only a second or two, she let me kiss her. Her lips were full and generous and sweet tasting. We kissed some more and touched each other, tentatively exploring. I almost forgot about Brady.

A nagging voice in my head told me I should have said something, warned her. But I argued with the voice. Maybe he wouldn't get there until after she left. I couldn't spoil our moment together.

I caressed her small breasts, so perfectly formed, and put my lips around her dark, hard nipples. She did the same to me, like we were performing a dance, exploring one another's body with each step.

Finally, she lay flat and spread her legs. I had a brief thought about Carl and how he had brought me to such exquisite heights. Could I do the same for Tamara?

"I want to please you," I said. "Tell me what to do."

She put her hands in my hair and guided me. "Here, and here, and here."

She began to moan with pleasure and the sound stoked a fire deep within me, bringing a surge of passion that made my skin hot with desire and the need to please her. When she moved under me and I tasted her, I felt my own climax building and I rubbed my hips against the rough sheet.

Tamara stiffened suddenly. For a moment, I thought she was ready to climax and increase the pressure. Instead, she grabbed my hair and yanked me off her. I sat up, came face to face with Brady. With an awful jolt of anguish, I turned back to Tamara. The bare, hate-filled look that screamed betrayal crushed my whole world in that instant. She screamed and scrambled backwards until she was plastered against the headboard. She pulled a sheet to cover herself.

"No!" Tamara screamed again. "No, no, no!"

"Tamara, wait!" I cried. "Listen to me."

She ripped off the sheet and dove off the bed, grabbing her clothes. Chest heaving, her face twisted in fury, she pointed a shaking finger at me. "How could you?"

I felt like the dregs at the bottom of the garbage. "I'm sorry," I whispered. "I was going to tell you, but I didn't know how."

She froze and stared at me like I had turned into a cockroach. Her voice turned cold. "You planned this? I told you I don't like men. You knew better and you lied. How could you do this to me?"

Brady didn't move. His face turned into a mask of bewilderment and indecision.

Tamara spun to face him. "Get the fuck away from me. Don't even look at me."

Tears filled her eyes as she zipped up her skirt and pulled her sweater over her head. She bent her head, hiding her tear-stained cheeks from me, and searched the floor for her shoes. She flung a scalding glare my way. "I'll never forgive you for this. Ever. I hope I never see you again."

I wanted to die.

Tamara didn't bother putting on her shoes. She picked them up and stormed out the door, slamming it behind her. I stared at the empty space where she had stood. *God, what had I just done? I destroyed a friendship. How could I ever face her at work again? Johnny was right. I was no good.*

Brady eased next to me as I sat, unable to move. "Well, that didn't work out well."

I stared at him in disbelief. His words, spoken casually, ripped into me. God! Was he that insensitive? Did he have no idea how I felt at that moment? Did he even give a shit?

I wanted to scream at him. Tell him to go away and never come back. Dammit! I should have locked the door after I'd let Tamara in. I wanted to crawl under the bed, curl up, and forget this ever happened.

Without saying a word, Brady pushed me back on the bed. I glowered at him, pushed against him, shaking my head, while tears spilled over my cheeks. Despite my resistance, he lowered his naked body on top of me. "Forget her," he growled. "You have me."

I went sort of crazy then. I fought him, slammed my fist into his chest, my nails clawed at his face. He gripped my wrists and held them down. His tongue thrust down my throat and when I stopped struggling, he let go and his fingers massaged the spot Tamara never had a chance to find with her lips. I squeezed my legs shut, but he forced them open. He dipped one finger, two fingers, three inside me. I scrapped my nails down his back. He smothered my sobs with his tongue and teeth. I just wanted to forget what happened. I was bad. I was evil. I was the devil.

When I shut my eyes, I saw Johnny's face. His triumphant grin was a cruel taunt. His lips moved. With sudden clarity, I knew the truth. Johnny hadn't died from my hand. He was alive. Whatever that meant, I couldn't think. I didn't want to think anymore.

"Fuck me. Hard. Hurt me!" I screamed. "Deep and hard."

Brady's punishing strokes penetrated deep inside me until I crashed over the edge, and Johnny's laughter faded into the night.

CHAPTER 16

I rode the bus to Center City Monday night, determined to put the day's nightmare behind me. My watch showed five-twenty when I hopped off at the corner of Chestnut and Seventeenth. The August breeze warmed me as I found the narrow, brick-paved street half a block away and turned into it. It looked more like an alley to me, but I continued to walk until I reached the door to Dreamscape.

My excitement rose as I looked up at the stage that was built into the second floor. Background music played a prelude to the show that would soon follow, the show in which I would play a part. Dreamscape had a different atmosphere from the other bars I'd worked. From my first step inside, I felt like I'd come home.

The nod that greeted me belonged to Joe, the bartender. He didn't complain that I was half an hour late, instead asked how my day had been. I lied because I didn't want to think about the worst day of my life since that awful evening.

Tamara had moved her work to another desk on the other side of the room, refused my apologies, and wouldn't talk to me. I had wrecked our friendship in the most humiliating way possible. My day job was now a hellhole where I had to listen to tapes dictated by psychologists who described even more aberrant behavior than my own.

But I would leave all that behind when I entered this world of make-believe. The audience didn't give a crap about how I got there, only how I could entertain them. They didn't care who I was or what I had done before.

I sat at the bar and asked Joe for a scotch and water.

Joe reached for a short glass. "Need a shot of courage?"

I nodded. "First nights are always the hardest."

"You'll get over it," Joe said. "Maggie's upstairs. She's been around the longest. She knows you're here."

No sooner had he spoken than I heard a noise behind me and turned to see a dancer prance down the stairs wearing a red fringed bikini. Her straight brown hair reached her waist and bangs grazed her eyebrows. Without a word she sat down on the stool next to me.

Joe poured her a glass of ginger ale over ice. "Meet the new girl, Maggie. Can you show Erin around?"

Maggie gave me a bored stare. "Sure." She swallowed half her drink and slid off the stool. "Where's your costume?"

I opened my canvas bag so she could see inside.

She headed for the stairs, drink in hand. "Come with me. Dressing room's upstairs."

I followed her. "Are we the only dancers tonight?"

"Rachel should be here. Others come in around nine, about the time you leave. I work the whole shift and get here early so I can relax a little before the crowd barges in." She leaned forward and lowered her voice. "Get in a few tokes. Can't talk to some of these jerks unless I'm high."

"You smoke pot here?" I couldn't keep the surprise out of my voice.

"Shhhh. I don't drink the real stuff here so when I puff my own poison, they look the other way."

The dressing room behind the stage didn't look much different from those in other clubs. Narrow and rectangular, with a long mirror running above the counter, clothes hooks on the wall at the opposite end. This one had a real door instead of a curtain. Classy.

Maggie lifted a cigarette out of a pack she pulled from her bikini top and lit up. "Joe tell you about sitting downstairs after your set?"

"Yeah, what am I supposed to do? How do I get them to buy me drinks?"

She gave me a pitying look. "Honey, you don't got to do nothing. They see a girl dance, they figure they're lucky if they get a chance to feel one up. Just get them talking about themselves. Keeps 'em too busy to mess with you."

I laughed. "That really works?"

"Up to you. Men's egos always need stroking. Better that than their body parts." She grinned.

A second girl entered the dressing room. Glossy black curls piled atop her head made her slim figure look tall. She towered over me with the help of pink stilettos. She shook off a tan trench coat to reveal a one-piece leotard of pink silk that showed more skin on her dancer's body than either Maggie or I showed in our bikini costumes. Black net stockings covered shapely legs.

"Hey, Maggie, what's up?" the girl in pink said.

"I'm Erin," I said, not waiting for Maggie to introduce us. I assumed she was Rachel, the other dancer Maggie mentioned.

She looked at me like I was standing in her way. I backed away so she could have the mirror while I quickly changed into my costume.

She studied her flawless skin in the mirror. "Where'd you dance before?"

I shrugged like this was old hat to me. "The usual. Kit Kats, Mod Girls, the Palace—"

She interrupted, "They're okay, but they just dance over there."

"Have you worked here long?" I asked.

Rachel rolled her eyes. "Too long. But next year? Vegas, baby."

Maggie stood by the door. "See, Erin? Bitch here thinks she's too good for us."

"Now, Mag, no names. I am a professional...dancer."

Maggie drew on her cig. "She thinks the rest of us are sluts."

If it wasn't for the teasing tone, I might have expected a fight.

Rachel grinned. "Honey, we're all sluts. Deny it and you're lying."

"Hell, I'm damn proud of it." Maggie punctuated her words with a pelvic thrust and laughed out loud.

I squeezed between them and peered in the mirror. My lipstick needed another glossy coat, and I didn't know what to do about my hair. Gravity and humidity had won out over the curls, and my hair looked like a brown waterfall.

Not in a good way either.

I felt Rachel's eyes on me and looked at her reflection in the mirror. "Any suggestions?"

"Honey, I have the most luscious hair stylist in the city. Any time you want a makeover, he's the guy. Don't even have to go to his salon. He'll come to your residence. But don't get any ideas. At night he's on the prowl and it's not for girls, if you know what I mean."

That didn't matter to me. "How much does he charge?"

"For a style? Twenty. But you need some color, honey. Blonde or red, I'd say. Something that'll make you stand out."

Rachel lifted the hair off my neck and swirled it high on my head. A few bobby pins in the right places and already I saw improvement. A makeover was just what I needed.

"You're on, kid," Maggie said, when the music volume turned to loud.

I shook off my initial jitters before I stepped out on that stage. After all, Joe or Lewis hadn't yet seen me dance. I went through the motions, keeping with the beat of the music. I kept eye contact with the men downstairs, something I'd learned during my apprenticeship.

I watched from the sidelines as the others followed me. I wanted to see my competition. I knew I was a better dancer than Maggie, who two-stepped across the stage and two-stepped back. Maggie had her admirers, though. I heard a few clapping hands when she trotted off stage.

On the other hand, I was a long way from coming close to the brilliance of Rachel's performance, which stirred up the few in the audience who'd fallen asleep watching Maggie.

I took my turn next and got the newbie attention I knew to expect. Shyness overcame me when I went downstairs and found a stool at the bar. To gain courage, I ordered a scotch and water. Joe fixed the drink, but the look on his face when he set the glass in front of me came as a warning.

I saw Maggie sitting across from me in deep conversation with an older man, and she drank as quickly as the man could add up his tab

Rachel bounced from one customer to another until

she found deep pockets in a corner. Last I looked she was practically in his lap.

I scanned the faces around me looking for a mark and found instead a pimply-faced kid, who couldn't have been twenty-one, staring at me. He dropped his gaze and took a large gulp of his Coke, before venturing another look my way. I smiled at him. Too young to be in here, I wanted to tell him.

Joe put his hand on my arm as I started to get up. "Don't bother with the kid. He doesn't have any money. Comes here, orders a Coke, and just looks."

"Okay."

"Try the guy with the orange shirt."

I nodded, went over to Joe's customer, and sat next to him.

He had a large, chunky body, with muscled bulges under his jacket. Short sandy hair combed to the side. A round face with small eyes, a thin mouth and a scar over his left eyebrow sat atop a thick neck.

I hadn't the least idea of what to say. In my sweetest voice, I winged it. "Hi. Do you come here often?" I didn't know the hard sell, whatever that was. I played the scene using instinct and tact.

"Often enough." He looked me over without being too intrusive. "Your first night?"

"Is it that obvious?" I looked right into his eyes and gave him a playful wink.

He gave me an appraising look. "I thought I knew all the girls. I'm Charley."

"Erin, and I'm just breaking in." I glanced down, as if embarrassed, then raised my eyes to meet his again. I kept my hands on top of the bar. "Guess you can tell that already."

"You're all right. Can I buy your first drink, Erin?"

It was that simple. Keep up the conversation. Show

some interest in the man. Flirt a little. I relaxed a bit.

Charley waved Joe over. "The real stuff, Joe. No ginger ale or that cheap watered down shit."

Joe didn't miss a beat. "Sure, Charley. I wouldn't cheat you."

What the hell? I was going to drink real scotch all night? What happened to Joe's lecture? Good thing I could hold my liquor, thanks to Johnny and the many hours we spent in bars. Crap, who was this guy? A good customer or a bad cop? I decided it might be best to treat him like he was made of gold.

"You ever work in a place like this?" Charley asked.

"All stages look the same after a while," I said, not rising to the bait. "So do the faces."

He looked amused. "Do you know who I am?"

"You're Charley. What else do I need to know?"

"That depends," he said.

Joe set a fresh scotch and water in front of me and took Charley's money.

I downed the drink in one long swallow. "Can I have another?"

I had to give the man credit. He didn't blink or change expression, but waved to Joe again. "Do her again."

Joe went through the motions without glancing my way until he put the drink in front of me. I thought I caught a smirk before he walked away.

I turned back to Charley. "What do I need to know about you, Charley?"

He shrugged. "If you're around long enough, you'll find out." He glanced up to the second floor. "Do you know what happens in the rooms upstairs?"

I faked innocence. "What rooms?"

"Don't act stupid, Erin, it doesn't become you."

I felt my neck hairs quiver. "I have never been in those rooms. And you don't know me."

He gave me a wry smile that only made me more nervous. I raised my half empty glass.

He put a restraining hand on my arm. "Take it easy. You'll last longer."

I wasn't sure what he meant by that remark, but I met his eyes and took a long swallow to finish off my drink. "I plan to last as long as it takes."

He smiled. We seemed to have reached an understanding. About what, I still had no idea, but Charley bought most of my drinks that night, and I didn't have to find out what went on in the rooms upstairs. When Charley finally left, I looked around to see if the kid had hung around. I was curious, not interested. But he'd left, replaced by someone older.

I stayed until almost ten. Joe seemed pleased with me. I didn't see Lewis at all that night and later Maggie told me he came in only occasionally. The night was early enough that I could catch the bus home. I slipped my street clothes on over my costume and breathed in the night air.

The kid was standing across the street opposite the door. He smiled when he saw me and approached without hesitation.

I thought about going back inside and asking Joe what else he knew about him. But the kid seemed okay. I noticed he was carrying a paper cup from one of the take-out places.

"You were the best dancer up there," the kid said.

"Thanks, but Rachel is much better."

"No, you're wrong." The kid spoke in earnest. "You have something she'll never have."

"Oh? What is that?"

"Heart. And the guys in there? If they can't see that,

they're really dumb. I've seen lots of dancers. I know what I'm talking about."

Jeez, he's seen a lot of dancers? How does he get into these places?

"I appreciate that." I turned up the street toward Seventeenth.

"Watch out for that guy you were sitting with."

I frowned. "Who?"

"That guy Charley. He's not a nice man."

"And you know him from where?"

"I seen him before. He manages another club." He held out the paper cup. "I bought you this. Thought you might need some coffee when you were done. It's still hot. I didn't know if you took cream or sugar so I told them black."

Was this kid for real? "That's nice of you. What's your name?"

"Ray. Hope you like coffee."

"Love it, and you guessed right." I took the steaming cup and sipped gingerly. Too late I wondered if he'd mixed in anything else, but it tasted right. I continued walking toward the end of the street, which seemed emptier than before.

"Where are you going now?" he asked.

"Bus stop. It's been a long day. I work two jobs."

"You shouldn't have to do that. It's too much." His protest came out in a high-pitched whine. "I'll walk with you. It's not safe for ladies to walk alone out here."

My stomach tightened. Who *was* this kid? I didn't want him following me home.

"You don't have to, Ray. It's a short walk to the bus stop and I'm used to going home this time of night."

I stepped up my pace. Too late to run back inside Dreamscape. I had already reached the main street. Besides, I told myself, he hadn't done anything wrong. Yet.

But this pimply-faced kid was starting to give me the creeps. He should be at home watching television or talking on the phone with a girl his own age. And why was he warning me about Charley?

I breathed easier when we came to the intersection. All kinds of traffic sped past, and I thought I saw a bus coming, still several blocks away. I walked quickly to the bus stop, thinking Ray would finally give up. But no, he'd followed me. I gave him a thin smile and drained the cup.

"I'll take that," he said before I could find a receptacle.

"Sure, thanks." I handed it to him. He didn't move.

The bus neared, and I stepped toward the curb. When I looked back, Ray was gazing lovingly at the lipstick mark I had left on the cup.

CHAPTER 17

The Zodiac Club became my stopping off place during the week when I worked the early shift at Dreamscape. Between the hospital and Dreamscape I was able to stash away a bundle for the attorney each week, pay rent, and treat myself to a few nice clothes. As long as Kramer got his money, he promised I had nothing to worry about. My record would get expunged as long I made my payments to him on time.

The club gave me something I didn't get at work or with Brady. I could dance any way I wanted without worrying about getting drinks off customers afterward. Nobody looked down at the way I danced, not like Johnny would if he showed up one day. I couldn't deny the possibility of that happening. But by now the fear that Johnny would reappear, either in print or in person, became the sliver that wouldn't go away, but stuck under my skin without the constant pain.

I flirted like crazy and danced dirty. To hell with anyone who might object. Not that anyone did. I was a free spirit. By the time I got home, I was ready to toss back a nightcap and be asleep by the time Brady got off work. Usually I made it on time to my day job the following morning.

I met up with other dancers I had worked with in the past and made a few new friends. Most of the time, I hung out with regulars like Marty and Dani from the Foxy Lady. I didn't like Dani's boyfriend, Bix, the bartender at their club. He came off loud and obnoxious most of the time.

I could never figure what she saw in him. Dani reminded me of my old self, before I met Johnny. Young, insecure, and vulnerable. Not hard enough yet for the business, but she put on a good act. I rarely saw her when she wasn't laughing and dancing.

Until one night I found her crying in the ladies room.

She was wearing a sheer top over a sequined bra and short shorts and had kicked off her high heels. As I approached her, I saw the bruises on her arms. When she turned I saw the black eye.

"Shit, Dani, did Bix do this?"

She started at the sound of my voice and swiped at her face. "Erin, thank God, it's you. Don't tell Bix you saw me. Please?"

"I won't," I said. "But, sweetie, you can't let him get away with hurting you."

"He didn't mean to," she said. "He just lost his temper."

I'd heard that before. "Yeah, and next time he might kill you."

She bit her lip. "It hurts. I'm scared to go back out. What should I do?"

"You could file charges against him. Have him arrested." I knew better, of course. No one who danced on Locust Street ever went to the cops, unless they were bleeding to death.

Her eyes widened. "I can't do that. He'd kill me. If he didn't, my boss would."

Her boss would protect the guy who hurt her? That really steamed me. "Who's your boss?"

"Tony Corelli. Nobody crosses him. Nobody."

I remembered now that she had mentioned him before. The Italian mob guy who owned Foxy Lady and a few others. The guy who had "auditioned" me when I first came to town.

I picked up Dani's purse from the floor where she had dropped it and handed it to her. "You need to stay out of sight for a couple of days. I have plenty of room at my apartment. You can hide out there."

For a moment, I saw a hopeful light in her eyes. Then they dimmed. "That would just make Bix more angry."

"He doesn't know where I live. Please, Dani, you can't go back out there."

She stood and went to the sink. As she splashed water on her face, I saw small angry red circles on her back under her sheer top.

I lifted the material. "Jesus. These are cigarettes burns."

She straightened suddenly. She turned toward me and I saw old scar tissue on her stomach.

"Dani, you've got to get away from him. A man who does this doesn't know how to love a woman."

She shook her head wearily. "I work with Bix. He's the bartender. If I ran away, I wouldn't have a job or money or anything." She put a restraining hand on my arm. "He gets jealous if I smile at a man unless I'm working. Worse, if I dance with someone. But he'll be over it by morning. He never stays mad for long."

I took both of her hands in mine and made her look at me. "Listen. I've been through the same thing you have. I've just left my ol' man because he thought he could control me. I know what it's like. We'd be eating at a restaurant and if I happened to look up and see a man standing in front of me, he'd accused me of flirting. He would time me when I went to the store for him. If I took longer than he thought necessary then I must have been meeting someone. Same as when I was waitressing and I didn't come out the second the restaurant closed. It's a rotten way of life, Dani. But I left him and you could do the same. I'll help you."

She looked hopeful. "Do you really think so?"

"Yes, I know you can. Talk to Joe, my boss at Dreamscape. He's a cop. He'll make sure Bix won't bother you again. He'll even give you a job so you don't have to work around Bix."

"He would do that?"

"Yes, Dani. Trust me. Come stay with me. I can use a roommate since Melanie left." I saw fear and hope in her eyes. I smiled encouragement. "I'll help you, Dani. You have lots of friends who care about you. They'll all help. We just want to see you safe."

On impulse, I reached into my bra where I kept cash and drew out a bundle. I peeled off three twenties.

"Do you have a pen and paper with you?"

She shook her head.

"Wait here."

I slipped out the door and went to the bar and snagged a napkin. I borrowed a pen from a waitress.

Back in the ladies room, I wrote down my address and phone number. I gave Dani both the money and the napkin.

"The money will get you to my apartment. That's the address on the napkin. If you can't make it there or need to leave town, here's enough cash to get you a train or bus ticket. Promise me you'll do something for yourself for a change."

Tears filled her eyes as she took the bundle. She gave a little nod.

When she walked back out to the bar, I wondered if she would take my advice, or if I would ever see her again.

CHAPTER 18

Paul Lincoln arrived at my apartment on a Friday afternoon two weeks later. I'd taken the day off from the hospital to see Kramer, but the lawyer rescheduled to Saturday morning at ten. Instead of going back to work, I called the number that Rachel had given me.

True to Rachel's description, the hairdresser could have been a male model. He brought all his paraphernalia in a huge duffel bag. I felt doomed when I saw all the shit he brought.

He positioned a stool in the kitchen and told me to sit. He spread the contents of his bag along the counter, then turned to me, comb in one hand, scissors in the other. He immediately set both down and lifted my straight brown hair with one hand. "This has got to go, darling."

"What?" I said, alarmed. "My hair?"

"No, you silly goose, the color. You're an entertainer. You must look like one. Not like a country mouse. Once I'm done, nobody will recognize you."

He thought I looked mousy? Not very flattering, but what if he was right about people not recognizing me? Like Johnny. Might be what I needed.

"You know I'm right, darling," Paul continued. "But

don't worry. Paul is going to fix you up. I have just the
color to match your complexion. I brought makeup as
well. You really do have beautiful eyes, love, but who
could tell unless you highlight them. Leave your appearance in my very capable hands, and when I'm done, you
won't know yourself."

Too bad hair color and make up couldn't camouflage
my past. It couldn't forgive what I'd done to Johnny. Or
to Tamara.

"I hope what I'm paying you is worth the benefits. I
have pressing debts to pay." I had to bring Kramer the
rest of what I owed. It amounted to far more than what I
had socked away. He had been able to keep me out of
jail, but the hearing was set for next week and Kramer
wouldn't represent me without his fee.

Paul crooked his head to look at me. "Darling, when
I'm done with you, Dreamscape's customers will fall all
over each other for the privilege of buying you those fifty
or hundred dollar bottles of champagne. What you do afterward is strictly up to you. Just remember, the more you
do, the more they tip." He gave a sly grin. "Tips you
don't have to report to Joe or Lewis."

The thought of what went on in the shadowy corner
tables or learning what happened in the private rooms
upstairs sent a pang of discomfort to my stomach, but I
didn't let on to Paul. I would force myself to do whatever
I had to do to make enough for Kramer.

Four hours later, Paul pronounced me ready for the
evening's performance. He offered me a hand mirror, but
I chose the full length one on my bedroom door instead.
My head felt heavy, my eyes stung from all the chemicals
that had blistered my skin and scented the air.

I stepped in front of the mirror, not knowing what to
expect. I gasped. I stared. I hardly recognized the reflection.

The color of my hair nearly blinded me. Sparkling Sherry, Paul used. That shade of red no one would find natural. Large burgundy spools were swept up away from my face and cascaded from the top of my head to the nape of my neck. Arched eyebrows and thick black lashes brought out the flecks of gold in my tortoise shell irises—Paul's words, not mine. My cheek bones looked higher than natural and were brushed with a light shade of peach. My lips were fuller and painted a bright coral.

I turned to Paul. "I hope you're coming over every night. I could never copy this look."

He had the good sense to laugh. "Darling, that's why you pay me the big bucks. Call me when you need me again." He started collecting his tools. "You are off to work, and I have a date with a very rich client who blesses me with extraordinary jewelry when I let him take me out on the town."

He raised his right hand to show off a huge diamond-encrusted emerald ring. On his left wrist was a gold bracelet. I crossed his palm with three tens.

"You be careful, Paul," I admonished. "Some gifts have thorns."

He lifted my chin and air kissed me. "Same warning back at you, princess. Work your customers in Dreamscape and never take your business home. I learned that the hard way. I keep telling myself that someday, Hollywood will call, and I'll be gone. The same applies to you, fancy dancer."

I watched him leave then went into the bedroom to collect my dance costumes. I slipped on a mini-sundress and paused before the mirror to study myself once again, this time with more critical eyes. I searched for the old Erin, but all traces of her seemed to have disappeared. The eyes that batted lashes so long they seemed fake, sparkled not with gold flakes, as Paul proclaimed, but with slivers of steel hard enough to pierce through lies and bullshit. The painted, curved mouth pursed a kiss.

I tossed my head—not enough to disturb the hair-do—but enough of a fuck-you-world gesture that made me feel stronger than the girl who'd run away from a nightmare.

I wondered how Brady would react. Would he see that I wasn't the same girl who bent to his every wish and desire?

Who are you, kidding, Erin? A new look? You'll never change the past that made you what you are.

No, I'm different. See that face in the mirror? See that strength, that courage?

To my horror, a tear squeezed through and threatened the artful mask. I blinked before the destructive emotion destroyed Paul's artistic brush strokes. Before I let myself become vulnerable again, I swept up my dancing clothes, shoved them in my bag and rushed out the door.

Thirty minutes later I arrived at the bar. As always, Joe glanced up when I came through the door, but this time he did a double take. I pretended not to notice. I felt his gaze follow me as I swept past. Maggie was sitting on a stool near the stairs. She almost fell over backward when she saw me. Ten seconds later she captured me in the dressing room.

"Shit, girl. What happened to you?"

I forced a grin and exchanged my sundress for the costume I'd put together that morning. This one had more sequins and beads than fringe. High cut bottom, low cut top.

"You should try Rachel's hairdresser sometime," I said.

"He did that?" Maggie couldn't stop staring at my hair. "Out of sight. Not my style, but it sure looks groovy on you. You're working until closing tonight, aren't you?"

I nodded. I'd switched my schedule to full time on Friday and Saturday nights, knowing I could sleep in the next day.

"A few girls I know are coming to my place tonight. You're welcome to come along."

"Far out," I said.

I had a brief thought about Brady, but dismissed him. He still had his own apartment over the bar and, though he had a key to mine and kept clothes in my closet and showed up most nights, I wasn't changing my life for him. My more urgent concern was keeping my appointment with Kramer. But I could meet him without sleep as long as I brought the money I owed.

Rachel burst in at her usual last minute arrival time. She cast a glance in my direction. "Good, you saw Paul. About time. He's as good as I said, isn't he?" She stopped and took a closer look. "Good look for you. Like it?"

"Hell, yeah," I said.

"I heard Max Factor in Hollywood puts out feelers. I doubt Paul will be with us for long."

I groaned. If Paul left, how would I ever find anyone to replace him?

The volume of the music rose. Maggie took her cue and left the dressing room for the stage.

I picked out my music on the jukebox and psyched myself up for the show. By the time Maggie finished her set, my hands shook and my mind raced. I took a deep breath and stepped out on stage, light-headed despite the bouncing curls.

The faces of the men who filled the barstools were a blur, but I smiled down at them, licked my lips slowly as the first drum beat played to "Hang on Sloopy." My feet and hips moved in sync with the rhythm. I knew how to translate the words to sexy as my hands moved down my body. The music swelled and I turned to my audience and beckoned them to *Come on!* The music and my hips became more frenetic to "Shake It, Shake It, Shake It," as I danced to every man at the bar. The dance became personal between audience and me. I knew the moment we connected. When the music stopped, all the faces were looking up at the stage. I ended the set with Led Zeppelin's "Whole Lotta Love." I really turned loose on that one.

I didn't expect applause or whistles. Dreamscape wasn't that kind of joint. The men usually showed their admiration by the number of drinks they bought between sets. If I turned them on and handled them right when I came downstairs, I controlled the action. What I first noticed was the way they reacted to the dance. I recognized a few of the regulars, some of them could be cool. But tonight, I needed to see them for what they were, some woman's cheating husband or boyfriend looking to get their rocks off, or a lonely soul craving for someone to listen and understand, and willing to pay top dollar for the privilege. I played the part, adjusting to each man's fantasy. I couldn't afford to waste Paul's handiwork by ignoring even one who bought me a drink.

When Rachel's favorite customer chose me, her blue eyes turned cold as icicles. Bart wasn't anything to look at—short, thin and bald—but his money was green and plentiful. I felt bad for Rachel, but I couldn't turn him down. Joe would have fired me if I did. Besides, I needed the money more than she did.

Bart ordered his usual bottle of champagne, and we sat in a shadowy corner booth. After an awkward attempt at conversation, he unzipped his fly. I hid my initial revulsion as he put my hand on his cock. I felt Rachel's eyes on us and felt the heat rush to my cheeks. I wished she was sitting here instead of me. I made myself remember Tamara and told myself this was my punishment, the knowing I was capable of anything.

Bart groaned and I realized that I was stroking and pulling on his cock. I withdrew my hand.

"You better order us another bottle, sweetheart," I whispered into his ear.

He tried to slip his hand between my legs but I moved out of his reach. He made a frantic gesture to Joe, who promptly brought another bottle and two fresh glasses. I took a sip of the wine and ginger ale mix that passed for champagne, and let him guide my hand back to his lap. I swung one leg over his to give him better access. His eager finger felt rough. I gritted my teeth and tried to smile, but Bart didn't seem to notice. He grabbed a napkin and covered his cock, grunting as he came. Finished, he slipped me some bills which I stuffed inside my bra. I left the booth after making sure he paid Joe.

I'd just become a whore in my eyes. Did Rachel go through this every time? If this went on in the booths, I wondered what happened in the rooms upstairs. A customer would have to pay a lot more than Bart to ever get me to accompany him to a room.

I sat at the bar and ordered a scotch on the rocks. I figured I deserved it after what I went through for two fifty dollar bottles. My plan was to drink enough the rest of the night so I would sleep through until morning without the usual nightmares. Not only did I have to contend with Johnny coming back to haunt my sleep, but now I had Tamara, and I supposed Rachel would follow.

Of course, getting drunk would mean seeing Kramer while suffering a hangover. So what?

"You're up," Joe said, setting the drink in front of me.

I tossed the highball down, felt the warmth settle in my stomach, and stood. All my anger and frustration played out as I danced the last two sessions. The men I sat with between sets expected the same treatment they'd seen me give Bart. Since they weren't willing to buy the bottle, I wasn't willing to put out what they wanted. They just got the tease, but that still paid off plenty.

At the end of the night, Rachel cornered me in the dressing room. Her lips curled into a snarl. "Bart is mine."

"He's a customer," I said, trying to remain calm. "Not my fault, Rachel. He told Joe he wanted me. You want me to say *no* to Joe?"

"You seduced him. That's why he asked for you."

"How?"

"The way you danced."

"Oh come on, Rachel. You dance better than I do."

Rachel stammered something I couldn't understand, and finally said, "You flirted with him."

I shook my head. "I'm the new girl. Men, they like variety. He'll be asking for you next time."

I left her to pack her stuff, while I pulled on jeans and a T-shirt. I reached inside my sequined bra and felt the money. With my back to Rachel, I withdrew the twenties and counted five of them. No wonder she was pissed. I stuffed the bills back.

Maggie said she'd meet me outside, but when I went out the door it was Ray, the kid at the bar from my first night.

"You worked late tonight." His tone was accusing.

"It's a weekend, Ray, and I have a ride," I told him.

He looked disappointed. "You're not taking the bus?"

"Not this time."

"Oh." He stared at the ground for a moment then

brightened as he pulled something of his pocket. "I saved this to remind me of our first walk." He showed me the torn piece of the coffee cup from the other night. The piece that had my lipstick smeared on it.

"You know what I'd really like?" he said softly, staring at the ground. "A pair of your panties. One you've worn."

"What?" I couldn't believe what I'd heard. "No. What's the hell's the matter with you?"

"I'm not a pervert," he whined. "I just want something that's been close to you."

"That's sick, Ray. I'm not giving you my panties."

A cab took up the space in the dark street, motor running. A minute later, Maggie danced out of the bar. I saw Ray slink back out of sight.

I smelled the marijuana smoke before I saw the joint cupped in Maggie's hands. I was glad she invited me. I hadn't drunk enough, but now I could get high instead.

Maggie waved at me. "Come on, this is our ride."

"Is Rachel coming?" I asked, hoping for another chance to soothe hurt feelings.

"Nope," Maggie said. "Not invited. She never comes anyway. Come on, let's get out of here."

Maggie lived on the first floor of a row house not far from my apartment. She had decorated with futons and bean bags, strings of beads for doors, black lights, and candles. Walls were filled with Art Deco, knives in box frames, and a variety of music posters. Dylan and Baez and music from *Hair* played alternately in the background.

Maggie's two roommates, Joyce with straight blonde hair and blue eyes, and Rena with dark tangled waves fanning her face, joined us. We sat cross-legged on the wooden floor. Maggie rolled one and we inhaled and held the smoke in our lungs. We passed around a bong and

Maggie began rolling another. Smoke bloomed around us.

"I saw that kid was back," Maggie said after we were all relaxed. "He's hanging around in the street now? Hope you're not encouraging him."

Her roommates both looked at me.

"No." I said, feeling mellow.

"He's got a thing for you," Maggie continued. "Better watch yourself. Kids like that are impulsive. You don't know what they might do."

"He's a sick little puppy," I said. "He gave me a cup of coffee one night and tonight he shows me the piece of the cup with my lipstick smear. He'd cut it out and saved it. Now he wants my used panties."

"Eeeww," Joyce said. "What did you say?"

"No, of course. That's gross."

Maggie shivered. "He's a creep."

"He's probably just lonely," I said.

"He could be crazy." Joyce passed the bong to Rena. "Like that guy they been talking about on the news, killed those women. And that serial killer they caught a few years ago, the Boston Strangler."

Yeah, right. Like Ray had anything in common with a serial killer. "I'm not worried. The kid's so scrawny I could have him doubled over in two seconds if I wanted."

Maggie picked the seeds from her stash. "That's probably what they said about DeSalvo before he started killing."

"Girls, you're freaking me out," I protested. "I can handle the little punk."

"That's what the first victim probably said," Joyce said, pressing the point.

"Enough," I laughed nervously. "Don't bring down my high." I blanked out their voices and tuned into the music. "Man, I could really get off on Dylan."

Maggie lit the joint and inhaled, closing her eyes and letting her head roll back before she passed it to Joyce. "You seem to get off on a lot of things, like that action with Rachel's guy. That was so cool I almost creamed my pants."

Rena giggled. "You got to Bart? Wow, that's primo. Wish I'd been there."

I turned to Maggie. "I thought you liked her."

"Girl thinks her pussy's gold. Time someone put her in her place."

"Oh, she's all right," I said. "She's got ambition. Nothing wrong with that."

"She better get used to a little competition if her sights are on Vegas," Maggie said.

"How is Joe about two dancers feuding?" I asked.

Maggie howled. "Joe? Shit! He loves it. Says when girls fight, there's action. Where's there's action, money flows. That's all he cares about."

The joint was passed to me. I took the smoke into my lungs and held it, feeling sleepy and horny at the same time.

"As for me," Maggie went on. "I don't care who you let fuck you under the table. It ain't none of my business, but if you want my advice, you'll take it slow. Make 'em spend the dough to get it. They'll spend a fortune to get you upstairs."

"I didn't fuck anyone. Christ, Maggie, he just wanted a hand job." I handed the joint back to Maggie. "What exactly goes on upstairs?"

"Hell if I know. Never been. Men buy me drinks enough to keep Joe and Lewis happy, but that's as far as I go. They can get laid on Locust Street, and that's one place you don't want to work. I know some of the girls over there. It's a rough crowd."

"You know Dani who works at Foxy Lady?"

"Dani? Hell, yeah. Sweet kid, but she got a mean boyfriend. She was my first roommate before she got tangled up with that guy. I guarantee she won't last a year. Where'd you meet her?"

I told her about the party and how I'd seen her several times at the Zodiac Club. "I warned her about Bix. The last time I saw her she had a black eye and I saw scars where he'd burned her with cigarettes. I told her I needed a roommate and she could move in right away. I haven't seen her since. I've been worried about her."

Maggie looked skeptical. "She's probably gone back to Bix like always. I swear he acts more like her pimp than her boyfriend. He thinks he owns her."

"But women can get away. I did."

"Yeah, but you're not Dani. What I'm interested in right now is whether you're going to go upstairs with a guy. If you do, you got to promise you'll let me know what happens. Deal?"

I laughed. "Sure, I'll do that, when and if." Then I laughed some more and couldn't stop. Everything Maggie said seemed hysterically funny. The other girls caught on and soon we were all giggling like school girls.

We passed the bong around again and Maggie offered me a button the size of a dot on a piece of paper, promised I would be flying and see the most wondrous sights in minutes.

But I was already relaxed enough to sleep and a glance at my watch showed it would be daylight in a couple of hours.

"I got to split," I told my newfound friends. "Brady might be waiting."

"Who the hell is Brady and why should you care?" Maggie sat and crossed her legs in the lotus position. She had finished rolling another joint. "If you're not going to fly a little with me, take a toke on this and make him go away. It's Saturday already and you don't have to work until I do."

"I got to meet someone in a few hours." I looked down at Maggie's roommates who were both asleep on the floor mats. I was tempted to stay, even go to psyche-delic heaven with Maggie, but my mid-morning appointment with Kramer forced me to put on the brakes.

"Party pooper," Maggie murmured, sounding sleepy. "The phone's over there. You can call a cab."

Thirty minutes later, the breaking dawn painted a red smudge above the trees and the downtown skyline. I climbed out of a cab in front of my apartment. I only had a few hours to get ready for my appointment. I trudged upstairs and unlocked the door.

Brady sat at the kitchen table. A half bottle of scotch perched in front of him and he held a full glass. His eyes widened as he took in the new Erin. Clearly he hadn't expected to come face to face with a redhead.

"What did you do to yourself?"

"I didn't do anything. A magician named Paul waved a wand over me and a new Erin appeared. Like it?"

Without answering, he swallowed more scotch. His eyes never wavered and I felt the hostility brewing inside him. Fuck him. I knew how to appease him and I was in the mood. The marijuana had me horny as hell for the past hour, a condition I'd hoped he would satisfy. I took his glass away and drank half.

"Have you been up all night?" I sat on his lap facing him and unzipped his fly. I nuzzled his neck and let my tongue dart inside his ear.

He grabbed both my hands roughly and pushed me off. He stood and backed me against the wall. "Where the fuck have you been all night? You been screwing around with a customer, haven't you?"

This sounded like an echo of Johnny. The accusation, coming from Brady, brought back all the hurt and anger from the past. I twisted violently out of his reach. "If I had been, what would I be doing here, you drunk sonofabitch? I wouldn't need you, would I?"

His open hand smacked the side of my head. Hard. Spots appeared in front of me. The high from the marijuana vanished, replaced with a sudden fury so strong it took over every cell of my being. I eyed the drawer where I kept the knives. His gaze followed the path.

"What are you going to do? Knife me in the back?"

Between clenched teeth, I said in a low voice, "You don't know what I'm capable of, you stupid prick bastard. You better get out of this house right now. You sleep here, you may never wake up again."

His eyes narrowed and he took a step back. "You threatening me?"

"I'm telling you what I'm capable of. Ask Johnny if you don't believe me."

A strange expression crossed his face, and his arms dropped to his sides. "I've always wondered how you got away from him. What did you do?"

Too late I sensed I'd crossed a dangerous line. I waited until my breathing slowed to normal. "Forget it."

I turned to leave the room, but Brady grabbed my arm and forced me to face him. "Bullshit. You're not going anywhere. Not until you tell me what happened between you two."

A flash of rage shot through me. "Let go of me."

"Or you'll do what in my sleep? Same thing you did to Johnny? Was he asleep or unconscious?"

"Get off me," I warned again. "You better get the hell out of here." I pushed my fists against his chest, but not hard enough. "I'm not giving you shit to use against me."

"I'm not leaving." He gripped my hands. "Should I stay awake all night?"

He wanted something and I wasn't sure what. How far could I manipulate him?

I glanced over his shoulder as the sun appeared in the window, a reminder that my appointment with Kramer was only a few short hours away. I twisted my hands to get away.

He tightened his hold and pushed me against the wall again. He pressed himself against me and I felt him hard against my abdomen. With a finger he tilted my head up and his lips smashed against mine. I parted my lips so his tongue could gain access and ground my pelvis against him. If anything could divert his attention from a dangerous subject, I knew a quick fuck would do it. Sex always worked with him. Didn't matter how drunk he got. My high had disappeared, but that didn't matter either. The fight had aroused me and now the power play was in my court.

He lifted me onto the table and, in seconds, had my jeans stripped down, followed by my bikini bottoms. I'd almost forgotten about the money stuffed in my bra. I pulled his head down to mine and his hands grasped my buttocks as he worked inside me. He came quickly and, as he staggered away and stumbled to the sink, I removed the cash Bart had given me. I pulled up my jeans and stuck the cash in my pocket, along with the nickel bag Maggie had given me.

CHAPTER 19

Brady passed out in time for me to grab a cold shower before I headed to the lawyer's office. My hair looked like hell. I didn't have time to do anything but brush it back into a ponytail. I probably shouldn't have partied so late, but hell, Kramer had given me a Saturday appointment so what did he expect? I was going to pay off the lawyer. My little mess with the stolen credit card would finally be over. Then I could sleep.

At exactly ten o'clock, I strode into Kramer's office dressed in my jeans and a red silk blouse Maggie had lent me. His secretary didn't recognize me at first. Then she gave me a broad smile and buzzed her boss.

Kramer didn't look happy when I walked into his inner office. "What's with the change? Are you still working at the hospital?"

"For the time being, but I'm making more money at night." I withdrew two hundred and forty dollars and plunked the lot on his desk. "I didn't make that at the hospital."

He glanced down at the money. "Brady good with what you do?"

What the hell did Brady have to do with anything? "He knows I dance. He encouraged me." I pushed the money forward. "That covers the rest of your fee so we're set to go to court, right?"

He picked up the bills and slid them in a drawer. "That almost covers it. You're still two hundred short because I had to talk to the judge to reset the court date. But I trust you'll get the rest in a timely fashion, then I'll confirm the date and call you."

I couldn't believe what I was hearing. "What do you mean another two hundred? You gave me your word this would be the final payment."

He shuffled papers on his desk before he looked up. "I never asked you for a retainer. I knew you didn't have it, but I had Brady's word that you would cover the fees as they were incurred. The two hundred covers time with the judge to get the criminal charges off your record. To do that, I had to file a continuance and get a new date. That's what you want, isn't it?"

"Yes, like we agreed, and what I've already paid you for, or so you led me to believe."

"No, getting your record expunged was separate."

"That's not what you told me." I felt steam rise off my cheeks. Who needed to apply blush these days? "This is bullshit. Do you know what I had to do to get that two hundred?" Tears stung my eyes. I blinked them away, furious that I'd showed this man any weakness.

"I can guess," Kramer said dryly. "Do you want your record cleared or not?"

I gritted my teeth. "I'll get the two hundred."

"When?"

I wanted to slap that complacent look right off his face. "Don't worry. You'll have the money by the end of the week."

"I'll set up the court date," he said. "As soon I have the full amount."

"What assurance do I have that there won't be another surprise?"

"You'll have to trust me, Erin." He leaned back in his chair. "By the way, how're you doing at the hospital?"

"The pay is lousy, and it's boring. What the fuck difference does it make?"

"I hope you're not thinking of quitting just yet. The judge wants to know that you hold a respectable job. If he knew what you do at night, he might think you're prone to criminal acts."

I leaned across his desk. "I wouldn't be surprised if I saw the judge where I work every night. Maybe he's one of my customers. Wouldn't it be funny if it turned out he was paying me your fee for sucking his cock?"

I hoped that would get a rise out of him. I straightened and folded my arms.

Kramer grinned. "Wouldn't surprise me."

I glared at him. "Yeah? I haven't seen *you* in there yet."

"Not my style."

"No? Just what is your style? Men? Young boys?"

"I go home to my wife," he said stiffly.

"I'll bet." I crossed my arms. "You know what I listen to every night? 'Erin, my wife doesn't understand me. I wish she was more like you.' It's so pathetic."

"You should stick with the hospital, Erin," Kramer said. "Your night job is making you cynical."

"Hah," I returned. "Men, not the job, made me cynical a long time ago. The job didn't change me, just made me more aware of how life really is." I clutched my pocketbook to my breast. "You'll have your money. You set up the court date. No more surprises."

I marched out of his office with my dignity in shreds and stood outside his door, shaking with fury and humiliation. I had planned to go home and take a nap before getting ready for work, but I knew sleep wouldn't come in my agitated state. Kramer's office was in Center City and I decided to walk off my anger and window shop. It didn't work. I gazed at the beautiful clothes on display that I could have bought with Kramer's money. I became more worked up and my steps picked up speed.

An hour later, I arrived at a bar and went inside to cool off. I sat at the far end and ordered a vodka and tonic with lime. There were few customers that time of day and the solitude slowly relaxed me. After a second drink, I left and took a bus home.

To my disappointment, Brady was there getting ready for work.

"Where you been?" were his first words.

"Fuck off."

He followed me into the bedroom. "What did you say?"

"Leave me alone. I'm going to take a nap."

"You see Kramer?"

"What else? You knew about the appointment."

"What happened? Are you set for court?"

I kicked off my shoes and stretched out on the bed. "He wants more money."

"What the hell for?"

"To get my record cleared. Would you please stop with the questions and leave me alone?"

"You're still mad about last night, aren't you?"

I rolled over, ignoring him.

"You gonna stay mad?"

I didn't answer.

A few minutes later, the door slammed and the room went finally quiet.

I dozed off and on. By late afternoon, I was able to drag my body out of bed. I had to go back to work, make more money to give the lawyer. When this was all over and my record was clear again, I planned to splurge on a new wardrobe.

I arrived at Dreamscape thirty minutes early, dressed in a low cut mini-dress. There were a few potential marks at the bar and, I figured, why not get a head start on earning Kramer's fee? The night passed quickly and without incident. No one bought champagne that night, but the customers were talkative and friendly between dance sets. I tried to make each of them feel special. Rachel ignored me despite my apologies, but Maggie was her usual carefree self.

Ten minutes after two, I changed back into my mini and left Dreamscape. To my surprise I found Brady outside with a waiting cab.

Remembering the fight we had earlier, I suspected him of spying. "What are you doing here?"

"I wanted to surprise you. Why the attitude? Are you doing something I wouldn't like?"

That clinched it. I strode away. "I'll get my own cab home."

"I was kidding." He hurried after me. "Wait. Please, baby. Don't be like that I came here tonight to surprise you and take you to an after-hours club."

I paused, softened by his pleading tone. I was curious. What kind of after-hours club?

He caught up with me and pulled me to him. His lips nuzzled my neck. "Come on, babe, I know I was being a prick last night. Let's get adventurous. Get the good times back."

I still wasn't sure where he planned on taking me. "Good times" and "adventurous" had many meanings when it came from Brady. When it came to sex, I was weak and he knew it. Tamara had ended in disaster. Now we kept our adventurous sex between us and used location for variety. The more risks we took, the more intense the thrill. Once we did it on the pool table at Moe's after he'd locked up for the night. Another time in an elevator and, on a dare, behind a shelf of books in a library. We even did it in a public alley in Center City at night.

As I followed him to the cab, I looked across the street. The kid was there. Ray with the pimples. Ray who wanted my used panties. Shit. He was fucking stalking me.

I took Brady's arm before he got into the cab and openly kissed him. Strictly for Ray's benefit, but Brady's pleased reaction was also worth the impulsive kiss. I hoped this would discourage Ray once and for all.

The cab drove us to Camac Street and let us off at a two-story building. Brady led me upstairs to the second floor where he knocked on a closed door and a peephole opened. Brady showed ID and after a few seconds we were led inside. The club took over the entire space with two large rectangular bars.

My first impression was that I was underdressed. I saw gorgeous women in full make-up, wearing gowns that would fit in at a fancy ball. A live band played in a corner and a decked-out singer poured out a song of ill-fated love.

We found two stools together at one end away from the stage. Brady ordered two scotch and waters from the voluptuous blonde behind the bar. I was admiring the women when Brady whispered to me that most of them were female impersonators. I had to look twice, even three times, and I still couldn't tell.

"You're kidding, right?" I whispered. "This is what I think it is?"

He grinned. "Thought you'd like it."

I found myself staring. I wondered if Paul came here. No, he came right out and told me he was a male prostitute at night. Nevertheless, he could have designed the hairstyles or wigs these men wore.

"I wish I looked that good," I said.

Brady looked at me with those blue eyes I first fell in lust with. My hand moved to his crotch. Brady slipped his hand under my dress. Brady's familiar touch soon had me hot and wet. A beautifully gowned man with cocoa skin came up behind us. He put an arm around Brady's shoulders and the other around me.

"You two got it going," he whispered huskily. "Need any help? We got a back room."

Already in a heightened state of arousal, I would have said "yes" to anything. Brady and I slipped off our stools and followed the slender man/woman to the other side of the room and through a door that opened to artificial candlelight and a lounge chair made for two. In the background, I recognized a Rachmaninoff piano concerto from the days my father played in a symphony orchestra.

Was this going to be another threesome? He seemed more interested in Brady than in me. I wasn't sure I was ready to take on two men at the same time and I was about to telegraph that to Brady, but then I saw him slip our host a few bills and Brady and I were alone again.

"So this is your idea of adventurous sex?" I whispered in his ear. "I like it. Show me more."

And he did.

CHAPTER 20

By the time Brady and I left the after-hours club it was Sunday morning. My plans included sleeping until evening, then slurping spaghetti with Brady at our favorite Italian restaurant. The phone call that awakened me at noon shot that idea all to hell.

An hour later, I met Maggie in the lobby of the county hospital. Tears had ruined her makeup, and she looked like she wanted to kill someone.

"I didn't know who to call," Maggie said. "I remembered you said you were friends with Dani. Marty's already gone up to see her."

I gripped Maggie's shoulders to calm her. She'd sounded hysterical over the phone. "What happened?"

"She's been beaten real bad."

Fucking Bix. "She'll be all right, though, won't she? What did the doctors say?"

"She's unconscious and they don't know if she'll come out of it. Fuck! I need a toke for my nerves." She broke away from me and rubbed her arms.

I could've used a hit myself. "Did they arrest Bix?" Why hadn't Dani listen to me? I tried to tell her creeps like Bix never stop. I'd seen the cigarette burns. In my experience, violence only escalates.

"They haven't found him yet," Maggie said.

"He ran? What a coward. Are the police looking for him?"

Maggie shrugged. "I don't know. Cops don't care what happens to us dancers. Dani won't file a complaint. She never does. If she wakes up…" She bit her lip and took my hand.

I nodded, and squeezed her hand. "Will they allow visitors?"

"They said only family, but she doesn't have any-one."

"Come on," I urged. "Let's check again with the doc-tor. Maybe they'll have better news."

We took the elevator to the fourth floor. Marty came out of the waiting room when he saw us. His face was pale, eyes reddened.

"God, what's wrong with this world?" he said. "What did Dani do to deserve this?"

"She didn't do anything," I said. "Except pick the wrong guy. What does the doctor say?"

"She's in a coma, that's all I know. That sonofabitch put Dani in a coma." Marty's voice choked up. He took a breath. "You need to see her. You won't believe what he's done." He turned. "I'll show you to her room."

I watched him hurry down the hall and hesitated. "The fool's in love with her." I didn't realize I'd said that aloud until I saw Maggie's expression.

She nodded in agreement. "Yeah, we always pick the one who'll hurt us."

"Isn't that the truth?" I thought of Johnny and the years I'd put up with him. Was I any different from Dani? Yes, I escaped.

"Come on, let's go in," Maggie said.

The nurse looked up as we passed the station, but she didn't try to stop us.

Nothing prepared me for what I saw. Dani's face was unrecognizable. What wasn't hidden by bandages and tubes was horribly discolored. Thankfully, a sheet covered her body.

After a second or two, I had to leave. A cold numbness crept over me. Flashes of Johnny came back in short clips. Johnny behind the wheel, revving the motor as I tried to dodge the car on foot, with him missing me by inches. Johnny accusing me of cheating on him, trying to force the truth out of me. Knowing I was never good enough for him, could never compete with his beautiful and rich ex-wife. What did he ever see in me? But I'd got even, hadn't I? And unlike Dani, I left Johnny with my body intact, if not my soul.

Maggie's voice penetrated through my spiraling self-pity. "Shit, Erin, you okay? We're here to help Dani, remember?"

I blinked as she came into focus. "I'm all right." I shook off the bad memories. I'd come a long way since leaving Johnny. I couldn't slide back.

"What should we do?" Maggie said. "Marty wants to go after Bix right now, but he's no match for that asshole. Bix will kill him if he gets the chance."

Maggie was wrong. Marty was a bouncer with broad muscular shoulders. He looked plenty able to take care of himself.

But I didn't care about Marty right then. My head cleared as I remembered the cash I had given Dani the night I found her in the ladies room of the Zodiac, and the napkin with my address written in ink. The idea of cops or anyone else snooping in her apartment and finding the napkin worried me. I didn't want to be on the cops' line of sight.

As for the money, I doubted Dani would miss it, if she hadn't spent it already.

I needed to lose Maggie and Marty.

"I think you should go with Marty," I told Maggie.

"Really?" The light came back in her eyes. Here was something she could do after all, instead of waiting for Dani to come out of her coma.

"Definitely," I said. "You know them both, and no one's better at stopping a fight than you."

She looked doubtful. "You should come with us."

"Bix doesn't know me at all, unless he heard how I tried to help Dani. In that case I would only make the situation worse."

Maggie frowned in thought. "What are you going to do?"

"Keep an eye on Dani." *Act casual.* "Bring her some clothes so she'll have them when she wakes up."

Maggie nodded in agreement. "That's a great idea. Do you know where she lives? I still have an extra key from when we were roommates, if she hasn't changed the lock." She opened her purse. Stopped with her hand still inside. "Maybe I should go with you."

I smiled and waved my hand, like it didn't matter. "Don't be silly. Marty needs you more. I can handle this and be back to check on Dani before you and Marty finish seeing Bix."

Maggie hesitated. "Why don't you wait until we get back?"

I tried not to show my impatience. "You do trust me, don't you? I'm not going to steal anything from her apartment. "

Maggie's jaw dropped. "I never thought any such thing. Of course, I trust you."

I held my breath, until finally she dug out her key ring, unhooked the door key and handed it to me.

My fist closed over the cold metal. "I'll get her a few clothes and other personal items. When we both get back, wouldn't it be wonderful if we found her sitting up in bed?"

I knew that wasn't going to happen. Maggie knew it, too. But voicing the idea seemed to make it easier to leave. She found a pen and wrote Dani's address on the palm of my hand and gave me a hopeful smile.

Marty staggered out of Dani's room and for one horrible moment I thought we had lost our friend. Maggie rushed to him, but he nodded and they spoke briefly. I sucked in a breath. I needed to get out of the hospital. *Now.* The overwhelming sickly smell, the stark white walls, blinding overhead lights, all crashed in on me. I punched the down button next to the elevator.

To my relief, the elevator doors opened right away. I didn't wait for Maggie and Marty. The doors opened to the lobby and I broke into a trot, eager to smell fresh air again, to breathe. Before I could reach the front door, Tony Corelli marched in. His expression grim, his eyes focused straight ahead, I was sure he wouldn't notice me. Before he reached the elevator, he gave a quick glance my way. His step faltered. I rushed out the door and didn't slow down until I reached the corner.

He'd come to check on Dani, I told myself. He was her boss. There couldn't be any other explanation. I know he saw me, but did he recognize me? It had been months since our encounter. He must have seen hundreds of waitresses and go-go dancers following that afternoon in his apartment. Paranoid. That's what I was. My nervous laugh drew stares from other pedestrians.

I caught the first cab that came along and gave the address Maggie had written on my hand.

A blast of humid air rushed at me when I climbed out of the cab in front of Dani's five-story brick apartment building. Like most of the buildings on the street, the structure looked old enough to have been built in the

1800s. A canopy of trees swayed over the narrow street.

Children played hopscotch half a block away. An elderly gentleman walked an overweight poodle. No one else stood out, but a chill hit the back of my neck already wet with sweat. I turned around and saw Ray, the stalker from Dreamscape, loping up the street toward me.

What the fuck was that creep doing here?

"Erin?" His voice cracked. "Is that you? What are you doing here?"

"I was about to ask you the same thing," I said when he reached me. "Do you live around here?"

"No, but my friend, Dani does. You know her, too? 'Cause that's a real coincidence, all of us knowing each other."

My head pounded with a million questions. How did he know Dani? Did he hang around Foxy Lady before he found Dreamscape? Did he ask for her used panties?

"I heard she got hurt," Ray continued. "I was hoping to see her. She was my friend. Like you, Erin. She danced real good." He added quickly, "Not as good as you, though."

How could I get rid of the little bastard? I needed to get inside Dani's apartment, but not with him watching.

I shook my head slowly, as if in mourning. "I came to see Dani, too, but I just found out from the super she's hurt bad. They've got her in the charity hospital."

His face reddened in alarm. "What do you mean? Did something else happen to her?"

Something else? Besides getting beaten up? What the hell was he talking about?

"She's in a coma, Ray. She may not make it."

"You mean, she might die?" His voice went up an octave.

"That's right. I'm sorry."

His face drained of color. "No, that can't be. Wait.

Please. Wait a minute. I got to go see her." He backed up, stumbled then righted himself.

No longer watching me, his wild eyes darted right and left. He circled awkwardly, then plunged forward in a half run, half jog, arms churning.

I watched until he disappeared and relaxed a little. I turned and faced Dani's apartment building and prayed that Maggie's key fit.

The vestibule smelled damp and moldy. I noted the names on the mail slots. Dani's apartment was on the third floor. An unlit hallway led to the elevators. An "Out of Order" sign barred the way. Didn't bother me any. I was used to climbing stairs at my apartment, which didn't have an elevator either.

To my relief, the key turned easily. I slipped inside and closed the door. At first glance, Dani's tiny apartment could have been a replica of mine. The living room was spare with dusty worn furniture that looked secondhand. One sofa, a pine table with scattered movie magazines and two empty cocktail glasses. Who drank from the second glass? Bix? I tossed cushions off the sofa and dug inside the crevices. Went so far as to lift one end and move it in order to sort through candy wrappers, a pizza box and potato chips.

I moved to a desk and a chair with a pair of stiletto heels discarded underneath. I rummaged through the desk drawers first. All I found was a rental contract, bills, and a checkbook with a balance of forty dollars and sixty-three cents. No hidden cash and no napkin with my address.

Her small kitchen looked lightly used. Rinsed dishes for one were left in the sink. The refrigerator contained a quart of Absolut Vodka, a container of orange juice and cartons of leftover Chinese food. I checked the cupboards and drawers. No money, no napkins, new or used.

I investigated the bathroom next. Shoved in the cabinet behind the bathroom mirror was a pharmacy of various drugs, plenty of uppers to get through the day and downers to help her sleep. I checked behind the toilet bowl. Clean.

Only one room left. It was the logical place to keep cash in the apartment, unless she had the money with her, which meant it could be in the pockets of the clothes she'd been wearing. I still had to make sure my address wasn't lying around.

A bedroom tells more about a person than any other room. I expected a messy bed, clothes scattered, and somewhere in the mess would be the napkin. The money, if she hadn't spent it, would be a bonus.

I smelled dried blood before I reached the door, but I still wasn't prepared for the sight that met me. Knocked-over table lamps, crooked window blinds, clothes strewn across the floor told its own story. I forced myself to look and choked back a scream at the sight of the bed, the blood soaked into the sheets, the blankets twisted in an unforgiving struggle. My knees buckled. I reached out and touched only air.

I might have fallen, but a hard-edged voice rang out and I stiffened.

"Find what you were looking for, Erin?"

Shock waves went through me. I spun around and came face to face with the dark-suited, angry-eyed, rigid form of Tony Corelli.

CHAPTER 21

My shock at seeing Tony Corelli almost took my mind off the state of Dani's bedroom. He must have followed me from the hospital. But why? What could he want? I was surprised he even remembered me.

The first words out of my mouth were meant to be flip. "*You* weren't on my list of things to look for." In moments like these a good act could be used as a good defense. I jerked my head toward the bedroom. "Not that scene either."

Corelli brushed past me and entered the bedroom. There he stopped. His temples throbbed. His body went rigid. I expected him to say something, but he didn't.

He slowly turned to me. His eyes were dark holes. His jaw tightened. He seemed to be holding himself together like a robot. Finally he spoke. "What are you doing here?"

The room felt sucked dry of air. I moistened my lips before speaking. "I came for Dani's clothes. She'll need them when she comes out of her coma." I glanced down the hall toward the living room. "I should go now." But his eyes held me in place.

"Who gave you permission?"

I didn't have a good answer, so I winged it, hoping I looked tougher than I felt. "I didn't break in if that's what you're thinking. I have a key. What are *you* doing here?"

He held up a ring holding a single key, identical to the one I had in my hand. Maybe Dani wasn't just a dancer to him. I doubted he kept an apartment key for every one of his dancers. Maybe he paid her rent.

"Does Bix know you have that key?" I really pushed my luck now.

"You know about Bix?" His eyes narrowed. "I didn't realize you and Dani were such good friends. Dreamscape is miles from Locust Street and the Foxy Lady."

Crap. He remembered my name. Knew where I worked. "If it's any of your business, I met her months ago. She came to my housewarming party. I see her often at the clubs. How the fuck do you know so much about me?"

A knowing smile thinned to a cruel line. "You think I'd forgotten you, Erin?"

A dagger of fear pierced my stomach. I reacted with rancor. "Why not? I'm just one of many you must have auditioned, fucked, and forgot. I'm nothing special."

His dark gaze transported me back to that fall afternoon in his bed. "Ah, Erin, you underestimate yourself."

I shivered, fighting the memory. "I don't need this bullshit. I'm getting out of here."

Despite my threat, I didn't move. Sonofabitch knew I wouldn't leave. That made me even angrier.

Corelli walked past me and approached the bed. He looked down at the bloodied sheets. "You've seen her?"

"Not my brightest moment," I said. "Whoever did this belongs in jail."

"I agree." His answer surprised me. He circled the bed. "It happened here, but this isn't where Dani was found."

"No? Then where?" My stomach cramped. Did I want to know?

"Behind Foxy Lady. Tossed in the alley like a sack of garbage."

I shrank from the room.

He glanced up sharply, and read my expression. "I didn't do this, Erin. Dani is like a daughter to me."

Something in his tone made me want to believe him. "What do the police say?"

He looked as if I'd made a bad joke. "You're thinking they're investigating? Do you see crime tape anywhere? Grow up, Erin. Think about it. Bar girls get beaten up every day, like prostitutes. Dani's not the first. She won't be the last." So much for his opinion of Philadelphia's finest. "One cop said she must have asked for it. Another called her a whore. I'll have his badge for that before I'm finished here." He turned back to the bed.

I felt sick. If he was right, then what happened to Dani could happen to any one of us. I could be next. Except, in Dani's case, it seemed more personal. "What are you going to do about it then? Are you going to fire Bix?"

He jerked his head up. "Why would I do that?"

"I've seen what he's done to her before, the bruises, black eyes, cigarette burns. Obviously, he went too far this time. You say she's like a daughter to you? And you're going to stand around and do nothing to him?"

He faced me. "He said he didn't do this, swore to me." He took a step closer to me. "If I thought for one second—"

"So you believe him?"

He rubbed his temples. "Yes."

I glanced down the hall, wondered if I could leave quietly without him stopping me. Corelli reminded me of a bull in a ring ready to charge. I almost expected him to paw the ground and blow steam from his nostrils. I didn't want to be in his way. Whatever questions I had could wait. I stepped out into the hall.

His voice, without changing pitch, stopped me. "I came here to talk to you."

He *had* followed me. I felt his stare even before I turned back. Corelli's eyes were flat, black buttons that revealed nothing. "You did not come here to get clothes for Dani."

The implication infuriated me. "No? You think I came here to steal something?"

He frowned, clearly irritated. "Cut the innocent act. Who do you think you're kidding?"

"Obviously not you. And what, pray tell, am I guilty of."

He reached into his jacket pocket and dug out a crumpled napkin and spread it open.

"Missing this?"

The napkin with *my* address. My mouth went dry. "How the hell—Gimme that." I made a grab for it, but Corelli was too fast. Back it went into his pocket. "Where did you get that?" I wanted to smash the smug expression off his face.

"From Dani. Didn't someone tell you? Nobody keeps secrets from me."

His superior tone only fueled my anger more. "So what? Why the fuck would you care where I lived? We met once. What's the matter? You didn't get enough ass for one afternoon? You haven't got enough whores to satisfy you?"

I swung at him, but he caught my wrist. His face came within inches of mine. "Shut up," he ordered.

We glared at each other for long drawn out seconds. I spoke first. "What do you want from me?"

"I want you to tell me about John Champion."

I stared at him in silence and felt all the fight drain out of me. *Johnny*? Hearing his name, spoken aloud by this man, sent shock waves from the past. I felt as if he'd punched me instead. But on another, deeper level, I wasn't surprised. That was more worrisome.

"You told me his name. Remember? I asked you if he was your boyfriend. You said he wasn't. Not exactly a lie, since I did refer to present time. It was, however, a lie of omission. That's why I wanted to know more about you. One reason anyway." His gaze broke away.

I looked at him coldly. "I don't understand. Do you know Johnny?"

"In a manner of speaking."

"Are you being vague on purpose?"

He smiled with an air of superiority that made me want to slap him. "I couldn't believe my luck when you wandered into my bar that afternoon. When you happened to mention Johnny's name, I thought the pope had blessed me." He paused for affect. "You see, I'd been looking for him ever since he eluded me in California."

I saw red dots in front of my eyes as the truth hit me. I should have expected this moment would come someday, but not yet, not today. I reached for the wall to steady myself. "That was you?"

"Every time I spotted the two of you together, you disappeared again. Changed names. Disappeared to another city or state. I don't know how he knew when I was onto him, but he always managed to get away. When I saw you here, in my city, I knew my fortune had changed. So I had you followed after you left. I thought you were going to lead me to him. But that wasn't the case. So I had you watched, kept waiting for you to meet up with Johnny."

"But I had left Johnny."

"I didn't believe that. You know why? Because after

seeing you two together I became convinced that Johnny wouldn't let you go." His expression changed, as if the truth suddenly came clear. "But he didn't let you go, did he? You ran away."

He waited for me to explain, but I said nothing.

Then he continued. "You moved rather suddenly. Something happened that changed everything. Maybe he found you. I had to know. So I paid a visit to your friend, Carl, and he filled me in on certain details."

"Carl?" Now he had gone too far. "You bastard. If you threatened him or hurt him in any way—"

"What? You'll kill me?" He held up a hand in protest. "I did nothing to the man, Erin. I did wonder why you chose to live with a black man. These times are much too racially charged, even for a free spirit like yourself. You could have put a man in Carl's position in potential danger."

Furious, my words tumbled out in a rush. "You threatened my friend in order to find me? Why? You wanted Johnny, not me. So you said. You're the liar, Tony Corelli. Watching me all this time? You just wanted another fuck, isn't that right? Admit it. Well, all you have to do is ask, you bastard."

As if to prove my point, I ripped off my T-shirt and threw it at him.

He caught my shirt with one hand. My fingers went to the zipper on my jeans. He stopped me and gripped my chin, tilting it so my face was inches from his. His dark eyes flashed with the first sign of emotion I'd seen in him. "Shut up. You think I'm some local schmuck? I give the word, and you will not exist."

The threat should have scared me, but at that moment I didn't care. "Fuck you. Take your hands off me." My head pounded. I knocked his hand away hard. I wanted to break his wrist.

He stepped back, raised a fist. I glared at him, daring him to hit me. Instead, he patted the pocket holding the napkin. A little reminder of what he knew.

"Carl didn't tell me your address," he said in a tight voice. "I found you through the clubs where you danced." He tossed my T-shirt at my chest. "Put this on. You're coming with me."

I jammed my arms and head through the holes and yanked the hem down to my hips. "I'm not going anywhere with you. I'm leaving right now, and if you try to stop me, I'll scream until someone calls the cops."

He pointed to the bedroom. "Dani didn't have much luck with that, did she?"

Oh god, maybe he did do this.

He must have seen my expression. With undisguised contempt, he said, "I meant the cops. I never touched her. Not ever." He grabbed my arm and propelled me down the hall toward the living room.

My heels skidded on the hardwood floor. "I am not going with you."

He stopped with an exasperated sigh. "Yes, you are. I'm not finished talking to you."

"Finish now then," I said, planting my feet.

"Not here. Not in Dani's apartment."

Not within smelling distance of her blood. "We have nothing more to talk about."

He looked at me with tight eyes. Then he said the words that changed my mind. "Don't you want to know what happened to Johnny?"

CHAPTER 22

Corelli walked me to his car and shoved me into the passenger's seat. Thirty minutes later, he unlocked the front door of his house and we went inside. Not much had changed since my first visit.

Corelli opened the maroon drapes to expose a lush garden and a pond. At the bar area, he reached for a bottle of scotch on the shelf behind him, and poured two glasses.

He handed one to me. "Your drink of choice, I believe?"

I accepted the glass and swirled the amber liquid. "Did Carl tell you that, too?" I couldn't remember if Carl knew. "Or did you plant a spy where I worked?"

His eyes widened. He caught himself and his expression went blank. "It's my business to know everything about my target."

"I'm your target now?"

He didn't answer, but indicated I should sit on the sofa.

I ignored him and chose a straight-back chair with a flowered cushioned seat. Corelli shrugged and moved to stand by the empty fireplace, drink in hand.

His thick wiry brows sprouted silver threads that

gleamed when hit by a ray of sun streaming through the window.

"I should have recognized you the day we met," he said.

I watched him warily.

He smiled. "I saw you for the first time in Mexico. Johnny was fishing at the end of a rocky pier. I could have shot him there, but that meant dealing with the locals. And there was a witness. You were on the beach, reading, looking incredibly young and beautiful. How did Johnny do it? I kept wondering why you were with a man Johnny's age. You were what? Eighteen? Johnny was fifty, according to the information I was given. I couldn't imagine what attracted you to him."

I wasn't going to help him. But the memories returned like it was yesterday. Johnny, with his mane of silver hair, his six-foot-two frame molded with wide, muscular shoulders, slim waist, and craggy-boned, tanned face with deep-set blue eyes. The man represented the hero in all the romance books I'd ever read growing up. Frank Yerby. Sidney Sheldon.

The fact that he was crippled when we first met in the Santa Monica bar made him all the more irresistible. I let him fuck me in the back of my car after we left the bar. We did it despite the casts on his legs. From that moment on, I became his redeemer. I was the reason he walked again without a limp. I was his lover and constant companion. I thought he would tell me everything. He never told me that the mob was after him. Never explained about the accident that happened before we met. Never said who was chasing him when he jumped three stories to cement and fractured both feet.

I felt Corelli's eyes on me and stared back.

He went on. "I caught up with him again in Key West. You were working as a waitress at the end of Duval Street. Johnny was working on a lobster boat. You got on a bus one day headed for Miami. You were leaving him."

I looked away. Stared at a fish tank that took up half the space against a wall opposite the window.

"Why were you leaving him?" Corelli asked. When I didn't answer, he mused aloud. "I thought to myself, Tony, you don't need to kill Johnny to fulfill the contract. This girl is doing it for you." He shook his head. "I never saw a man so destroyed. He came after you."

Oh, Johnny. The bus had rattled into the Miami station and, even before I got off, I heard my name called over the intercom. I knew then he wouldn't let me go. Even when I hid in a bar until dark, found a two-dollar-a-night room and a Chinese restaurant that hired me the next day, I knew my freedom wouldn't last.

Aloud I said, "He found me on the street two blocks from the bus station. We went to a fancy bar overlooking the city and he told me he would be dead if I didn't come back with him."

Corelli nodded.

"Why didn't you take your shot when you had the opportunity?" I asked him.

Corelli took a poker next to the fireplace and pushed coals in a pile. "I think he always sensed when I was around. He would disappear so quickly, it was like he was never there. It's the Apache in him. You know his mother was full-blooded."

I remembered the story he told me. "His father was murdered in front of his eyes. They killed him because he was married to an Indian." I looked up at him. "Johnny was nine years old. Didn't speak to a soul for two years. Did you know that?"

He shook his head.

"Can I have a cigarette?" I asked.

He went to the coffee table and lifted the top off a ceramic dish and took out two cigarettes. He lit both and handed one to me.

We smoked silently.

"Why did you leave him in the end?" he finally asked.

I thought about this, wondering why I should tell him anything. Maybe it was my need to let the truth air out into the open. Somehow it didn't seem strange to unload to the man hired to kill the man I had so desperately loved and hated. I could never confess to anyone else.

I took a large swallow of scotch. "Johnny became increasingly paranoid. After a while I couldn't take his jealousy and suspicions. He would belittle me, call me stupid and common. I could never compete with his beautiful ex-wife. Every two months or so, we had to move. I thought he was having paranoid delusions."

I glared at Corelli, wanting to put all the blame on him. "But obviously I guessed wrong. He knew you were closing in on him." I took a deep drag off the cigarette. "We lived in six different towns in Florida before we spent a summer in New York and before we moved to New Jersey. I got a job to support us. He stayed home. When we first met, he got money from some attorney. But that stopped.

"He couldn't work. Didn't have a social security card. I thought the police were after him. He would never say. Except once, he told me his ex-wife was Sicilian and he didn't get along too well with his brother-in-law. Tried to kill him, he told me one day. It didn't take long to put it together. Not the police."

Corelli watched me from his stance near the fireplace. He still held the poker in his hand.

"We started having terrible fights. He could drink like it was water. From morning until night he put it away. Most of the time he was a quiet drunk. But the alcohol began to feed his suspicions. He didn't believe I could stay faithful to him. Then he announced that he was moving us to an island. He had it all arranged, he said. An island, where we would see nobody but each other. I was already a prisoner. He told me he'd never let me go."

I took another drag.

Corelli replenished our drinks. "So you ran away."

"No." I flicked ash on his carpet. "I decided to kill him."

CHAPTER 23

Corelli's spewed out scotch and the spray landed on his cigarette and shirt sleeve. He laughed out loud. "You? You were going to kill him?"

I spoke as calmly as if telling him the sky was blue. "I thought it all out," I said, as if reciting a script. "I'd wait until he was drunk and asleep, then use our iron skillet on his head. After he was dead, I would drag him to the car, put him in the trunk and drive to the bridge that crossed the river. There I would throw him overboard. We had a small house on the lake, the nearest neighbor lived a mile away, and no one knew us. No one to question his disappearance. It seemed like a perfect plan and the perfect getaway for me. I would finally be free."

Corelli observed me with quiet meditation. I sipped my drink and smoked my cigarette. My hands shook slightly, disobeying my will. Finally he spoke. "It didn't go as planned," he concluded.

I looked at him. "How do you do it? Is killing so easy for you?"

He took his time answering. "It's a business. If I am paid to do a job, I do it, because if I fail, they will kill me. I much prefer doing what I do now. Running the bars on Locust Street."

I thought about what he said. "You were paid to kill Johnny, but you didn't."

"Neither did you," he pointed out.

"That's not the same thing."

"Yes, it is. Just the motivations were different." He drank some more. "Johnny was supposed to be my last job."

"So why are you still alive and allowed to own bars?"

He smiled in a strange, offhand way. "First tell me what happened to your plan?"

I contemplated the golden swirl in my glass. "It turns out that it isn't as easy as I thought it would be. Things go wrong." I paused.

He rolled his hand for me to continue.

I sipped. "Johnny got drunk and fell asleep on the couch. That much was according to plan. I paced up and down. I chewed my nails. I kept thinking, I had to do it. I had planned it, now it was time to finish. It would be my only chance." I looked up at Corelli, hoping to see his reaction to my words. But he only stared at the coals in the fireplace. "I got the skillet and I poised it over his head. Then I brought it down. He yelled out and started to sit up and fell back down again. I think I must have dropped the pan. I don't remember. I panicked and ran. Ran as fast as I could until I finally came to a shed where I hid inside. I huddled down in a corner, shaking so hard I thought I'd shatter into tiny pieces. I stayed there all night, horrified over what I'd done. I'd never be able to live with myself. I wanted to be the one who died."

I heard nothing but silence when I was done.

Finally Corelli's voice reached me after what seemed an eternity. "Erin." His hand touched my shoulder and I jerked away.

I realized I had curled up in a ball and was shaking and sobbing.

Corelli sat beside me until I was cried out. I looked up, expecting to see scorn or disgust in his eyes.

Instead, I saw a very human emotion. Warmth. And, did I dare say it? Understanding. I forced myself to sit up straight.

"He wasn't dead," he said.

I slowly shook my head. "He was gone. Disappeared."

"That's when you ran away."

I looked up at him, seeing my reflection in his eyes, and immediately shut out the sight. "Until now, I couldn't remember what happened. I kept having dreams about raising that skillet over his head and in those nightmares I was hitting him over and over, unable to stop myself. But that couldn't be what happened. He would have been dead." I shook my head.

"Was there blood?"

What? Blood? I tried to think back. "I don't remember." I tried and tried, but the blood image wasn't there.

"Erin, look at me."

I did, after some effort, manage to meet his eyes.

"If you had cracked open his skull, there would have been copious amounts of blood. You would have blood splatters all over you. Is that what happened? Is that what you see?"

I tried again to visualize the scene of my crime. No blood. No blood anywhere.

Relief swept over me, like a baptismal. "I really didn't kill him, did I?" Then doubt crept in. "But I did strike a blow. What if he died as a consequence much later?"

Corelli shook his head. "You aren't a killer, Erin."

"All this time," I mused. "I really thought…" I

looked at him then, easing away from him. "Why didn't your boss kill you?" I had a terrible thought.

He smiled in that strange way he had. "The man who hired me believes I succeeded."

I jumped up, but he was quicker. He gripped my arm. "I was able to fool him, Erin. The truth is, Johnny is alive."

"How do you know that?"

"I've seen him. He's in Atlantic City."

I sat back down. He let me digest this news. Finally I faced him. "I want to know all of it. Who hired you, and why?"

He started to shake his head, but changed his mind. "I supposed you've earned the right. You guessed correctly who put out the hit on him. Johnny's brother-in-law, Nico Franchetti, hired me. Johnny was married to a crime family. His wife didn't like him doing the demolition work for the oil companies. Said it was too dangerous. But that isn't what threatened his life. Niko wanted to use his talent for blowing someone up."

"Some*one*?"

"Yeah. But Johnny's no fool, and he's no killer. He knew he would be the scapegoat when all the ashes settled. So he threatened to go to the feds. Nico had to shut him up."

"So Nico hired you. Didn't you own the clubs back then?"

"Nico knew me when I was a soldier for the Family. I owed him a few favors and he called it in."

I finished my drink and poured another one. Corelli watched me. His story was going through my head, trying to make sense of it all. I joined him by the fireplace.

"Why now?" I asked.

He frowned in puzzlement. "What do you mean?"

"Why come to me now? You've known about me for

the last several months. You've been following my career, as it were, but staying in the background. So what's happened that changed everything?"

Corelli threw back his head and laughed. When the sound died, he raised his drink and saluted me. "You are smart. I knew you were special the first time I saw you. Some things you can just tell by the way a person moves.

I waited.

He scrutinized me. "First, a question. Do you want Johnny dead or alive?"

I stared at him. "What kind of joke is that?"

"No joke. A question. Answer it." Sounded like an order.

"Alive. I don't want him dead. I don't care what he does to me, but I want your word that he does not die by unnatural means."

"Are you willing to do anything to prevent his murder?"

"Yes, anything. Name it."

He nodded approvingly. "Nico is coming to Atlantic City," he recited like a news reporter. "He has the idea he can take over my casinos."

"What's that got to do with Johnny?"

"It's what you can do to save him." Corelli watched me. "I told you Johnny was in Atlantic City. Niko has become suspicious. Someone's whispered in his ear and told him Johnny was still alive. Now he is blackmailing me. My casinos or he tells the bosses I never made the hit. If he sees Johnny there, he'll demand a hit on both me and Johnny. If Johnny sees Nico, he'll want to kill him."

A chill ran down my spine. "What do you want me to do?"

"Nico doesn't know you. Doesn't know anything about you. I'll send you down to dance in one of my casinos. I'll introduce you to him. You show him the sights. Keep him occupied. I'll do the rest."

"I'm supposed to trust you to keep Johnny safe?"

"You don't think I can do that?"

"I guess I will find out. What happens to Nico?"

"Depends on him." Corelli took our empty glasses, rinsed them, and put them away. It was time to go.

I was sure I wasn't getting the whole picture, and maybe never would. The thought of seeing Johnny again sent a whole different set of goblins to rattle my cage. I wasn't sure if I was ready.

"You'll be paid for the gig." Corelli was suddenly all business. "A thousand. That should take care of your lawyer and give you pocket change."

He knew about my arrest and the lawyer? Of course, he would. Nobody kept secrets from Tony Corelli.

CHAPTER 24

Carl's apartment had changed little since I'd moved out. There was a musty smell in the air I hadn't noticed before, like worn shoes and dirty socks. The room seemed smaller. He still kept up the place, very little dust on the furniture, the dishes washed and put away.

Carl had aged. I took in the tightness around his eyes, the thin lips pressed together, and the deep furrows between his eyes. It made me sad to see him that way.

He didn't look surprised to see me.

"Something's wrong." Carl studied me. "Are you sick?"

I sighed, "No, Carl. I came to apologize."

"For what?"

"I saw Tony Corelli this afternoon. He told me he paid you a visit."

Carl's shoulders slumped. "Yes, he came here. Looking for you. I didn't tell him anything he couldn't easily find out. I never told him where you lived."

"I know. I'm not blaming you."

He turned away from me and rummaged under the sink. He straightened, holding a saucepan. "That man knew about me, Erin, knew where I lived, where I came from. I never met the man, so how did he find out about *me*?"

"I didn't tell him anything about you. He had me followed that day after I left him."

Carl's face turned a shade of gray and he slumped into a chair. "I been careful, stayed low like they told me."

"Did he threaten you?" The thought sickened me.

"My dear, men like him don't have to threaten. He knew all about me. That's all it took." He shivered.

"Carl, I'm so sorry. Listen to me. I didn't know he'd come here. He just told me today. He already knew who I was. My fault, my big mouth. He explained he was just getting more information. You should have told me. But I'm here now to convince you not to worry. He's not interested in your past association or how you're living now."

He looked at me with rummy eyes. "You—you brought me happiness the short time you lived here. You know that, don't you? I wouldn't take those days away for all the peace in eternity."

"And I will be forever grateful to you for taking me in." I assured him.

He patted my hand "I need some coffee. Would you join me? I still remember how you like it." He measured the instant coffee and when the water boiled, filled the cups and added milk to mine. He set them on the table and sat across from me. "How is the boyfriend?"

"Brady? He's okay. I'm not looking for marriage."

Tired eyes scrutinized me. "You are worried. I can see it in your face."

His concern made me feel worse. He got threatened, but he worries about me.

"I'm going to dance in Atlantic City. Johnny may be there."

He looked surprised. "Your ex?"

"Yes, the one I was running from. But it's okay. What I want to know is, can a man like Tony ever be trusted to keep his word?"

He gave a low chuckle. "You will have to decide that for yourself. I am no judge."

"Can you tell me anything else about him?"

Carl brought his cup to his lips and blew the steam off. "I checked around after our talk. I still know some people who will talk without hurting me. Tony is only a part owner in the Philly clubs. What I hear about his partner, he's the more dangerous of the two."

"What's his name?"

"Charley Rossino."

The name threw me. I rose up from my chair, bumping into the table and almost knocking over our coffee. "Shit. I know him. He's been coming into Dreamspell, buying me drinks."

"Perhaps he's spying for Corelli."

Of course. It fit. That's how Tony knew so much about me. How I drank scotch, for instance.

"Sit down and drink your coffee," Carl advised. "Let's talk about this. Between the two of us, we know quite a bit. Let's try and help each other out."

I sat back down again. One thing I knew for sure. Carl knew a lot more about the mob than I did, and I needed to learn all I could.

CHAPTER 25

The next morning I hustled over to Kramer's office. I stormed past his secretary and barged into his inner sanctum. Without a word of greeting, I plunked two hundred dollar bills and a fifty from the cash Tony had given me on Kramer's desk. "I want my court date."

The lawyer glanced down at the bills. "I knew you'd come through."

"Really? You knew that, huh?"

His eyes hardened. "What I didn't know was how connected you were. You're due in court Friday morning. Nine o'clock. Don't be late."

I stared at him in confusion. "Wait a minute. How long have you had the date? And when were you going to tell me?"

"I knew you'd be in this morning."

"You were that sure I had the money?" An ugly suspicion nudged me. "Or did you already have the date when you asked for more money?" *I should have waited to pay him.*

Kramer shoved the cash in his top drawer and locked it. "You act surprised."

"I am." I leaned on his desk, anger rising. "What did

you mean when you said you didn't know how *connected* I was?"

He waved his hand as if it didn't matter. "You're a smart girl, Erin. You've proven that. You make the right friends."

"I don't know what the hell you're talking about. What friends?"

He put his elbows on the table and shifted his weight forward until his face was a foot from mine. "You don't fool me. Oh, I admit you had me in the beginning, playing the innocent victim, but you sharpened up quick."

"I don't know what connections you think I have. You're the lawyer and the only one I know of that can get me off this rap. What the fuck am I paying you for? If you know something, tell me. I'm the goddamn client here."

"Watch your mouth, and lower your voice," Kramer snapped. He jabbed his forefinger at me. "I'll tell you what I think. Someone talked to the judge. You don't know anything about that?"

My knees felt rubbery and I sank into a client chair. "No, I do not."

Kramer sat back. His lips thinned. "Your appearance will be a walk on. The judge will acknowledge you, accept your 'not guilty' plea, and your record will be expunged. Tell me you didn't already know that."

I sat there silent, not knowing how to reply. I thought back to my encounter yesterday. Fucking Corelli, interfering into my business, thinking he owns me now.

Kramer went back to shuffling his papers, a signal that I'd been dismissed.

I stood. "Since everything's been taken care of, gimme my two fifty back."

He gave me a stony look that told me I'd never see that money again.

"I'll be quitting my day job this morning," I said.

He didn't bother looking up. "Thought you already had."

I left with my emotions boiling over. I should've been glad the case was over, but I hated the way it was handled. Fuck Corelli.

The money that was left after paying Kramer called to me from the depths of my purse and cried to be spent. After all, I'd earned it, or would as soon as I went to Atlantic City. I needed something flashy to wear to get the attention of Nico. First, I'd give my notice. Center City and the shops would be my next stop. If I was still around to see winter, I would need a good fur coat and boots, and some new dresses. I definitely needed a good conservative suit to wear to court. I didn't want to look like one of Corelli's girls. I'd show all of them.

I wanted to forget about Corelli for now, but once I hit the street, I remembered Dani. I stopped at a phone booth and called the hospital. The nurse told me there had been no change in her condition, but they had a guard at her door. That made sense since her attacker was still free to try again. Maybe the cops were on it after all.

I arrived home shortly after five, humming a happy tune. Shopping always picked me up. Bundles of clothes in boxes and bags weighed me down, but I felt as light as the autumn leaves that drifted in my path. Facing the grim office manager at the hospital had taken the sting off my visit with Kramer. She accepted my resignation and couldn't resist telling me that the hospital was better off without me. I gave her a generous smile in return and told her I agreed completely.

Brady was getting ready for work when I carried my purchases inside. He came out of the bathroom with half his face clean-shaven and lather dripping off the other half. He stared at the boxes and the clothes bags.

"Where the fuck you been all day? I tried calling you at work and they said you weren't there."

"I quit." I brought the boxes into the bedroom and piled them on the bed, draping the dress bags next to them.

His jaw tightened. "Why?"

"I felt like it. I make enough at Dreamscape, and if I need more I could dance the lunch hour. I can make more in two hours than I could ever make typing all day." I stepped up to him and placed my forefinger on his chest and dripped sarcasm into my voice. "Then I'd have free time to spend with you, darling."

I turned my back on him and shook out a shimmering gold evening dress from the protective bag and slipped it on a hanger in the closet. Hung up the coat with the fur collar next.

"Where'd you get the money for all this?" Brady asked. "Did you pay off Kramer?"

"Yes, I paid off the asshole. I've worked two jobs, remember? You didn't help." I took several pairs of silk underwear and nylons from the box and set them in the drawer.

His mouth set in a thin line. "What else did you do?"

I turned slowly and faced him. "What do you mean?"

"You didn't have that much money this morning. You spend all day shopping? Or did you make the extra some other way?"

With difficulty, I kept my voice calm. "If you want an argument, it will have to wait. I have to get ready for work."

"You didn't answer my question. Where were you all day?"

"I already told you."

"You get a court date?"

"Friday morning." Before he could say another word,

I said, "Aren't you going to be late for work?"

He scowled but returned to the bathroom. I heard water running and by the time I finished hanging up my new dresses, he came out, smooth-faced, his thinning hair slicked back. He would be bald in a couple of years, I guessed. Maybe it would look good on him. I wondered whether I would stick around long enough to notice.

He stood there watching me. "I'll see you tonight, then?"

I shrugged. "Maybe."

I knew he'd have something to say to that, but I didn't wait. Instead, I went into the bathroom, locked the door, and turned on the shower. I ignored the sounds coming from the bedroom.

Maybe it was time to live alone. I hoped he'd be gone by the time I finished in the bathroom.

CHAPTER 26

I arrived at Dreamscape on time, my costume stuffed in my new duffel. The regulars who came early turned bored looks my way before going back to their drinks. The music was low, the lights no brighter than they would be in an hour when the crowd drifted in. When my eyes adjusted to the darkness, I slid onto a seat near the stage and motioned to Joe. He ambled over polishing a highball glass.

"I quit my day job," I said. "I'm free to dance at lunch if you've got an open spot."

"Free is good," Joe said with a grin.

"Not what I meant."

"Thought you quit the hospital a long time ago."

"Wanted to, but couldn't until now."

"Come in tomorrow around eleven-thirty." He put away the glass. "We got a new girl starting tonight. Trixie. Be nice to her. She's got talent for bringing in the customers, or so she tells me."

"Swell." More competition.

He peered at me. "You look like you can use a drink."

Wasn't sure how to take his meaning. Did I forget my makeup? I shrugged. "Thanks. It's been a rough day."

Joe grabbed the bar scotch and poured generously. He watched me swirl the liquid. I knew he wanted to ask a question, but he held back.

I thought about Carl's suggestions, along with his warnings, and finally set the glass down. "You seem to be good buddies with Charley Rossino. At least you knew him well enough to put me with him on my first night. What's his story?"

Joe gave me a quizzical look. "He manages the Foxy Lady. Don't know why he keeps coming here." He gave me a knowing wink.

"Ever wonder why he's so interested in me?"

Joe smiled. "Looked in the mirror lately?"

"Get real, Joe. All the girls who work for him at Foxy Lady are drop-dead gorgeous, and he comes here to talk to me? Come on, does that make a lot of sense to you?"

"Well, when you put it that way…" He leaned his elbows on the bar. "If he's giving you trouble, you give the word and he's out of here. He don't spend enough to cause my girls to worry."

"No, and don't say anything to him about this." I took a sip of my drink. "Doesn't Tony Corelli own the Foxy Lady?"

"Half owner." Joe corrected. "Now there's a guy you need to stay away from. Charley can be bad enough when he's drunk, but I can control him in my own bar. But Tony, he's another story. Hey, he's not trying to get you to work for him, is he?"

"You know I'd never leave you for Locust Street. Do I look the type?" I didn't dare mention Atlantic City to him.

He grinned. "No, sweetheart, you're class all the way. But hear what I'm saying about Tony. He's connected, if you know what I mean. So's Charley, for that matter, but lower in rank."

I needed to change the subject before Joe got suspicious. "Tell me about Trixie. Why do you need someone new? Is she a better dancer?"

Joe laughed. "No, she's cut from another cloth. Wait until you meet her. You watch she don't steal Charley from you, or any other customers."

"She can have Charley." *After I'm finished with him.* I downed the drink and slid off the bar stool. "Better get changed. Thanks, Joe."

"For what?"

I waved my hand in response as I moved up the stairs.

I closed the door and sat on the small stool in front of the mirror. After staring into space and trying to empty my mind, I dropped my head into my hands. Carl had suggested I might be able to smooth talk Charley into giving up some information about the Atlantic City clubs. But he also had reservations.

"He's like a fox," Carl had said. "Don't let him know what you're doing. He's a mean one."

Mean like how? Mean like whoever beat up Dani? I wondered if Bix had been found yet. I thought of my own situation and the deal Corelli offered me. I had no doubt that the story Corelli had given to me was only half true. I'd agreed to save Johnny, but what if that wasn't the only reason Corelli wanted me there. Carl thought I should go to Atlantic City, have a face-to-face with Johnny, and warn him about Nico. Why even bother with Charley? Get this whole thing over with. Shit. When did life get so complicated? Yeah, right. When wasn't it complicated?

Tony knew where I worked because he got Charley to spy on me. I got that part. There had to be a way to use that information. Charley made it clear a few times that he wanted more than conversation from me. If I could dangle that fruit in front of him, maybe he'd loosen his tongue and give me something I could use in Atlantic City. Since working at Dreamscape, I'd come to the conclusion that any man could be manipulated with sex.

I heard female voices coming from downstairs and hurriedly changed into my costume. While I checked my makeup, a woman charged into the dressing wearing bright red lipstick, vibrant blue mascara, and a costume of white ostrich, or at least that's how it looked on her. A fan of sparkly white feathers licked her breasts from below, barely covering her nipples. Her hair was a shade more white than blonde and layered the top of her head with big curls. She was taller than me by a good four inches, and I'm five-four.

Rachel and Maggie followed her in. The girl I figured to be Trixie laughed good naturedly at the three of us.

"Girls, it's a pleasure, really it is. Y'all don't mind if I go on first, do you? I like to warm up the crowd before I go down and pleasure them with my company."

Rachel, Maggie, and I exchanged glances.

"Do your worst," Maggie said. "Don't bother me none. I'd be happy just dancing."

"But the money is downstairs," Trixie said. "All they care about is getting their dicks hard and getting off. They come in here and they know they gotta pay."

"Tell us something we don't know," Rachel said, looking bored.

"You've never seen the expert at work," Trixie countered.

"Some can get a little rough," Maggie said, changing into her costume.

"Oh, honey, I got that covered."

Trixie reached into her boot and pulled out a leather sheath. The blade, when she drew it out for us to see, looked sharp enough to split hairs. "Nobody get rough with me, honey. Like nobody gets my black ass honey man unless I'm with him." She slid the blade back, put on another coat of lipstick, flipped a tail feather and flounced out.

Rachel turned to us. "Did she say what I think she said? Was she talking threesomes? With a black man?"

Maggie shrugged. "Could be. I just heard black ass honey man. I'm hot already." She gave a short laugh. "Yeah, right."

I kept my mouth shut and tried not to think of my own experience in a failed threesome.

Early in the night, Rachel and I both lost Champagne Bart to Trixie. I watched for Charley, but he didn't usually show until late.

I tried to relax in the meantime by drinking and flirting with other customers.

It was almost eleven when I saw him come through the door. Mr. Big Bucks. Mr. Lucky Corelli's partner. I kept my distance until he settled at the bar. I made eye contact and walked slowly up to him, swinging my hips, but without exaggerating the movement.

Trying to be subtle and seductive at the same time, I continued behind him and reached his other side when his hand shot out and he wrapped his fingers around my arm.

"Where are you going?" he asked.

"Right here, honey." I sidled up to him, still standing. His hand didn't let go of my arm and when he pulled me closer, my breast brushed up against him. Expensive cologne soured with his whiskey breath.

"Sit down. Have a drink."

"If you insist."

He loosened his grip and I slid onto the seat next to

him, showing as much cleavage as my push-up bra could expose.

"Scotch on the rocks, right?"

"With a splash of water," I said.

Charley got Joe's attention and gave him the order.

I felt movement behind us. I turned to find Trixie pressing against Charley's back.

"Hey, baby, I've been waiting for you."

He swiveled in his chair to face her. "Trixie. I'm busy here."

Trixie didn't even glance at me. She kept her eyes on Charley. "Oh, I didn't think you were *that* busy. I just stopped by to see if you needed some relief."

Charley snarled. "I said get lost."

Trixie's smile faded. She backed off.

"She work for you at Foxy Lady?" I said to Charley.

His jaw tightened. "Where'd you hear that?"

I shrugged. "Seemed obvious she knew you."

"Okay, yeah. How'd you know about Foxy Lady?"

"Oh, you know, word gets around." I pretended not to notice his frown and forged ahead. "Do you have an interest in the Atlantic City bars, too? The reason I asked is I'll be working there next weekend."

"Yeah? Says who?"

"Your partner. Tony Corelli."

A shadow fell over his face. "Oh?"

"Maybe you could help me. I've never worked in Atlantic City before. Is it different from here?"

His expression made me want to follow Trixie. But I stuck with my plan. I wondered how to ask him if he knew about Johnny.

Before I could come up with anything, he said, "The dancers, they go topless."

I pushed a drooping curl off my forehead. "Not me."

His upper lip curled in a sneer. "You think you're better than the other dancers? Is that it?"

"Yes, I am better. You know I am."

He watched me for a long moment. "Tony told me about you."

Along with his orders to find out more. "What did he say?"

"Said he got plans for you."

"Really?" I tried to act casual, but my insides were churning. "Plans other than dancing in Atlantic City? I'd like to hear it."

"I bet you would. What are you doing after you leave here?"

"I have a date," I lied. Well, not really a lie, if you consider my arrangement with Brady.

"How about we go upstairs and we can discuss it over a bottle of champagne. Joe would like that, wouldn't he? I've never taken anyone upstairs before. Trixie thought she'd be the first."

My palms felt wet and I could feel my heart beat against my chest. This wasn't included in my plan. Charley always made it clear he'd never pay to take anyone upstairs.

I could almost hear Carl whispering in my ear to shut down the strategy we'd discussed. But would I ever have another opportunity like this one? If I could get Charley as an ally, get him to tell me exactly what Tony's plans were for Johnny and for me—shit, I'd even give him a blowjob if he asked.

I barely breathed while Charley ordered the champagne. He handed the flutes to me while he kept the bottle. I dared a glance at Trixie who stared daggers at me. If she only knew, I would give almost anything if our roles were reversed.

Men crowded the bar at this hour. The smell of beer

and whiskey collided with the scent of perfume, sweat, and cigarettes. Glasses clinked, drunken eyes leered at the dancers. Rock-and-roll jammed through the speakers. The pounding of dancing feet on the stage reverberated through the room.

I looked down on the scene from the top of the stairs where I lingered for only a moment and wondered what the hell I had talked myself into. This wouldn't be the same as auditioning for Tony in his bedroom. I realized that when the door closed behind us and Charley grabbed me. He mashed his lips against mine and then forced his tongue inside my mouth.

"Ah, yes," he whispered hoarsely in my ear. "I knew you'd be sweet as sugar."

I tried to shove him back using both hands on his chest. But he didn't budge. Didn't seem to notice my efforts. His kissed me again and pressed his hands on my ass until I could feel the lump in his pants against me.

"This isn't Locust Street," I said when I managed to gasp a breath. I silently nixed the blow job and anything else Charley wanted.

He laughed at me. "You think you're better than girls like Trixie? I've watched you and talked to you since your first night here. You think you're so special, but you're not, bitch. What do you think the girls do up in these rooms? Play patty cake?"

"I'm not that naïve," I said, steeling myself.

He grinned. "That's better. You want information about your role in Atlantic City? You'll have to work for it first. Call this a preview of what to expect when you get down there. I want to see if you're good enough for Nico Franchetti. He's expecting the best."

That wasn't what I signed up for. Corelli didn't mention the part of doing Nico. Before I could react, Charley's lips came down on mine again. He grabbed my hand, put it against his crotch, and rubbed the lump through the wool material of his slacks until I felt moisture. I closed my eyes, tried to imagine he was someone else.

He slid his hand inside my bikini bottoms, rubbed me until I felt the wetness betray me. He kept stroking me and entering me with one finger then two. I caught my breath and pushed against his hand. He gave a triumphant smile. Then he slipped his hand out and unzipped his fly. He took out his cock, oversized and purple, and pushed me down to my knees. I closed my eyes and took him in my mouth.

He held my head with both hands and grunted as he fucked my mouth. He held my head even as I gagged and tried to pull away. He held me as he spilled his juices and made me swallow. I gagged again and fell to the floor, spitting him out.

This made him furious. He grabbed my hair and twisted it and slammed his fist into the side of my head. The blow almost blinded me, and I lay there fighting my way through the pain. But before I could get to my feet, his boot plowed into my stomach.

I screamed, brought my knees to my chest, and rolled away from him. The sound seemed to shake some sense into him. He dropped his arms, but his face was suffused with color.

"Shut up, whore. I said, shut up!" He pushed his member back inside his pants and zipped up.

I crawled backward, staying as far away from him as the room would let me, and struggled to my feet.

I saw both his fists clench as I stood panting against the wall and spoke fast. "You hit me again and you'll have the whole police force here. This isn't Foxy Lady. I'm not your punching bag. Joe and Lewis are cops and you're in trouble."

"Shut up," he bellowed. He took another step toward me, but second thoughts stopped him. Without another word, he turned unsteadily and groped for the doorknob.

We both heard footsteps coming up the stairs. I saw him hesitate and took advantage of the distraction to rush past him and open the door.

Charley was faster. He pushed me aside and I landed on the floor. His heavy footsteps took the stairs like a man half his size. He flew past the figure coming up the stairs and disappeared into the dark hollows of the bar.

I struggled back to my feet, waiting for whoever came up the stairs to appear. When no one did, I ventured out to the hall. I was alone.

My legs felt too weak to hold me up. I went back inside the room. For the first time I took notice of the red lounge chair and the small table and chairs. I limped to the lounge and eased down. When my breathing returned to normal, I reach for the champagne bottle and filled an empty flute. I downed it, wishing it held something stronger than ginger ale. My head pounded and I felt like throwing up. I put my head between my knees. After several minutes, the nausea subsided and I was able to get back on my feet. I went out to the railing and looked down.

There was no sign of Charley or any disruption he might have caused. I limped to the dressing room, wanting to hide there for the rest of the night.

I inspected the damage to my face. The redness would soon turn purple. I thought about killing Charley and pictured all the ways that would hurt him the most. As I stared at my reflection, I remembered Dani. What had happened to me was nothing compared to what someone did to her. Maybe the police were looking in the wrong direction after all. Right then I could think of only one person capable of such damage. Charley Rossino.

CHAPTER 27

I couldn't hide forever so I lathered more makeup on my face, hoped the darkness and smoke below would hide any traces left by Charley's fist. I left the empty dressing room and went downstairs. Nothing seemed different. Trixie was on stage. A few eyes were on her, but as usual most of the men were either drinking, masturbating, smoking, or all of the above. Yet, for me everything had changed. I lingered at the bottom step and looked for Charley. If I saw him, I would have Joe arrest the bastard.

I sat by myself in a corner under the stage, thinking what I needed was a stiff drink. Joe was busy with a group at the other end of the bar. While I waited for him to notice me, I kept busy imagining Charley behind bars. I knew that wouldn't happen. Not to Tony Corelli's partner. Corelli knew judges. He'd proven that with my case.

Tony wouldn't let anything interfere with his plans for Atlantic City. He made that plain enough. He was in trouble and I was the oil that would grease the kinks to smooth sailing. Once he found out I willingly went upstairs with Charley, he'd say I deserved whatever I got. He might even look at the incident as a betrayal. I'd gone behind his back and possibly made Charley a threat to his plans. How stupid could a girl get?

Joe noticed me after about five minutes. His eyes narrowed and his jaw tightened.

"Charley Rossino stormed out of here like the devil himself was after him. Never knew he could move so fast." He leaned closer. "Did he do that to you?"

"Let it go, Joe."

"No way," he said. "That asshole hit you. You can't hide the bruises with makeup."

"It's no big deal. I can handle it."

"This is my bar. I'm a fucking cop. We don't allow that kind of rough stuff here. I'm going to let Tony know that his boy will be arrested if he sets foot in here again."

I panicked at the thought of him talking to Corelli. "No, Joe. You can't do that."

"Oh yes, I can."

"No, please, don't. Not yet. I have to work something out with Tony and if you start a fight, it will screw things up. Please, let me take care of this. It was an accident. Please, Joe."

He frowned. "I don't know what you have going with Tony. I've warned you about him before. What you do on your own time is your business, but this place is mine. Charley is eighty-sixed here, Erin. Nobody gets away with hitting my girls."

I sat back. "Can I have a scotch?"

He poured a shot glass and set it in front of me. I downed it and felt the warmth hit my stomach. A breath on my neck caused me to jump. I turned. No Charley. A stranger, offering to buy me a drink. I didn't feel like talking, but being as I was paid to be there, I might as well work and get my mind on someone else besides myself.

"I'll take another," I said to him.

A noise at the door distracted me. I looked up saw a man stumble out. He lurched and caught his balance. I inhaled sharply when he turned, and I saw his face.

Brady? What the fuck was he doing here? Did he see me go upstairs with Charley? Oh, shit, no.

He couldn't have. Fuck. Was that him on the stairs? Joe had already shown that he hadn't gone up.

I downed my drink and asked for another. I needed a bottle at that point. My customer looked at me funny, probably seeing my face for the first time instead of my tits.

"Yeah, why not," the stranger said. He waved to Joe and pointed to my glass.

Trixie finished her set and came down to join the drunks. She stopped behind me so my customer couldn't see her. She leaned in close and whispered, "You are so dead. Charley will kill you for what you just did to him."

What *I* did to *him?* I whirled around to retort, but she was already sitting with the next customer. She flashed me a look of pity and then chose to ignore me.

I kept hearing her words in my head as the night dragged on. By two o'clock my head felt ready to explode, but I wasn't in any hurry to get home. Not in any mood to deal with Brady, who was likely even more drunk and pissed.

I trudged upstairs, almost crashed into Maggie when she flew out.

"Sorry," she yelled over her shoulder. "Got a date. See ya."

I watched her leave before going inside the dressing room. Rachel was putting on her coat.

She stared at my face. "Girl, what happened to you?"

"Rough customer," I said.

She frowned. "You were with Charley, weren't you?"

"You know him?"

Her expression turned somber. "Not really, but I've heard stories. He's got a temper."

"No shit. Guess I pushed a few wrong buttons, the way he reacted." Thinking of Dani, I asked, "He's really hurt other girls? You know that for sure?"

"Yeah, from what I hear. So watch yourself." With a wave, Rachel disappeared out the door.

Watch myself. Yeah, right. Before I ended up like Dani.

I changed clothes and met my cab outside the door. I had a standing date with the taxi company when I worked until two. It beat waiting for the bus. More important, it discouraged customers from thinking they had bought me for the night.

Inside the cab, all my bravado seeped out of me. I felt the injured side of my head. Still tender, but not as painful as it could have been without the amount of liquor I'd consumed. I gave my address to the driver and lay back against the seat. I closed my eyes, trying to sort out the evening's events. But I gave up before the taxi pulled up to my apartment.

The minute I walked inside I smelled a strange odor. A burnt hair smell.

Brady was in the kitchen drinking a highball. He smirked when he saw me. "Come here. I want to talk to you."

My chest tightened. "What the fuck's your problem?" I sniffed the air. "And what have you been burning?"

"You'll see," he said. "First I want to know what you were doing in the room upstairs with that guy."

My stomach clenched. "That *was* you on the stairs."

"Yeah, that was me." His words slurred and he wiped his mouth with his sleeve. "Thought I'd better check on you since your other boyfriend called me."

"My *what*?"

"Your boy, Ray. He told me to stay away from you. Why didn't you tell me you preferred whiny little punks to me? Or have you discarded him for bigger fish. Sure you can handle Charley Rossino?"

I hadn't gotten past his mention of Ray. "Ray, the kid who waits outside the club for me? Are you crazy? He's delusional."

"You must have encouraged him." His voice grew louder. "After what I saw tonight, I wonder how many more guys believe that shit. Does Charley?"

"How the fuck do you know Charley?"

"Because he comes into my bar," he shouted.

"I wouldn't know that because I don't check up on you," I shouted back. "What the fuck were you doing at my work? What happens there has nothing to do with us."

"You'd like to believe that, wouldn't you? Maybe you can separate the two, but I can't. You think I haven't noticed how you've cooled off the last few days? I took the night off so I could see if you were all right. But you were sucking dick with a customer who paid with a champagne bottle. You get a tip from him, too?"

"Fuck you."

"No thanks, don't want any sloppy seconds." His lips curled in a snarl. "I know what goes on upstairs in those rooms."

"You're drunk and I'm tired. I'm taking my shower and going to bed."

I stalked off toward the bathroom, wondering what else he was going to accuse me of doing.

I opened the door and the smell hit me like a noxious wave. Stronger than what I'd smelled earlier. I felt a sick stab of pain go through my stomach as I looked into the bathtub. My new clothes filled the basin. The clothes still smoldered from the fire. On top of the pile, the blackened fur on the hood of my new coat stood out.

At first I felt numb. Then a surge of hot fury raced through me. I turned and charged at Brady, fists pounding on his chest. He raised his hand and hit me on the left side of my face so hard I staggered, but didn't fall. I ignored the pain and went at him again, butting my head against him, punching, but he didn't seem to feel the blows. He finally got a grip on me and dragged me by my hair to a stool in the middle of the kitchen. I saw the scissors in his hand, and screamed. I kicked at him and tried desperately to squirm out of his hold.

He wrapped his hand around my hair and twisted violently. "Don't move," he warned. "Don't want to cut you unnecessarily."

Fear and the way he held my head kept me from moving while I felt, more than heard, the clips and snaps of the scissors. I saw my red curls, my act's trademark, fall to the floor.

Brady was panting hard by the time he finished with me. I could smell his sweat. He stepped away when he was done. "Now see how much the men will love you."

I sat on the stool, unmoving, savoring the fury and hate that curdled inside of me.

Finally, with a deliberate calm, I slid off the stool and walked back to the bathroom, one measured step in front of the other.

I didn't look at the clothes again. My reflection stared back at me. Only it wasn't me. Not without my hair, my most prized asset. Short spikes now sprouted on my scalp.

I turned away from the mirror, raised my skirt and sat on the toilet bowl, peed with the door open. I flushed, left the room and headed for the bedroom.

At the door I turned and saw Brady standing there

with the scissors still in his hand. His face had turned red and he was breathing hard.

"Get out," I said in a low growl. He didn't move. Then I was screaming, "Get out! Leave!"

"I'm not going anywhere," Brady sputtered. "What are you going to do that would hurt me more than I already hurt?"

"You're hurt?" I gave a harsh laugh. "You don't know hurt yet, motherfucker." My hands curled and my nails bit into my palms. I wanted to smash his face and might have if he hadn't been holding the scissors. "Believe me, if you decide to stay, I advise you not to go to sleep tonight. Remember what happened to Johnny."

I slammed the bedroom door and sat on the edge of the bed shaking, watching to see if he'd break in. I reached under the bed for the baseball bat I kept for protection and laid it across my lap. A few moments later, I heard the apartment door slam. I waited a few more seconds listening for footsteps. Hearing none, I took the bat and went back into the kitchen and locked the front door. Tomorrow I would have new locks installed.

When my heart rate slowed to normal, the pain in my stomach returned to remind me of Charley's vicious kick. A little higher and he could have cracked a rib or two. I also became aware of my headache, throbbing worse from Brady's punch. Panic set in when I remembered my deal with Tony. How could I perform in Atlantic City feeling and looking the way I did, and what would happen to me and to Johnny if I didn't keep my end of the bargain?

CHAPTER 28

It was almost noon when I awoke. Late morning sun streamed between the blinds delivering a sharp pain to my eyes. I covered my face with my hands. Rolling over to avoid the light brought more pain, this time to my gut as well. My head felt light and my fingers crawled to the straw ends that used to be my hair. Tears of fury blinded me all over again. For a moment I felt paralyzed. Gritting my teeth, I rocked slowly over on my back. I stayed in position for several minutes, out of breath.

Slowly and carefully, I forced myself up on my elbows. Took a breath and pushed down with my hands until I ended up in a sitting position. So far so good. I wasn't terminal. I didn't hear Brady moving around the apartment. Smart man. He better stay away. Maybe he realized he wasn't safe here. I should have used the bat on him before he left. I thought of Trixie's dagger. Maybe I should get one.

I avoided the bathroom mirror before I showered, but had to look at myself to apply makeup. I cringed. The bruises on my face had turned purple. Every time I touched my skin, I wanted to scream.

My hair made me look worse than shit. I needed a wig to cover this mess. A vise-like pain squeezed my head and my eyes stung from crying. I found aspirin in the medicine cabinet, downed four with water, and forced myself to look through my closet for something to wear. Nothing sexy would match my hair style or the way I felt. I pulled on jeans and a sweatshirt.

Work was out of the question until I could figure out what to do with my appearance. When was the Atlantic City gig? I couldn't think straight. Next weekend? Or did I have an extra week to recover and plan? I had to think of something quick. Tony wouldn't listen to any excuses, but I couldn't perform looking like this. As for entertaining Nico Franchetti, forget it. He wouldn't look twice at me and that would upset whatever Tony had planned. Explaining what happened would only make matters worse. There was no question whose side he'd take. His right hand man and partner might embarrass him, but that would be the end of it. He'd protect Charley over me.

I had to concentrate on solutions. My hair problem had to be fixed first and I knew the only person who could help. I found Paul's number in my wallet and dialed. He answered groggily. "Who is this and what the fuck time is it?"

"Wake up," I said. "It's Erin. I need your help."

"Erin? My dancer babe? Call back in an hour."

"Paul, this is an emergency. Listen to me."

"Oohh, my head. Don't yell. Okay, hold on. I just got home an hour ago. Hangover city."

I heard shuffling noises, then water running.

He came back on the line, sounding every bit as groggy as when he picked up. "What's so important that can't wait until later?"

I gave him a brief rundown of what Brady had done. "I need help. Fast. Where do I find a good wig?"

"Your hair? He did what? Fuck. Hold a sec." He left again.

I waited so long, I thought he went back to sleep. Minutes later he came back on the line with an address. He told me to meet him there in an hour.

With a scarf over my head, I met Paul at a wig shop not far from where I lived. Paul was waiting inside when I arrived. He didn't look as hung over as he'd sounded over the phone. He blanched when he saw my face. A clerk started toward me, but he motioned her away.

I approached Paul and let the scarf drop.

He staggered back a step, and frowned. "Jesus. Not just your hair, but your face."

"I told you my asshole boyfriend went off on me." I left out the part about Charley.

"Babe, that's downright criminal. Time to get rid of that fucker. If you want, I know a guy with a solution." He winked.

I shuddered. "You're a good friend. All I want is for you to fix this." I patted my head.

"No fixing that, sweetheart. You were right. You need a wig. Only thing to do is cover up that mess until your hair grows out again. And it will grow out."

But not in time, I thought. I paced the floor looking at rows of shelves that held wigs on Styrofoam heads. Full-sized mannequins stood in every corner. I studied the various styles and colors until I was dizzy. "Help me pick one."

He ignored me. He knew exactly where to go. He stopped in front of a tall mannequin and slipped off a waist-length wig with luscious curls almost the same shade Paul had chosen for me the first time he'd colored my hair.

He grabbed a stool out of a corner and made me sit. Tilting my head up, he capped the wig over my hair. It felt tight, but Paul said it was a perfect fit and wouldn't fall off while dancing. He turned me toward a mirror. I sucked in a breath, relieved and amazed at the instant transformation. The shade of red made my skin glow everywhere, but on the bruises. Behind me, he twirled the curls and finessed the fake hair into a show piece.

"This is your revenge," he pronounced.

"Revenge nothing. It may save my life."

"I wouldn't go that far, darlin'." He frowned. "Or are you referring to something more serious than a haircut? Give, sweetheart. I'm all ears."

I took a deep breath. "I'm dancing in Atlantic City."

"Color me jealous." He stepped back to inspect his handiwork. "How did you land such a plum gig?"

"Not my idea or my choice. What do you know about the Lucky Lady?"

"The topless club? Girl, you're making me crazy. You don't dance topless. Why Atlantic City? Who's sending you?"

"Doesn't matter. Come on, I need info, not more questions. I know you hang out there all the time."

"Well, let's see." He strolled around me, checking out the wig from different angles. "So who is it? Not Joe or Lewis. Those guys need you right where you are."

"No, not them," I said.

He narrowed his eyes. "Lucky Lady is one of Tony Corelli's joints."

"I know."

Paul came to a stop in front of me and crossed his arms. "This sounds serious, babe. What are you involved in?"

"You don't want to know," I said.

"Maybe not, but tell me anyway. Corelli know you're dancing at his club?"

I just looked at him.

"Corelli is sending you?" His jaw dropped, but his voice rose in alarm.

A surge of panic went through me. "You can't tell anyone, Paul."

"Why? Is he threatening you?"

"No, it's not that. There's someone else involved. Don't ask me anymore."

Paul shook his head. "Damn, girl. Does this have any thing to do with your boyfriend? Is that why that coward chopped off your hair?"

"No. Brady doesn't know about this."

"Then he's a worse prick for messing you up. Jealousy makes a man crazy. "

"I know."

"Why haven't you told him about your new gig?"

"None of his business. He can go hang himself for all I care." I glanced at him. "What do you know about Charley Rossino?"

"Tony's manager and partner in the Philly clubs. Is he involved with the Atlantic City gig? I heard he wants to buy the clubs there."

I hadn't heard about that. Charley's interest in the clubs brought a new prospective to the picture I already had. I wished I'd known this before last night. Damn Tony. He could have mentioned it.

Paul fingered the wig again. "Stay away from Charley. That's my advice."

"He's one of my customers."

He shook his head. "Be careful. You don't want to get on his bad side."

"No kidding."

He stepped back and frowned. "I saw what you tried to cover up. I thought Brady did all of that."

"Not all of it," I admitted. "Some happened earlier at the club."

"Fuck. You've really gotten yourself into some shit."

I couldn't tell him about Johnny, but he already told me more than enough about Charley.

"I know a few guys who know a few guys who might know a little more," he said finally. "Let me check around. You working tonight?"

"I'm supposed to."

"I'll bring over some theatrical makeup before you leave. Nobody will know what happened to you after I get finished. Unless they get too close. In the meantime, get yourself some Vitamin E cream, and put ice on it, helps with the bruising. Are you sure you're able to dance?"

"No, but I have to anyway."

"Don't worry how you look. You'll be all right on stage. Lighting's dim on the floor, so you shouldn't have too much trouble there either."

I thanked him and paid the clerk who packed the wig in a hat box. Paul and I said our goodbyes on the street and he took off. I reached my apartment fifteen minutes later. To my relief, Brady hadn't returned. I locked up and hid the box in the closet. I was determined he would never see me in the wig, if he was crazy enough to tempt fate by coming by again.

I was so glad to be alone that I could hardly keep my eyes open. Maybe a quick nap would revive me for tonight's shift. I lay down, but couldn't sleep. I ran over different ways to get revenge on Brady, but none seemed harsh enough.

I soon tired of Brady and my thoughts drifted to Tony instead. The memory of that afternoon when I'd walked into that bar haunted me. Must have been a real jolt for Tony to hear me say Johnny's name. He thought he'd fooled the mob and Nico into thinking Johnny was dead. All his lies were coming back to bite him. Was Johnny the threat to his own existence? Or was I?

I thought about our confrontation at Dani's apartment and afterward at his place. The way his eyes bored into mine. Had I imagined the sexual heat that fired up between us? He'd been watching me from afar. Even back when he was hunting Johnny he was also watching me.

My head pounded anew. I had to figure a way to handle the Atlantic City gig without anyone getting hurt—including me.

I finally dozed off only to be awakened by the shrill ring of the telephone. I glanced at the clock. Three thirty-five.

Paul's voice brought me to a sitting position, a more painful maneuver than I experienced earlier. "I'm on my way over. Got some more information for you."

CHAPTER 29

Paul arrived with a suitcase full of makeup, combs, curlers, and hairspray. I directed him into the kitchen where he opened the suitcase on the counter.

"Watch out for Charley," he said without preamble.

I couldn't help laughing. "No shit. I learned that the hard way."

"Girl, you learn everything the hard way." He removed an artist palette of makeup from the case.

"You said you knew something more."

"Darling, please, let me tell the story my way. You're so impatient." He saw me fume and grinned. "When I left, I was thirsty anyway so I went to have a drink at one of the joints on Locust. They open early, and by noon the place is already smoking with girls dancing on the stage. I prefer watching young men dance, but that wasn't happening. I take what I can get."

He put dots of a liquid base coat, a shade darker than my skin tone, on my forehead, cheeks and chin.

"Wait," I said. "You went to Foxy Lady?"

"Sweetheart, give me credit. I'm not that obvious. There is more than one bar on Locust Street. Well, to tell the truth, I considered Foxy Lady, but on the way I stopped in a few other joints and as luck would have it, I found a mutual friend. Marty, the bouncer from Foxy Lady was having a drink with his buddy, Bix."

I grabbed Paul's arm. "He found Bix?"

"Don't get excited, sweetheart. That's want I wanted to tell you. Bix didn't hurt Dani."

I let go of his arm. "How do you know?"

"Bix's got an alibi." He smoothed the base coat with a feathery touch. "Marty and he were both upset after hearing what Charley did to you. Now they're convinced Charley hurt Dani. I told them to be cool and not freak out. Didn't want them alerting Charley about our suspicions yet."

Even Paul's light touch made me pull back in pain when he covered my bruises. "I wonder if Tony knows," I said. "You'd think he'd want to hurt whoever sent Dani to the hospital."

Paul raised an eyebrow.

I explained. "I mean, Dani must be his favorite if he's got a key to her apartment."

Paul nodded. "Yeah, he would. Tony and Dani's mother used to be an item before she overdosed."

"Poor Dani. Was her mother a dancer, too?"

"One of the best. Could have gone to Broadway if she hadn't fallen for the wrong guy. Instead she became a heroin addict."

"That must have been awful for Dani," I said. Another thought came to me. "Do you think Tony's her father?"

Paul chuckled. "No one's accused Tony that I know of, and he ain't saying." He applied blush then picked out what looked like a different artist's brush and went to work on my eyebrows.

"Okay, so back to Charley and Atlantic City. What did you find out?"

"I knew both Marty and Bix were crazy about Dani, and they'd had quite a bit to drink before I saw them."

I glanced at the clock. "Bottom line, Paul. I don't need the whole story. What did you find out?"

He looked crestfallen. Paul loved to ramble on for hours. "You know Charley owns half of the Philly clubs with Corelli. He also owns a half interest with Tony in the Atlantic City clubs."

I was disappointed. "I guessed that already."

"Okay, then you might not know that Tony is meeting a buyer from California who wants the whole lot." He saw the look on my face. "Okay, you heard that, too. Did you know Charley borrowed loan shark money to buy out Tony's interest when he found out about the California buyer?"

Corelli evidently didn't confide the whole story to Charley. He didn't appear to know that the California buyer was Nico Franchetti.

I said, "Too bad for Charley. I don't think he's going to be part of this deal." I couldn't tell him the rest. Enough people were in danger without me getting Paul involved. He'd already asked enough questions on the street than was healthy.

Paul was watching my expression. "You know something you're not telling me."

I shrugged. "Nothing I can talk about. Thanks for looking into this for me."

"I hope it helps in some way." He finished with my eyebrows and took another brush and held it over pots of paint on his palette. My bruised skin radiated and pulsed. "Getting back to your immediate problem, what're you wearing tonight?"

I groaned inwardly at the thought. "I haven't decided."

"Girl, if you want to be color coordinated, you gotta

figure it out now. I'm about to pick a color highlight for your eyes. Something other than black and blue, please."

I picked up the hand mirror from the table and had to bite my lip to keep from crying. He had worked miracles covering my bruises. I slid off the chair and let him help me pick out a costume so he could finish with my eyes and my lips. The finale came when Paul fit the wig on my head. Curls fell loosely down my back. When I finally faced the image again, I saw a beautifully painted mannequin. Tears came to my eyes as I stared back at the mirror.

"Can she dance?" My voice broke in spite of all my efforts to keep up the bravado I had managed so far.

Paul turned my face away from the mirror and lifted my chin. "Like a Broadway star."

I gave him a weak smile. "One who had the shit kicked out of her."

"But that would never stop you. Now stop feeling sorry for yourself and let's go."

I blinked away tears. Paul would kill me if he had to redo my makeup.

"Are you riding the bus with me?" I asked.

He looked alarmed. "No, babe, I'm calling a cab. I'm not taking chances of having a hair out of place before you get to work."

"You're paying?" I said.

"Hmmm. I'll split the cost with you, darling. Do you have it?"

"I can dig up some coins." I went into my bedroom and found my purse. Took out enough for cab fare, threw on a coat over my costume and pulled on my boots. I gave the money to Paul. "We can catch a cab outside. There's always one this time of night."

We didn't have to wait long. The driver dropped me off at Dreamscape and left to take Paul to his apartment. I walked into the dimly-lit bar half expecting Joe to stop me before I reached the stairs. I felt rather than saw his gaze follow me, but he said nothing. When I turned at the top of the stairs, I saw him smiling up at me. That smile warmed me. It felt like a good omen.

Customers filled half the room. Smoke drifted upward. Ice rattled in glasses. Music blared. I recognized a few regulars, nobody threatening. The front door swung open and Trixie made her entrance wearing a white fur coat that swirled around her feet. A matching fur hat revealed wisps of white blonde curls. Stilettos clicked across the floor, her lipstick smile wide enough for all the men in the room.

She met me at the top of the stairs. We glided into the dressing room together.

"Honey, I just want you to know, there's no hard feelings about last night. Hell, glad it was you, not me." She peered closer at my face. "You don't look too damaged. I was afraid he'd really fucked you up, the mood he was in." She took off her hat and shook out her curls. "I should have seen it coming. I should have warned you."

"You did," I said. "You said he would kill me. Remember?"

Her eyebrows lifted. "Oh, *that* warning. It's true, he's capable. With Charley, you can never tell how he's going to be." She eyed me again, this time with a critical stare. "Wow, I want the name of your hairdresser. Did he do your makeup, too?"

"He does it all," I said. She wasn't getting Paul's name out of me, although she could obviously afford him. I wasn't in a generous mood.

She moved close behind me until we were both looking in the mirror. "My boyfriend and I are having a small party after work if you want to come over to our place. You can bring your boyfriend. He's real cute. I told him about the party. He acted like you'd both might join in."

She talked to Brady last night? So he wasn't above talking to another dancer or buying her drinks behind my back.

"What sort of party?" I said.

Trixie smiled and wet her lips. "A fun party that couples can enjoy together."

It wasn't hard to imagine what she meant. A foursome any other time might have rated a second or third thought. She had mentioned her black ass honey man, an enticement that brought back memories of Carl. But Brady's run as a haircutter cooled any thoughts of sex between us or anyone else.

"Sorry," I said. "I've got plans."

Trixie shrugged. "Some other time then. I got the impression that your boy would enjoy the experience." She winked at me.

Maggie strode in, which stopped me from punching Trixie and ending my career. By that time I didn't care about the consequences, and if Brady got stupid and showed up at home, I'd tell him to go fuck Trixie *and* her boyfriend. If he had the money last night, I bet he'd have taken her upstairs. Bastard.

For my performances, I picked slow, sexy numbers, like "Light My Fire" by The Doors so my body wouldn't suffer more than necessary while I turned on the men. My new look gave me more confidence at the bar. Wit and sarcasm seemed to come easily. To my surprise, the customers responded to the edginess. I didn't hold back, feeling the sharp bite of anger against all men simmering under the surface of every conversation. I peppered it all with the right amount of sexual innuendo. It was a game anyway. These men were nothing but cheats and liars and I knew how to play them to win.

Drinks flowed. Money changed hands. I didn't need

to touch a man's crotch or take him upstairs or even sit in a dark corner with him. Not even Trixie could take the spotlight from me. I felt drunk with power, or maybe it was the scotch Joe served me.

I was feeling better and dancing like my old self when the front door flew open. Even from the stage I could see it was Marty. He didn't look up. He didn't walk. He staggered inside.

Someone screamed. I watched in horror as he held his stomach and in slow motion sank to the ground. A red stain spread across his shirt.

The music continued to play, but I ran off the stage and almost tripped taking the stairs.

I saw Joe jump over the bar to get to him. When I got to the foot of the stairs, Lewis blocked my way.

A crowd gathered. Someone yelled, "He's been stabbed."

Another scream. Did it come from me?

"Let me through," I cried.

"Stay back," Lewis ordered.

His face meant business, but I wasn't having any. I ducked under his arm, pushed through the crowd surrounding Marty and fell to my knees beside him. Pain dulled his eyes, but they flickered and struggled for life. His hand gripped mine with strength I didn't think possible. He pulled me toward him. I bent close to his lips.

"Marty," I said, "the ambulance is on its way. You're going to be all right. You've got to hang on."

He blinked, his eyes became unfocused.

"What happened?" I begged. "Who did this?"

"Dani—" he whispered.

"What about Dani? Don't you die, Marty."

He squeezed his eyes shut. I put my ear next to his mouth.

"Stopped—a fight—" His eyes flew open and in a

last burst of strength, he said, "Came to warn you—be careful—"

His eyes rolled back in his head. His hand dropped from mine. Sirens screamed. Lights flashed. The door flew open again. Uniforms piled in.

I was lifted up. Shoved out of the way.

Helpless, I watched the medics hover over Marty. The Who filled the room at full volume, not quite drowning out the shrill of the siren from the departing ambulance. Cops took witnesses outside separately to give their statement. The rest of the customers turned on their bar stools, heads down, drinks in their hand, the dying man already forgotten. Rachel came on stage and danced like a wooden puppet. The only girl who continued like nothing happened was Trixie. She paraded her tits to a pair of customers, arms draped across their shoulders, carrying on for the rest of us.

Lewis approached me in the shadows. In the dark his eyes looked flat and unresponsive. Maybe he would fire me. Good. I would be free to leave. Go to the hospital. Get out of town. Run, run, run.

"You're up next," Lewis said, indicating the stage with his thumb.

I stood frozen for several seconds, undecided. Couldn't block out the sight of Marty, bleeding, dying in my arms.

Lewis sighed, put his arm around me in a fatherly manner. "Nothing you could do, kid. Just another bar fight. Happens all the time."

Thanks, boss. That's supposed to make me feel better?

Like a prisoner, I nodded without answering and trudged up the stairs, feeling heavy as if my shoes were dipped in cement, waiting to be thrown off a bridge.

I stepped onstage to a Beatles tune. Aspirin and

scotch had no effect on the side of my face, which felt like a swollen balloon. My body moved on auto to all three songs while my mind mingled with Marty's ghost at the front door.

The night seemed lost on Maggie and Rachel, too. They moved like shadows, insubstantial on the flashing stage. I didn't know Marty like they did, but he had been a fixture in the nightlife, always partying at the clubs with us, always full of gossip and news about who was new in town and who the big tippers were. We knew he loved Dani from afar, but was more like a brother to her than a lover.

I couldn't keep my attention on the customers. Marty's voice ran through my mind like a needle stuck in a long-playing record. What about Dani? Who should I be careful of and why? Had Dani died? Is that what he was trying to tell me?

CHAPTER 30

I tossed lacy underwear in my suitcase, discarding unwanted items on the floor. I heard the apartment door open and swore under my breath. A glance at my watch stirred panic and I felt my heart in my throat. I needed to catch the train in thirty minutes if I was going to arrive in Atlantic City in time. Two seconds later Brady stepped into the bedroom. I hadn't put on my wig yet and my hair spiked on top. That's how I wanted to look when he was around. I ignored him while I continued to pack. I threw in the wig at the last minute.

He stopped short when he saw my suitcase. "Where the hell are you going?" he said finally.

"Damn," I said, going to the closet. "I knew there was something I forgot. I meant to tell the manager to change the locks two weeks ago."

"I've given you time to cool down. I tried to see you before, but you wouldn't answer the door or my calls. You can't kick me out for good without listening to me."

"Of course, I can. You're not paying the rent." I threw in two shirts and slammed the suitcase shut. "Do you think I'd forget what you did? Takes more than a couple of weeks. What are you doing here? Looking for more clothes to burn?"

His face reddened. "You're still mad at me, aren't you?"

"No, Brady, that would mean I still had feelings for you. That went bye-bye with my hair."

"I came to say I'm sorry. I got jealous. Seeing you with other men makes me crazy. I'll make it up to you, I promise." He sidestepped around me and sat on the edge of the bed. "I heard about Marty's murder. I know he was a friend of yours."

I closed my eyes, trying to block out Brady's words. The image of Marty bleeding on that dirty floor never seemed to leave me. I blinked. "It was bad."

He pointed to the suitcase. "Where are you going?"

"I have a gig," I said, reminded again I was running out of time. I grabbed my jacket out of the closet.

He frowned. "Where?"

"Atlantic City."

"Dancing? You never mentioned that."

"Why the hell should I?"

"We used to tell each other everything."

I shot him a look of disbelief. "Really? When were you going to tell me about Trixie's offer?"

He had the nerve to act like he didn't know what I was talking about. He stood and blocked my way. I wasn't sure if he wanted to hit me again or kiss me.

I picked up my suitcase and held it like a shield. "We're through, Brady. As a matter of fact, I'm glad you're here so you can pick up your crap. Leave your key when you're done."

He stopped moving and his face darkened. "You don't mean that."

"After what you did? Look at my face and my hair. What the fuck do you expect?"

Brady winced. "I said I was sorry. You know I love you."

"That's the way you show it?" It felt good to see him miserable.

"I'll never hit you again, I promise. I'm really sorry about your hair."

He took one step closer, but I lifted my suitcase higher.

"All right," he said. "You're still angry, but let me at least protect you in Atlantic City."

"Protect me from what? Guys like you?"

"You'll be in a rougher part of the boardwalk."

I bristled. "How do you know where I'm dancing?"

"There are only so many clubs in Atlantic City with go-go dancers. Most of them are owned by the same group that owns Locust Street. Bad karma, babe."

I dropped the suitcase on the floor. "I'm no longer your babe. If I want your opinion on anything, I'll ask. Now get out of my way. I have a train to catch."

He paused, and seemed to come to a decision. "There's another way. We can take my car."

I stared at him in surprise. "What car?"

"Mine."

I searched his face for a sign he was lying. "You never told me you had a car." What else had he kept from me?

"There's no place to park in the city. I rent space in a garage. I only need it when I get out of town. I was going to tell you."

When? We'd been together for almost a year. Must be ashamed of the wreck. "What kind? Don't tell me it's a Volkswagen." I couldn't picture him as a hippy.

He laughed, sounding more confident. "A cherry red Camaro convertible."

My dream car. I closed my eyes and pictured the car I'd seen advertised on billboards. Awesome color, sleek, powerful. I imagined speed and muscle, my hands clasped around the wheel, my foot against the pedal. So tempting.

Damn Brady. Why was I so weak?

I glanced at Brady. He leaned against the door frame, arms folded, a smug smile on his face. So fucking sure of himself, thinking he'd won this round.

"Forget it. I'm taking the train." I glanced at the clock. If I didn't get to the station fast, I wouldn't be going anywhere. Tony wouldn't accept excuses if I didn't make it.

As if reading my mind, he said, "My Camaro will get you there faster."

I stopped, knowing I had to decide between rushing to the station, taking a chance on missing the train, or giving in to Brady and riding in his car. I stalled. "Don't you have to work?"

"I've taken a few days off," he said.

I took a deep breath. "I'll agree on two conditions. Number one, I drive."

His hands dropped to his side and he straightened. His face went ashen. "You?"

"That's the deal. The second condition is you stay away from the club. Get a hotel room, go see another show, I don't care. But stay away from where I'm working."

"You want to drive my Camaro?" He seemed fixated on that. I don't think he heard what else I said.

I stood firm. "Take it or leave it."

When he didn't answer right away, I picked up the suitcase and started for the door.

"You need a driver's license," he countered.

"I got a license." From California, but it was still a license. I glanced back at him. He rubbed his chin like it was genie's bottle. "I'm leaving now, so make up your mind."

His Adam's apple bobbed up and down. "You win."

෧ඁ෧

I wore a black mini with a white halter top, four-inch heels, and a black beret and felt like Twiggy in Paris. I anxiously waited for Brady to come around the corner in the red Camaro. Not the new model I pictured in my head, but a sleek muscle car nonetheless. Brady popped out of the driver's side. He strutted like a rooster to the passenger's side and opened the door. I picked up my suitcase and ambled down the stairs, focusing on the white bucket seats.

Brady brandished the keys in front of my face, clasping them in his fingers as if he didn't want to let go. He looked nervous. "Need lessons?"

I grinned. "Are you kidding? Wait until I get this baby out on the road."

The last car I drove was a Cadillac, a luxury Johnny talked me into buying with my inheritance. I drove us to Baja California for a six-month stay and back again only to trade it in for an Airstream.

Brady took my suitcase from me and set it in the trunk. He sank into the passenger's seat. I slid behind the wheel and took out the address Tony had given me.

Brady glanced over. "What's that?"

"My instructions. It says to drive and shut the fuck up."

I hit the gas. Brady wrapped his fist around the door handle as I grinded the gears and peeled out. I zoomed around cars and pedestrians. He kept glancing over at me, his knuckles whitening. I wanted to laugh, see the needle meet the hundred mark, watch Brady's reaction, but I wasn't ready to kill us.

Brady let the silence stretch out with the miles.

I let my thoughts stray to the job Tony was paying me to do. Not too different from my own purpose, which was to keep Johnny alive.

I felt a hand on my arm and shot Brady a look. "What?"

"You in a hurry?" He pointed to the speedometer. "I like to race, too, but the cops are out everywhere today."

I looked at the dial. Eighty-five creeping toward ninety. I eased my foot off the gas. "Chicken."

He lifted an eyebrow. No smile. No doubt he was regretting his decision to let me drive.

I gripped the wheel tighter. Maybe Nico wouldn't show and then all my worry for Johnny could fly out the window. No, the dumb bastard would be there because he knew the truth and he planned to make it pay off big. He would own the Atlantic City clubs. Maybe he was even more ambitious. Like owning all of Atlantic City. I could picture a transformation that would be something like Las Vegas.

Brady nudged me again. Pointed at the speedometer, shaking at ninety.

His voice rose. "What's the matter with you? You got something going on I don't know about?"

"I just want to get there," I answered.

"Yeah, me too. Alive."

I should have left him standing at the curb in front of the apartment.

Blackhorse Pike grew more congested as we neared the New Jersey border and I was forced to drive with the flow of traffic. It seemed to me the entire population of Pennsylvania was headed for the boardwalk.

When I inhaled the smell of the Atlantic, I knew we had arrived. I slowed and pulled over on a side street and checked the directions again. I might as well have followed my nose, we were that close.

Fifteen minutes later, I saw the sign. *Lucky Lady.*
I pointed. "There."

The bar anchored at the far end of the boardwalk. I parked on the street as close as I could get. Brady locked the trunk and rolled up the canvas top.

I watched the crowds stroll along the boardwalk, many disappearing into storefronts and restaurants. "I'll walk from here. Remember what I said, stay away from the club. I'll find you afterward."

"What if you get in trouble? Why can't I be there? I want to see you dance."

I stepped in front of him. "You agreed to this, Brady. You promised. That's one of the reasons I let you come with me. You owe me this favor." I saw he was conflicted and needed more convincing. "I'm working here. I'd feel self-conscious with you watching. I'll meet you on the beach at midnight. Please, do this for me."

His face slackened and he nodded reluctantly. "Okay, but I'll be close by."

I left him and strolled down the boardwalk. With him behind me and the sight of the sea to my left, my resolve strengthened. The air felt different, lighter away from the city. Several tourists had taken off their shoes to shuffle through the sand and get their feet wet as the waves lapped the shore. The briny smell off the ocean mingled with the sweetness of cotton candy and taffy from vendor carts.

Music drifted out from the cafes and bars. The sound of the Beatles singing "Sgt. Pepper's Lonely Hearts Club Band" echoed over the boardwalk. Farther down, Credence Clearwater Revival wafted out of a café that advertised *Fried Frog Legs* in block letters on the glass front. As I neared Lucky Lady, I saw young girls with big hair, wearing hotpants and mini-skirts, standing by the front door.

They drank sodas, smoked filtered cigarettes, and occasionally pulled in a customer. I loosened my shoulders, let my hips sway, and arrived at the bar's entrance.

CHAPTER 31

I pushed the door open and waited until my eyes adjusted to the darkness. A crowd packed the tables in Lucky Lady, their voices fighting to be heard. Cigarette smoke drifted like clouds above their heads and mingled with the smell of sweat and spilled beer, replacing any form of fresh air from the outside.

A long curved bar commanded one end of the room and most of the barstools were taken. Waitresses in black mini-skirts and gold tops that showed the swell of their breasts wove around tables carrying full trays of drinks to those seated.

A circular raised platform beside the bar served as the stage.

Sweat popped on my neck. I wanted to forget the whole show, or get it over with quick. I asked the red-headed bartender, who didn't look old enough to mix drinks, where I could find the manager. He pointed to a tall guy in a gray suit smoking a cigarette in the corner. The guy spotted me and motioned me over. I realized he had the advantage of being able to watch the room and everyone in it from where he stood.

"Tony Corelli sent me," I told him. "Said to tell you I'm dancing under the name Flame." Tony picked the name to go with my hair, the short version now hidden under my beret.

The manager eyed me as if fitting me for a costume. "I hope you're better than the last one who called herself a dancer."

"I am," I said, venturing another glance around the room. I wondered if anyone managed to impress this audience comprised mostly of men middle-aged or younger.

"You go topless?"

"No," I said.

He frowned. "How you expect to get these clods' attention then?"

"Watch and see," I challenged.

"You're one of those. Well, if you bore them, I'll notice, then you'll take off the top or you're out."

I shrugged. "I'm not worried. Where do I change?"

He pointed to a door between the bar and the stage.

"Thanks."

He stuck his cigarette between his lips and crossed his arms. He scanned the faces in the room. The music volume went up, and the dressing room door opened. A topless young woman with short black curls came out and mounted the stage. She had a curvy figure and showed it off with a black spandex bottom that hugged her hips. Large breasts too heavy to be called perky bounced without benefit of restraint. All eyes strained to look at Topless and her breasts. I observed the girl with the critical interest of a competitor.

What struck me was the way she never smiled or related to the audience. Her bored superior look reminded me of Maggie, but after a moment I decided I was being unfair to my friend. Maggie could somehow pull it off where this girl didn't.

I glanced again at the audience. Some of them still eyed the stage, but most returned to their conversation with their buddies or ordered more drinks. Others stared into space, as bored as the dancer looked. No enthusiasm in the crowd. After one look no one cared if her boobs were bouncing.

I scanned the room again, this time more carefully, looking for someone that matched the name Nico Franchetti. Tony's description of an Italian mobster didn't fit anyone I saw at the tables.

"Your turn in five," a voice said.

I whirled at the sound. The manager stood behind me, face stern, lips thinned.

"After this song," he said.

I hurried to the backstage door.

I changed fast. If Nico was in the audience, he was the one I needed to impress. I applied stage makeup and fitted the red wig on my head. My legs felt weak, my throat dry. I needed a drink.

Topless was taking the three wooden steps down from the stage when I walked out of the dressing room. A glance at the crowd told me nothing had changed while I'd been in the dressing room. The manager stood by the stage, a cigarette dangling from his mouth. He kept a close watch on me as I strode to the stage. How much had Tony told him?

The music of The Doors shattered the silence. I mounted the stairs, my confidence at risk. My only talent was dancing. I had nothing else. If I didn't stir this crowd, I'd have to take off my top. I needed to forget about Nico. Forget about Tony and Johnny. Only concentrate on what I did best. For the next ten minutes, nothing else mattered.

I closed my eyes and let the music absorb into every muscle, bone and sinew, the rhythm and beat taking over not only my body but my soul. I emptied my mind of everything but the connection between dancer and audi-

ence. I danced for them. I met their eyes, smiled, beckoned, and teased. I reacted to their responses. Just before
each song ended, I allowed a glance at the manager. The
same cigarette stuck to his lower lip. He never moved,
while his eyes glazed over. I proved my case. I bet I
could dress in a bag and still get more reaction than his
topless dancer.

My face felt flushed from dancing as the applause
followed me off the stage. In the privacy of the dressing
room, I stared into the mirror. My face shone with a rosy
hue that darkened my bruises, but much of the discoloration had faded over the weeks. My eyes glittered. The
heat prickled my skin. I whipped off the wig. The slow
moving overhead fan brought a welcome breeze to my
damp hair and scalp.

Dancing was the easy part of Tony's instructions. I
didn't look forward to entertaining Nico Franchetti.
Where was Johnny? Had Tony got the word to him? I
hadn't any contact with Corelli since we'd talked in his
apartment.

I wiped my face clean and applied fresh make up. I
changed into a white low-cut mini-dress, put on white
stiletto heels, and reset the vibrant red wig over my damp
head, letting the curls tumble down my back.

After one final check in the mirror, I left the dressing
room.

The bar was hot and smoke-filled. The wig fit snug
against my scalp. I strode to the bar and ordered ice water. I'd let Nico Franchetti find me.

A fat man with a round face and baby-smooth olive
skin approached after my first sip. The top of his balding
head barely came up to my chin. He beamed as he looked
me up and down. "I'm Nico Franchetti. You some swell
dancer. You are Flame?"

I leaned back against the bar in what I hoped was a

provocative pose. "You got it, honey. I'm your guide this afternoon."

"My pleasure," Nico said with a leer. "I like red-heads. Tony says you are smart girl. He no mention you were looker."

"Why, thank you, Mr. Franchetti." *Up your ass, Mr. Franchetti. Don't mistake looker for hooker.*

"Call me Nico. How come you no dance in Tony's Philly clubs? Seem to me he misses a good thing."

A charmer, this Nico. Too bad he was as ugly as a mole rat. "He doesn't want me to have too much exposure to start out."

"He plan something special for you. I knew it. Like you here, to please me." Nico winked. He patted my ass and gave it a squeeze.

I moved out of his reach. "Take it easy, honey. We have clubs to see. We have all night."

"His clubs can wait. You can't."

Tony hadn't mentioned whoring me out to Nico. "Tony says you need to see what you're buying."

Nico's mud-colored eyes focused on my cleavage. "I am looking at what I want to buy."

I started to set Nico straight when I saw Charley lurking near the entrance. My heart jumped to my throat. What the hell was he doing here? My fists clenched. I hadn't forgotten what he did to me upstairs at Dreamspell. My face burned at the memory. His gaze flicked over me without interest before leveling his stare at Nico. If looks could kill, I'd never have to worry about Nico again. But that would leave Charley.

Tony Corelli, who rattled me further, walked in behind Charley, looked all spiffed up in a black suit and white shirt. Not a sweat stain or a shine on him despite the sultry August heat. Tony hadn't mentioned he would bring Charley. Did he know about his partner's plans? Or about the loan shark money? How was he going to break the news to Charley that he was selling out to Nico? Maybe I was wrong. Maybe Charley already knew and had accepted the idea that he would be paired with Nico. Somehow I doubted that scenario.

Tony strode past Charley and carved a path toward us. Nico pulled out a cigar and bit off the end. He spit it out on the floor. He grinned at Tony and stuck the cigar in the corner of his mouth.

Tony shook Nico's hand. "I see you've met Flame. She taking care of you?"

Nico chomped on the cigar and placed his arm around my shoulders. "Better if we had a room." His laugh echoed through the room. "I'm a joking, Tony. Don't look so serious. Our business can wait, eh?" He pulled me closer to him, grabbing a tit in his sweaty hands.

I glared at Tony, not caring if Nico noticed.

Tony didn't react. "Sure, Nico. Have a good time. Have another drink and buy one for Flame. I have to see about something else right now, but whenever you're ready, have Flame go with you to the other clubs."

I watched Tony leave and extracted myself from Nico's grip. He grinned and waved to the bartender. "Two scotch and waters." He turned his head to me. "I hear that is your drink, Miss Flame. We gonna have us a good time."

I barely listened as Nico rattled on about how I could entertain him. Instead, I kept my eyes on Tony as he headed for the kitchen accompanied by Charley. Both looked grim. Oh, oh. I was beginning to think my first assumption was right. Charley didn't know what was going on and now he was going to find out.

I didn't want to wait for something to happen that I couldn't handle. No way was I playing along with this game anymore. I needed an excuse to get away without rousing Nico's suspicions. Spilling my drink would be too obvious, but a waitress spilling her tray wouldn't point to me.

I waited until one of the waitresses filled her tray at the bar and started to pass me. When the girl tripped and her tray wobbled, she juggled those drinks like a magician. I was impressed. Nevertheless, a strawberry Daiquiri was top heavy and spilled down my front.

I jumped back. "My dress!"

Nico sputtered for a few seconds before he picked up a bar napkin and made a few futile swipes at my dress. He succeeded only in grabbing another feel.

I pushed his hand away. "I'll take care of it." I left him holding the soiled napkin and rushed toward the kitchen. When I reached the swinging doors, I eased them open. The kitchen was crowded, noisy, and hot. At first all I saw were the cooks chopping and slicing and flipping meat on the grill. On my right, dishwashers stood before institution-sized sinks and sprayed dishes with high-powered hoses. One of them, tall and thin with his blond hair in a ponytail, saw the strawberry mess dripping off my dress. He pointed to an empty wash basin that held a hose with a spray attachment. I nodded my thanks and looked around for Tony and Charley. Had they gone out the back?

I heard their voices first, coming from inside a storage room on the other side of the wash basin. Because the dishwasher was watching me, I leaned over and sprayed the front of my dress. I gasped as the cold water soaked through to my skin and grabbed a towel off a six-foot-wide laundry basket on rollers a few feet away. The top of the basket reached my waist and the bottom dragged on the ground, heavy with dirty towels and aprons. The towel I picked was stained and smelly, but I had no choice. I had an excuse for being there if caught eaves-dropping. The dishwasher nodded and turned his attention back to his work.

I kept the towel pressed against my dress and inched closer to the storage room. If either or both men came out, I would be the first person they saw. I held my breath and strained to hear.

Charley's voice rose over the kitchen noise. "Why are you doing business with that thug? Let me get rid of him. You don't need him."

Tony's voice stayed calm but firm. "I'm handling it. Stop worrying."

"You promised I could buy you out. Those clubs belong to me. I borrowed money on your promise. How am I supposed to pay them back plus the vig?"

I knew from Carl that the vig was the loan shark's interest on the original amount of the loan.

Tony sounded disgusted. "That's your problem, Charley. I never told you to borrow money. That was stupid."

"You're selling me out, boss. What's Nico got on you, forcing you to sell to him? He's blackmailing you, ain't he?"

"That's none of your business," Tony said.

"Wait, this is about Nico's contract on Johnny, right? You didn't make good so now you're Nico's bitch."

"Watch it, Charley. You're going too far."

"Look, boss, Johnny's here. I seen him.

My heart was planted in my throat. Johnny had arrived at the club?

Charley continued. "If we take him out, the contract's done. Or we take Nico out. Or kill 'em both. Don't bother me none. Then we're clear. Tony, get smart. You want out of the bar business in this fucking town, I buy you out. Simple, boss."

"You get smart and stay out of this," Tony said. "I said I'll handle it."

"Oh shit. It's the girl, ain't it? Fucking whore. She screwed you up. She's why you didn't do the hit on Johnny."

I stuffed a fist in my mouth to keep from screaming. Since when did Tony get fixated on me? Why the hell was Charley blaming me?

"Leave her out of this," Tony said. "She's got nothing to do with the hit."

"You know what they do when a hit don't happen. They go after the hit man. You know how they are. They'll use me, Tony. In exchange for the loan and vig. What am I supposed to tell them? That you're too hung up on the girl to kill your target?"

Hung up on me? Bullshit. He'd seen me from a distance while he was stalking Johnny. That didn't mean anything. Johnny was too smart for him. That's the only reason he's still alive. Hung up on me? He didn't even know me. Not then, not now.

"I'm telling you, Nico will want me for the trigger man and I won't have a choice. They'll order me to wipe you out and for what?"

"Shut the fuck up, Charley." No mistaking the threat in his tone.

"She ain't worth it, boss. She's a real cocksucker. Ask me, I can tell you. She did me at that club where she works. Ask her if you don't believe me. Don't be a chump, Tony. Why you send her down here?"

The best question of all, I thought. My head swam.

Scuffling feet warned me they could burst out any moment. I was too far away to make it back to the bar. Instead, I sank behind the laundry basket.

I heard Tony's voice, low and threatening. "You touch her, you're a dead man. Understood?"

"Yeah, I understand all right," Charley said, his tone bitter. "But if you don't take care of this Nico business, I will."

One set of footsteps stomped past the laundry basket. I waited, hardly daring to breathe. Who left? I heard a door slam on the other side of the kitchen and hoped that Tony and Charley were gone.

The laundry cart moved, exposing me. I looked up to find the dishwasher staring at me. I glanced around as I got to my feet. No sign of Tony or Charley.

The guy frowned. "You all right? What happened?"

I indicated my stained dress. "I really messed up. If my boss sees this, I'll be fired."

He looked at the swinging door to the bar. "Yeah, I understand. I can get you to the dressing room without anybody seeing you."

He was suddenly my best friend. He led me to a lounge area with lockers on one wall and two tables in the middle, littered with ashtrays full of cigarette stubs. He pointed out two doors. "That one opens to the alley in back. The other gets you through the back of the dressing room. Comes in handy for the girls who want to leave without being seen."

"You're a life saver," I told him.

He might never know how true those words would be. I thanked him and let myself into the dressing room.

Topless was in front of the mirror spraying her hair. She eyed my reflection without turning. "What happened to you?"

"Long story." I stripped and rummaged through my suitcase, taking out a sleeveless mini. I shook out the wrinkles, slipped it on, and zipped up. I squeezed beside Topless in front of the mirror. The rich forest green of the dress flattered my skin color and burgundy color of my wig.

"Somebody was looking for you," Topless said. "Impatient guy."

"Not surprised." I stood with my hand on the door-knob.

"You gonna finish out the day?"

I turned back to her. "If not, I'm sure you can handle it."

"What does that mean?" she said, clearly annoyed.

I didn't answer. Instead of leaving, I opened my suit-case, rolled up the soiled dress, and stuffed it inside. My costumes and makeup followed the soiled dress.

"You're leaving?" Her voice raised an octave.

"As soon as I finish up some business," I answered.

"You're supposed to dance after me."

"Sorry," I said. "I don't think I'll make it."

CHAPTER 32

Charley was right about one thing. I didn't want anyone to die, but if Nico was bumped off, I wouldn't feel bad. With Nico out of the way, Tony wouldn't have the contract on Johnny. Johnny would be safe and I would be long gone. Or so I hoped.

I opened the dressing room door and stepped into the noisy, smoke-filled bar. Restless customers awaited the show. Behind me, Topless emerged from the dressing room and climbed onstage. The crowd clapped as she bounced to the accompaniment of The Monkees singing "I'm a Believer."

I stood behind the stage and peered around the side. Brady never listened to me. If I knew him as well as I thought, he would be here. But there was no sign of him. The one time I really needed him, he decided to listen and stay away.

Nico hadn't left the bar, but I could tell from a distance he looked annoyed. I didn't want him to see me until I found Brady. I eased back behind the stage.

A hand clasped the back of my neck. "What the fuck—" I started to turn but the pressure on my neck increased painfully. I reached around and sank my fingernails into a hand. Nothing happened except my neck jerked forward. I gritted my teeth and said, "Let go or I'll scream."

The pressure released enough for me to turn and look behind me. My knees went weak at the sight of the grim expression on his narrow, weathered face.

"Johnny? Oh my God, it's you." My heart beat like a bass drum at a rock concert.

Icy blue-gray eyes regarded me. "Well, well, Erin, how you've changed. Not enough and not for the better."

I swallowed at the all too familiar scorn that resonated in both tone and words. "Johnny, you shouldn't be here. Don't you know that you're still in danger?"

"What are you doing here?" he said in a low growl.

"You're still angry. Well, you've got every right. I was crazy back then—"

"Shut up. Not very smart to bring up the past. I could kill you for what you did to me, but we'll settle that later. Don't speak, just listen."

He stepped farther back into the shadows behind the stage, drawing me with him. I saw the man I'd run away from almost a year ago. He hadn't changed. The spotlight that hung over the stage glinted off his silver-gray hair which curled over his black turtleneck. Still powerfully built, the wide muscular shoulders I'd always admired sloped down to a narrow waist that showed not a hint of fat.

Nor was there a sign of the injury I'd inflicted on him with the iron skillet. Maybe the scar over his left ear. I winced.

Neither was there a sign of the injuries he suffered jumping off a roof to escape a hit man. The sheer strength of his will power to overcome the odds made him walk again when the prognosis said differently. That power that attracted me when we met affected me now.

He turned me around so my back was to him. He

kept his voice low and close to my ear. "I shouldn't care what happens to you, but I'm telling you go back to Philadelphia. Don't ask questions, don't argue. Leave and do it now."

I whispered back. "I know what you're trying to do, and it won't work. Why couldn't you trust me enough to tell me about Nico and the contract he took out on you? Don't you think I knew someone was chasing us?"

"How could I trust you? You trusted everyone but me."

This wasn't the time to argue. "Did you know that Nico and Tony were both here?"

"Of course. That's why I'm here. You must leave now. They're using you to get to me."

"I am leaving, packed and ready. You should, too, Johnny."

"You had nothing to do with this?"

I stood my ground. "Tony told me about the hit. I agreed to come here when he asked me if I wanted you dead or alive. I told him I wanted you alive and I would do everything it took to save you. I was crazy to try what I did to you. I've never forgiven myself. I thought I really did succeed. I came back. Did you know that? I wasn't going to leave. And you were gone. I didn't know what to think. So I ran."

He didn't say anything. Just stared at me. I felt worse than ever.

"Charley's the dangerous one," I said, trying to get through to him. "Think what you want of me, I'm trying to save your life. I overheard him and Tony talking in the kitchen. Charley won't hesitate to kill Nico or you or even Tony in order to get control of the nightclubs here."

"I'm aware of Charley." His lips formed a grim line. "I'm not that easy to kill. As you should know."

His words delivered a well-aimed ball of guilt that

collided with my own. I felt a current of air behind me. When I turned, Johnny was gone. I slumped against the wall behind the stage. I don't know how long I stayed that way, but I finally managed to move and stepped into the noise and the push of the crowd.

Tony plowed a path through the customers packed in the bar. I ventured a quick glance around the room for Johnny, but he had disappeared. Tony's dark eyes flashed in fury. When he reached me, he gripped my upper arm and kept his voice low so only I could hear him. "Where the hell have you been? Nico's been looking everywhere for you. Have you forgotten our bargain?"

I pried his fingers off my arm. "Get away from me. We don't have a bargain anymore. I don't like being used."

"What do you mean? We already had this discussion. You knew what you were getting into."

"Fucking Nico wasn't in the bargain. You let Nico think I'm for sale, too."

His eyes narrowed. "You are dead wrong." His tone dripped venom.

He looked up and I followed his gaze. Nico lumbered toward us.

I lightened my tone and addressed Tony loud enough for Nico to hear. "Didn't Nico tell you about my dress? A strawberry Daiquiri all down the front. As you can see, I had to change. Really, Tony, the club owes me a new dress."

Tony didn't seem to buy a word, but Nico apparently swallowed every syllable.

"Ah, you found her," Nico said. "Looking beautiful, just for me."

He took my hand and drew me away from Tony. Great. If Nico was Charley's target, I didn't want to be anywhere close to him.

Nico grinned, revealing a gold tooth I hadn't noticed before. "You show me the clubs now."

"If that's what you want," I said, wishing I could leave Atlantic City and get as far away as possible from all this crap.

I spotted Brady by the restrooms, trying to blend in with other customers. Thank God. I had to get his attention.

I turned to Nico. "I need to visit the ladies before we go. I'll be just a minute."

He frowned. "You just came back."

"One minute, Nico. It's the ice water. I can't help it."

Before he could protest further, I broke away. Brady looked hesitant as I approached him. I nodded in the direction of the ladies. He understood and planted himself by the door.

I paused next to him without looking his way and whispered, "Get my suitcase and purse out of the dressing room and put them in the car. Have the keys ready. I'll meet you as soon as I can get away."

Brady stepped aside, and I continued into the restroom. Minutes later I rejoined Nico, who paced in front of the bar, impatient to leave and join the crowd of tourists on the boardwalk.

Outside, the sea air filled my lungs, and we were surrounded by young families with children, groups of teenagers, couples holding hands. Several lined up to try their luck at "Shoot the Duck" or "Sink the Penny."

I tried to ignore the increased flutter in my chest and the tightness in my throat.

I glanced around to see if Johnny or Charley lurked in the shadows. I hoped Brady got to the dressing room without being stopped.

"Do you know where we are going?"

Nico's question threw me off balance. I stumbled.

Nico grasped my arm and propelled me through the crowd, forcing me to trot beside him.

"Nico, slow down. Why the questions?"

"Because I don't think you have ever been to Atlantic City. Yet Tony asks you to show me the clubs. Why is that?"

I tensed. "Tony doesn't explain anything to me. He offered me a job and I accepted."

Nico nodded his head. "That is funny. You never worked for him before. Is this not true?"

"Not in Philadelphia." My mouth felt dry. I didn't like the direction this conversation was headed. "Why should it matter? You're only interested in buying his Atlantic City clubs. I'm just dressing."

"You think so, Flame? Or should I be calling you Erin? You know what I did to the last chick who lied to me, *Erin*? I sliced her nipples off. I would find it much fun to do yours."

"Let go of me." I tried to pull my arm away, but he squeezed tighter. My hand grew numb. The crowd had thinned and I saw why. We were at the other end of the boardwalk and had almost reached the other two bars Tony owned, Dancers and Roxy. The familiar smell of beer and whiskey called to me. Maybe I'd be safe if I could lose Nico in one of those places.

I was out of breath from being dragged along, while Nico didn't seem the least bothered, despite his girth. He wasn't even sweating. He pushed me off the boardwalk onto the sandy beach and came to stand next to me.

"Erin Matthews," he said, with a look of triumph. "Did Tony not tell you about the deal we made to save his life? You and his nightclubs."

I tried again to wrench free. When I couldn't, I braked to a stop. "Fuck you, Nico. I am not for sale."

"You're already sold." A self-satisfied sneer spread

over his bloated face. "Everyone has a price. Even Tony Corelli. You are here because Tony has bigger worries than you."

"I know you're blackmailing him. You don't really want me. If it's the nightclubs you want, you can fight Charley for those, if he doesn't kill you first."

Too late I realized I had gone too far. There was a dangerous glint in Nico's eyes. I glanced past him to where the Atlantic Ocean tumbled in waves, and foam slithered up the shore. I wanted to jump in the water and swim away.

"Who is this Charley who thinks he can kill me? Tony's boy? A joke. Only good enough to beat up women." Something about the nightclubs behind me distracted him. Surprise and fury flashed across his face.

A man shouted my name and I recognized the voice. Brady was running toward me from the opposite direction of the boardwalk, his feet digging into the sand and leaving a spray behind him. As I tried to twist free of Nico, I heard a pop. I froze in horror as a bullet opened a hole between Nico's eyes. Brady tackled me from behind and shoved me to into the sand. I heard a second pop as I covered my head with my hands. The smell of death went straight from my nostrils to my stomach. When I lifted my head, Nico lay crumpled in front of me, eyes open, face frozen. The sand turned crimson. The smell got worse.

Brady pulled me to my feet, yelling, "Run!" I looked back and saw a figure darting behind the door to one of the other bars. I didn't bother to see which one.

Brady half-carried, half-dragged me away from Nico. My wig twisted, synthetic hair blew on my face and caught in my mouth. I yanked it off. My feet made contact with the sand and I ran alongside Brady.

We circled around to the boardwalk where the crowd

of tourists made heavy cover. I felt as if I'd raced up a mountain with no oxygen. Brady steered us under the awning of a gift shop where we stopped to catch our breath.

"He's not going to shoot us in this crowd," Brady whispered.

I panted. "Who? Was it Charley?" The second I spoke, I knew the name would mean nothing to Brady.

"Don't know. I put your stuff in the trunk. I've got the keys. Can you make it?"

Gasping for air, I could only nod. I looked back down the boardwalk, but couldn't see anyone chasing us.

"We should call the police," I said, panting. "They need to know about Nico."

"Later. Once we're away from here. "

"Did you get a look at the shooter?"

"No, the guy jumped behind the door. He shot at you, too."

I remembered hearing two pops, the one after Nico was down was meant for me.

"Come on." Brady pushed on my back. "The car's just ahead. If we stay close to the shops and people, maybe we won't be seen."

I wasn't sure about that. As I looked again into the mass of people behind us, I thought I could detect erratic movements.

We hurried along the storefronts. People stared at us. I looked down and saw drops of red on my dress. Nico's blood? Reality hit me hard. Panic gripped my throat and I ran faster.

"We're almost there." Brady reached in his pocket for the car keys. We veered left into the parking lot and dashed toward the Camaro. He opened the passenger door for me and hurried around to slide behind the wheel. The engine cranked and Brady peeled out onto the road.

I kept looking back as Brady swerved in and out of traffic. I couldn't see anyone following us. As we turned onto Blackhorse Pike, I started to relax.

"How did you know where I'd be?" I asked as he swerved into the fast lane and sped up.

"I didn't. When I saw you leave with Nico, I got a bad feeling. I went looking for you. I got there just in time."

"I'm so glad," I said, stroking his arm.

He managed a smile, but got distracted when he glanced at the rearview. The smile disappeared. Grim faced, he pushed the gas pedal down and we spurted ahead. I glanced at the speedometer. It shook at ninety and climbing.

"What's wrong?" I said, my stomach flip-flopping.

Brady's voice cracked. "We're being followed."

I turned to look. But the car wasn't behind us. It came up fast to the right of us.

"Keep your head down," Brady shouted and shoved me.

I heard the bullet whizz past. Brady's head exploded before my eyes. Blood splattered everywhere. The steering wheel spun to the left. I made a desperate leap across Brady's body to grab it. The wheel was slippery with blood. Cars rushed toward us. I looked up and saw a tree looming large before everything went black.

CHAPTER 33

I lay in bed, smooth cool sheets against my skin. Johnny sat at the foot of the bed. He was smiling.

"We'll take a cruise." His voice sounded calm and reassuring. "Go back to Baja, fly down to Cabo, sip margaritas on the cliffs and watch the waves."

I smiled, happy. Why was I ever afraid of him?

"I'll take you to Tahiti like I promised. We'll lie on the white sands and drink Pína Coladas. Come with me to Africa, to Australia, to Italy…"

Yes, I wanted to cry out. *I'll go with you. Take me away from here.*

His hand touched mine and I strained to raise my head, but I couldn't move. Pain everywhere. Pressure on my shoulder. I couldn't open my eyes. Johnny was fading and I didn't want to let him go. "Johnny."

"Erin, you're awake. Thank God."

The voice was familiar, but not Johnny's. I wanted my dream back. I wanted to fly away with Johnny.

"Erin," the voice said again, "can you can open your eyes?"

My eyelids fluttered. Bright light. Glaring. *No! Shut out the light.*

"Someone turn off those lights," the voice ordered.

I felt something cool on my forehead. I didn't want to wake up. Not yet. I became aware of cologne and another smell—hospital disinfectant. This wasn't my bedroom. Slowly I opened my eyes to semi-darkness.

A hand covered mine. "Erin, it's all right. You're safe now."

I turned my head toward the voice. The movement brought a wave of dizziness that made my stomach roil. I waited for the room to stop spinning before looking at the shadowy figure who owned the voice.

Tony Corelli.

No. I closed my eyes and pulled my hand away. *I want to go back to Cabo.*

"Erin, don't be afraid. Look at me. You're safe."

"Where's Johnny?" My voice sounded raspy.

"Johnny's not here, Erin," Tony said. "You were dreaming."

A dream? Or a ghost? Had Tony finally made good on his contract? Johnny's voice sounded so real. I attempted to lift my head and use my arms to sit up, but a sharp pain in my chest and left shoulder put me down again.

"Don't move," Tony said quickly. "You got broken ribs, maybe internal damage. Lie quiet now."

What was he talking about? What happened to me?

"Erin, do you remember anything about the accident?"

The accident. Yes, that must be it. The car must have crashed. That's why I was in the hospital. I closed my eyes and tried to remember. Brady and I were running.

Running from what?

"What do you remember before the accident?" Tony's voice was soft, coaxing.

The image of Nico flashed in my mind. "Nico."

"What about Nico?"

"Someone shot him." I opened my eyes. "He's dead, isn't he?"

Tony nodded somberly. "What do you remember about the shooting?"

"Nothing. Brady came. He helped me get away." I gripped his hand. "Ask him. Ask Brady. He'll tell you what happened."

Tony drew back in his chair, expressionless.

"Where's Brady?" I demanded. "Was he hurt? Is he here in the hospital? Why aren't you answering me?"

Tony bit his lower lip and looked as if he'd rather be anywhere but in this room.

My chest tightened, a sob swelling in my throat. My voice rose. "Tell me Brady's all right. Tell me the truth, Tony."

Slowly he shook his head. "I'm sorry."

The sob became a scream. My hands flew to my face.

The door opened. A nurse came in.

"Sir, you'll have to leave."

"I'll be back, Erin." His voice came from far away. "Get some rest."

My body convulsed with pain. The nurse stuck a needle in my arm and I welcomed the warmth of the chemical sleep. But my mind wouldn't let go. Brady was dead and it was my fault. I had blocked out the last image of him in the car. The reality was too horrible to face. I let the drug do its best and rock me to sleep. A dreamless, Johnny-less sleep this time. I was alone. All alone.

I awoke to silence and a darkened room with only a strip of light under the closed door. I turned my head slowly toward the window and gazed into the darkness of night. I welcomed the quiet because I knew it wouldn't last.

Where are you, Johnny? Where did you go?

The events before the accident began to run through my mind like a reel of film. Dancing at Lucky Lady. Meeting Nico. Listening to Charley and Tony in the kitchen. Nico threatening me on the boardwalk.

The shooting. Had I really seen Nico die?

What about afterward? The second shot after Nico was down. The one meant for me.

Why couldn't I remember the shooter?

I remembered Brady picking me up, running with me through the crowd to the car.

Then what happened?

I became aware of both my fists gripping the blanket, my body stretched and taut as a rubber slingshot aimed and ready. Tears streamed down my cheeks. My chest hurt. Brady died in the accident because of me. But I couldn't—or wouldn't—see it.

I lay awake for hours. I must have dosed off at some point because the nurse woke me to check my vitals and help me to the bathroom. A short while later someone brought breakfast. My bed was raised until I was propped up in a sitting position. I sipped bad coffee and tried the cold toast, but finally pushed the tray away and asked for the bed to be lowered. Outside my window, rain fell under a gray dome.

Tony appeared at nine o'clock sharp, clothes wrinkled, hair disheveled and there were bags under his eyes. I'd never seen him this way.

"You're looking better," he said.

"You don't," I said. "Did you sleep?"

"I had a busy night. How about you? Were you able to sleep?"

"Some."

He pulled a chair close to my bed and sat with his elbows on his knees. "Has your memory improved?"

"What part are you interested in?" As if I didn't

know. But a voice in my head warned me. What if Tony was the shooter? He had more reasons than anyone for wanting Nico dead. Without Nico, wouldn't his contract on Johnny cease to exist? If so, the mob wouldn't be after him. He'd be a free man. Or did the mob ever forget?

I thought again of that second shot. The one meant for me so I couldn't testify about Nico.

"The police will want to question you. They'll want to know about Nico's murder, and Brady's."

I stared at him. "Didn't Brady die in the accident?"

"You really don't remember what happened?"

I lifted my head. "No, I don't. What aren't you telling me?"

"You'll know sooner or later. Brady was shot. After that, the car went out of control and hit a tree."

I didn't want to believe him. If what he said was true, why couldn't I remember? "I don't understand. Why would someone shoot him? He wasn't involved in any of this mess."

"Maybe he wasn't the target."

I sucked in my breath. He was right, of course. I was the target.

Tony went on. "The cops will ask you about Nico, too. Who shot him, and what you saw."

I suddenly understood why Tony was there. A rising panic took over my breathing. He knew I must have seen the killer, whether I remembered or not. It was only a matter of time before my memory returned. He didn't care about me, only about himself.

"Erin, listen to me," Tony said. "I need to know what you saw."

"Go away. Leave me alone."

Tony lowered his voice, but the message was clear. "You've got to trust me."

I shrank from him.

"Erin?" He frowned.

I forced myself to breath normally. There was nothing threatening in Tony's expression, but that meant nothing. Tony was a master of deception. He'd proven that.

"I don't remember if I saw Nico's shooter," I said, my voice shaky. "I don't remember the accident. There is nothing I can tell the cops. Now go away."

"Calm down. I'm only trying to help. If you think of anything else, you'll let me know first. Understood?"

I nodded, not trusting myself to speak.

As long as Tony believed me, I was safe. Whether he had shot Nico and Brady, or had Charley do it for him, he would cover it up one way or another. As long as I had no memory of the shooter's face, I would stay alive. That is, until one of them decided that, as a witness, I was too much of a risk to live.

My heart beat faster. My body shivered as if a blanket of ice covered me. As Tony stood, looking concerned, a nurse came in. After a visual check, she stuck a thermometer in my mouth.

She looked at Tony. "Sir, Miss Matthews needs to rest."

"I'll see you later," he said. "Remember what I said. You'll be fine."

I felt only relief after he left. The nurse checked my blood pressure, adjusted my IV and gave me a shot that put me to sleep again. When I awoke, two police officers stood at the foot of my bed. They were joking about some drunk they had brought into the jail.

I pulled the thin blanket up to my chin.

One of them noticed, the taller of the two, and nudged his partner. "Good morning. How're you doing, Miss Matthews?"

Was it still morning? Or had another day gone by?

According to the direction of the sun streaming in my room, it was closer to noon.

"Groggy. And really shitty."

Both men were in uniform. Both looked to be in their middle thirties. The tall one was dark-haired and had an angular build while the other was blond, stocky, and needed a shave.

"I'm Officer Anderfelt," said the tall officer. "This is my partner, Officer Rennard. We need your statement concerning events leading up to the accident."

Neither held a pad and pencil. I didn't see any recording devices.

"I don't remember much," I said. "Did we hit another car?"

The officers exchanged glances.

"We want to know about the driver," Anderfelt said.

"Brady Case." Saying his name aloud brought a fresh stab of pain and guilt. I couldn't believe he was dead. He came to Atlantic City to help me, saved my life, and now he was gone.

I said none of this to the cops. They were going through the motions. Nothing I told them would make a difference. It wouldn't bring Brady back. Moreover, I strongly suspected whatever I told these officers would never go into a file. They were certainly on Tony's payroll. All I had to do was follow the script.

Rennard continued, "You were coming from Atlantic City. Is that right?"

I nodded.

"What was your business there?"

"I'm a dancer. I worked at the Lucky Lady."

"What about Brady Case? Did he work there, too?"

"No. He was my ride."

"What was your destination after leaving Atlantic City?"

"Home. Philadelphia."

"Had the two of you been drinking?"

"I had a few. I don't know about Brady."

Rennard looked at his partner.

Anderfelt took over. "Do you know why someone would shoot Brady?"

Now they were getting to the real reason they were here. But I couldn't help them. "I don't remember any shots, officer. Or what happened to Brady. Or the accident."

I felt completely removed from the room as if someone else was lying there answering their questions. I had never felt so alone. There was no one who cared. Brady was dead. Tony didn't want me to remember. Johnny still hated me.

"We found your purse and suitcase in the car," Rennard said. "Your ID and keys are in there, along with your wallet and money." He pointed to the closet. "We put everything in there."

"Thanks," I said.

Anderfelt pulled a photograph out of his front pocket. "Would you like to see what your car looked like after the accident?"

Not really, but I had the feeling I wasn't given a choice. I tensed, expecting the worst.

The picture showed Brady's red Camaro wrapped around a tree. I imagined the red paint turning to blood.

Anderfelt said, "You're lucky you survived."

"You okay, Miss Matthews?" Rennard said.

"I'm going to be sick," I turned on my side and pressed the call button for the nurse. The two cops backed up a few feet. Fifteen seconds later a nurse popped into the room, took one look at me and ordered them to leave.

Tony kept his word and returned the next day. I had nothing new to tell him.

I said. "You don't have to bother with me. I'll be fine."

His jaw tightened. "I'm not your enemy, Erin."

I turned my head away.

There was resignation in his voice when he spoke again. "I'll be back when you're feeling better."

I heard the door shut, and his footsteps faded down the hall. I was better off not trusting him. Even if he didn't pull the trigger, he would protect whoever did. I was expendable.

CHAPTER 34

For the next couple of weeks, I was given pills to help me sleep and pills to wake me up. There were doctors, x-rays, blood tests, and shots. The bruise to my chest from the steering wheel remained purple. I hurt like hell whenever I moved. During all that time, Tony stayed away. I had no visitors, but plenty of time to think.

On the morning of my release, a woman from the accounting office came to my room and informed me that my bill had been paid by my employer. She didn't mean Dreamscape. She gave me a copy of the paperwork.

I dug through my suitcase for the few clean choices I had left. The strawberry-stained white dress was still rolled up. The blood-stained green mini-dress I'd worn during the shooting had been stuffed in a plastic bag by the hospital personnel. I tossed both in the trash and chose a pair of orange bell bottom pants and a short-sleeved sweater to match. I pulled on my white go-go boots.

The process exhausted me and I sank down on the bed to wait. I had no idea if anyone would come for me. My shoulders tensed and my neck hurt. Maybe I had been completely abandoned.

The orderly finally came with the wheelchair and made small talk as we rode down the elevator. The lobby looked deserted. I tried not to cry as the orderly wheeled me to the outer doors.

The rain fell in a steady downpour. The sky was leaden. Tony stood next to a black stretch limo parked in the covered circular driveway. I gave in to a sob of relief, but quickly brushed away the tears and kept my head down.

"I'll take her from here," he told the orderly.

He reached out for me and I let him take my hand and help me out of the wheelchair. I tried to ignore the pain in my chest. My legs felt stiff and sore, I could barely move them. He noticed and lifted me as if I weighed nothing and set me in the back of the limo. Once I settled in, he leaned over and covered my legs with a multi-colored Indian blanket.

His face turned toward mine, inches away.

I looked down. "Either I must be someone special to deserve a limo, or you want something."

Amused, he said, "You don't like limousines?"

"They're pretentious."

"Yes, but it impresses most people." He backed out. "You're not most people, but even you are not opposed to comfort."

I let that pass. "I wasn't sure you would be here."

He straightened and his smile disappeared. "I told you I would pick you up. You still don't trust me?"

"You weren't completely honest about Atlantic City," I reminded him.

"I told you what I could while still protecting you."

I laughed at this, though I didn't see much humor in his words. "The only person you were protecting was yourself."

A flash of anger crossed his face and disappeared as quickly. "I couldn't foresee what happened."

"You didn't plan to kill Nico?" I said, and instantly regretted the words. I broke into a sweat despite the cold air.

Tony looked grim. He slid beside me and shut the door. The closed windows were covered with a dark tint so no one outside could see in.

"Is that what you think?"

I took a deep breath. "The contract. You would benefit the most if Nico or Johnny were dead," I said. "Now Nico is dead. I don't know about Johnny."

He sighed. "I didn't kill Nico. When your memory returns, you'll know the truth."

"You're safe. My memory hasn't returned." I said.

"But you decided I was the shooter."

"It could have been you, or it could have been Charley. He would have killed for you and for himself."

"And there is Johnny," he said, "who has been the target all along. There's motive."

I didn't respond, but I knew he was right. Johnny had means, opportunity, and motive.

"Are you still afraid?"

I shook my head.

As if reaching a decision, he opened the door, and climbed out. My heart beat faster. The window rolled down and he stuck his head in. "My driver will take you to your apartment. You will be okay there. I've had someone watching your place since you've been in the hospital. He'll be there until I can find a safer place for you."

"Where will you be?" I asked.

"I have business to attend to, but I'll be in touch." He straightened and nodded to the driver.

I didn't bother to ask what kind of business. He

wouldn't have told me. I peered through the privacy window that separated me from the driver. I didn't recognize him. He wore a black cap and crisp white shirt and faced forward. His stony eyes stared back at me from the rearview. The window rolled back up and Tony stepped away. At the same time, the limo glided out of the driveway and onto the street. I looked back in time to see another black car pull up in place of the limo. Tony opened the passenger's door and disappeared inside.

Did Charley drive the second car? No way to tell.

The rain followed us to Philadelphia. Two hours later I arrived at my apartment. The sky was painted several shades of gray. The driver got out first and opened my door.

"My orders are to help you upstairs," he said.

"You don't have to bother," I replied.

His face didn't change expression. "I have my orders." He lifted me out of the car.

"You're not going to carry me." When he made no move to put me down, I added, "You can help me go up without carrying me. That way you're still following orders."

I convinced him we could make it upstairs with his arm around my waist supporting me. On the short walk from the limo to the front door, the rain wet my hair and a puddle soaked through my boots.

Tony's words echoed in my head. He had someone watching my apartment. I took inventory of the street. I didn't see any strange cars parked along the curb and wondered where the so-called protection hid. Maybe he left for lunch.

The chauffeur waited until I unlocked the door before he wrapped his arm around my waist. Even with his help, my chest and legs burned with the effort of climbing the stairs to my second-story apartment. I fumbled in my purse for my keys. I stared at the black leather key holder Brady had given me for my twenty-third birthday. Tears wet my cheeks and the key holder blurred.

When I finally got the door open, my chauffeur waited until I locked the door from the inside. I heard his footsteps recede as I set the chain and pulled off my boots. When I reached the bedroom, I stripped off my wet clothes.

I stared at my reflection in the oval pier glass, the one piece of furniture Melanie had left behind that I actually liked. Not so much today, though. Dark indentations of the steering wheel were stamped on my chest. My legs were violet. My hair stuck out in clumps and I regretted the loss of the red wig.

I turned my back on the mirror and went into the bathroom. While the shower ran, I stepped under the hot water, closed my eyes, and imagined dissolving along with the sweat and hospital smell. When the water ran cold, I slipped on a robe and walked through the apartment. Two weeks earlier I would have been happy to have the place to myself, could have gladly lived alone without Brady. But now Brady was dead and I saw evidence of him everywhere I looked.

I strolled into the kitchen, located the bottle of scotch I had bought before leaving for Atlantic City. I found the bottle of Valium I had filled at the hospital, took both into the living room, and sat in the middle of the hardwood floor. The first gulp of scotch burned down to my stomach.

I opened the bottle of Valium and poured several into my hand. Tears started to flow as I remembered how the day in Atlantic City ended with Nico shot and dying in front of me. I thought of how I had been used as bait in his murder by his killer or killers.

I remembered the night I tried to kill Johnny. What

was wrong with me? I had set out to murder the man I'd lived with for five years. A man I both feared and loved, who brought out emotions I didn't know I could possibly feel. At the time, striking Johnny out of my life seemed the only way to be free. It didn't matter whether I'd succeeded or not. I had intended for Johnny to die.

I'd spent hours planning his murder. What if I had gone through with it? Tony once said I was no better than he. He was right. The fact that Johnny didn't die that night hadn't erased my guilt. That would stay with me forever. I was doomed to relive those moments the rest of my life. Now two more men were dead and I had been with both of them when it happened.

I sat on the floor, acting as my own judge and jury. I was to blame for Brady's death. I was meant to die in that car.

I took another gulp of scotch and two more Valiums. I pounded the floor with my fists and screamed out the agony I could no longer contain. The tears flowed with the scotch. The rest of the pills fell to the floor in front of me.

I alone was responsible for Brady's death. How could I go on living with that burden? I made a living dancing half naked in a room full of men, teasing and showing off my body so they would cheat on their wives or girlfriends. That's all I was. Nothing.

I brought the bottle up to my lips and drank. Tears followed. I picked up a handful of pills and rolled them around in my hand. Before I could shovel them into my mouth, my stomach rebelled. I tried to stand. The sudden movement caused the room to swirl around me. Sweat poured off my forehead, and I bolted, half stumbling, for the bathroom, reaching the toilet just in time. Booze and pills emptied out until only bile was left, leaving me drenched and exhausted.

I'd even failed at killing myself.

I staggered into the bedroom and fell across the bed, afraid to close my eyes, knowing the room would spin, trying to keep the nightmares at bay. I must have fallen asleep because when I opened my eyes, darkness surrounded me. Pain shot through my eyes. My temples pounded. A waterfall roared in my ears. My mouth felt sandy and tasted sour.

I pushed up to a sitting position and waited for the room to settle. Finally, I made it to the kitchen and poured a glass of water. I probably needed food, but the refrigerator held nothing edible, only sour milk, moldy cheese, a six-pack of beer, and a bottle of vodka. I found a can of vegetable soup in the cupboard and heated the contents in a small saucepan. I made a pot of tea, put on Miles Davis's "Kind of Blue" and ate in solitude.

I almost jumped out of my chair when I heard a rap at my door. I didn't move at first. Anger rose, my cheeks flushed hot. My visitor could only be one person. Tony Corelli, and I wasn't in the mood.

The knocking continued until it echoed the pounding in my head. A voice I didn't recognize at first came through the wood. Young and slightly familiar, the voice got stronger as he repeated my name. Curiosity and impatience to stop the noise overcame stubbornness. I went to the door and cautiously opened it with the chain on.

Damn. My stalker had found me.

CHAPTER 35

I left the door chain in place and peered through the two-inch gap. The teenaged face with the pimple scars belonged at Dreamscape, not at my apartment. Ray was the last person I expected to see. He wore a red T-shirt that covered a scrawny chest and brown slacks with sharp creases down the front. His straight brown hair stuck up in angles that didn't conform to his head.

"How did you find me?" I asked.

"Your boss."

"You're lying, Ray." I couldn't imagine Lewis or Joe giving out my address. "You followed me home one night."

Ray's face reddened. "No, I didn't."

I started to close the door.

"All right," he yelled, pushing against the chain. "Gimme another chance."

I let go of the door, and the chain snapped taut with a loud crack.

He spoke fast. "I heard about the accident and what happened to Brady, and I had to see if you were okay."

I wasn't okay. I hurt like hell, and standing made me feel worse.

"Do you need anything?" Ray said. "Tell me what you need and I'll get it for you."

I leaned against the wall next to the door. "I'm not ready for company, Ray. I just got home, and I feel like crap."

"I know. I saw the limo drive up. You had to be helped up the stairs. That's why I'm here—to help you."

A chill ran up my spine. "You've been outside all this time? Waiting?" Stalking better described it.

"It's not what you think," Ray said. "I got worried about you. All alone, it's not good."

"Go away, Ray." I couldn't stand on my feet much longer. The dizziness returned. I felt sick.

His hand came through the opening and closed firmly around my wrist. "Don't be scared, Erin. I've never hurt anyone. You can ask Dani. Let me help you. I'll do anything you say."

At the mention of Dani's name, my heart jumped into my throat. I hadn't thought about her since I'd left town. I had no idea about her condition, whether or not she had improved. I didn't want to think about the alternative. I didn't want to think about anything yet.

"How is Dani?" I said finally.

"When you're well enough, you should go see her."

"Is she still in a coma?"

"Go see for yourself."

Maggie once told me Ray was dangerous. He'd stalked Dani. In fact, the last time I'd seen Ray was in front of Dani's apartment after she'd been attacked.

The blood raced to my head. I tried to wrench my arm away, but his grip tightened. I raised my voice. "You don't have an answer because you don't know. They wouldn't let you into her room. Why is that, Ray? Because they know you hurt her?"

Ray's fingers flew off me like he'd been burned.

"That's not true. I'd never hurt her. Never. She was my friend." Tears welled in his eyes. "How could you be so cruel? I done nothing to hurt you or Dani."

His tears got to me. Maybe I'd been too hard on him. In my weakened state, I couldn't think straight. I slid the chain off and opened the door. My knees wobbled. "Oh, for Christ sake, come in."

He sniffled, but crossed the threshold without hesitation. His tears dried quickly enough. "I bet they'd let *you* in. I think she's out of her coma."

"I'll go and see her as soon as I'm stronger."

My legs were unsteady. Ray grabbed me before I hit the floor.

He supported me to the kitchen and lowered me into the chair facing the table. He surveyed the empty soup bowl and the remains of my cup of tea. Miles Davis played on.

"I'll fix you a fresh cup of tea," he said.

"Thanks." I was surprised he knew how. "Got a cigarette?"

He pulled a fresh pack out of his shirt pocket. My brand. He shook one out and handed it to me. Before I could ask, a lighter appeared in his hand and the flame touched the end.

He seemed at home in my kitchen, making tea, later clearing the table and washing the few dishes. But I didn't feel comfortable. My sanctuary had been invaded. Yet I couldn't find the strength to tell him to leave.

"You aren't planning on working soon, are you?" he said.

"I have to. I don't make money sitting here."

"Let me take care of you until you're well enough," Ray said. "You don't have anyone else."

How did he know that?

"You have nothing to eat in the refrigerator," he continued. "I'll go to the store and get a few things. Don't worry. I have money. You rest. Where's your key?" He opened my purse and dug through. Before I could protest, my key was in his hand. "Keep your door locked and don't let anyone in." He helped me to the bed, eased me down, and covered me with a blanket. "Be right back."

I felt like an invalid. When the door shut behind him, I wanted to get up again and put the chain on. But I couldn't move. I felt drugged. The Valium was still in my system.

"Brady," I whispered. Tears stung. I turned my head into the pillow and sobbed until I fell asleep.

I didn't hear Ray return. When I awoke, it was night and the smell of roast chicken reached me. My body felt like lead. I gave in to the lethargy and didn't move. I fell asleep again and woke to someone shaking me.

"Dinner time," Ray said. "I brought you a tray."

I opened my eyes to see a plate filled with a chicken breast, steamed vegetables, and mashed potatoes with gravy. It was accompanied by a glass of milk, napkin, silverware, and a single rose in a crystal vase. He helped me sit up and set the tray over my lap.

I surveyed the food with some reservation. My stomach rumbled.

Ray beamed at me, his face sweaty from the kitchen's heat.

"Aren't you eating?" I asked.

"Sure. Mind if I keep you company?"

"You shouldn't have gone to all this trouble."

"If you're going to get strong again, you have to eat," he said.

I was not used to dealing with Ray, the adult. Or eating a home-cooked meal. The chicken looked tender and smelled delicious. I decided the food hadn't been poisoned and wolfed all of it down.

"I need my key back," I said when he took my plate from me.

"You're not in any shape to take care of yourself," Ray said. He left the room and came back holding up a prescription bottle. "This bottle is empty. It's my guess you tried to kill yourself before I got here." I made a grab for the bottle and missed. "Do you think I want your suicide on my conscience?" he said.

My mouth fell open, but no words came out.

"You shouldn't feel bad about what happened," Ray said. "Wasn't your fault. You just got in with bad guys. Even Brady. I saw the way he treated you."

At the mention of Brady's name, I sat up. "Don't you dare talk about him. Brady loved me and I loved him."

Ray worked his mouth silently. Then, as if nothing had been said, he brightened. "Hey, I got a cake for dessert. Want some?"

"Jesus. No. How old are you, Ray?"

He hesitated. "Twenty-one."

"You should go home. Your parents must be worried."

"You don't tell me what to do. I'm a man. Anyway, my folks are dead. I only got my grandma."

"Sorry about your parents," I said. "Won't your grandmother miss you?"

"No. She don't mind me being gone."

"She must worry."

Ray's jaw tightened. "That's none of your business."

"You pry into mine."

"Because I'm taking care of you." His voice rose in agitation. "Better than anyone else."

"Is that so?"

He didn't answer and I was tired of arguing. I wanted to go back to sleep and not think about Ray or Brady or Atlantic City.

"I'm going back to work soon." I spoke into the pillow and pulled the covers over me. "I can take care of myself."

He didn't answer.

I sneaked a peak from under the covers. He was pouting. I sighed and covered my head again. Ray turned off the music and left the room. After several minutes, I heard him humming in the kitchen. I turned over and slept.

Ray stayed a week while I convalesced in my bedroom. I didn't have the energy to protest. He fed me, brought me cigarettes, and tried his best to take Brady's place. Without the sex. The idea of this kid getting close enough to touch me made my stomach revolt.

Not that he tried. Not even once. This did nothing for my self-esteem. Why was he taking care of me if it wasn't for sex?

Toward mid-week, I got weary thinking about Ray and why he didn't want to fuck me. I also didn't want to think about what happened in Atlantic City or to Brady. I'd never forget Brady, but I couldn't bring him back. Every time I thought about him, the flood of tears would come. I would slide under the blanket and close my eyes to block out his image, only for him to appear in Technicolor.

Two phone calls finally pulled me out of my depression. The first came from Tony.

"Who's that guy with you?" he asked without preamble.

"What guy?"

"Don't fuck with me, Erin."

"He's a customer from Dreamscape. He came to check on me."

"Why is he still there?"

"Because he's helping me recover from an accident. You remember the accident, don't you?"

"Don't be a wiseass. Get rid of him."

"Or what?" I said, annoyed with him giving me orders.

"Or I will." He hung up.

The second caller sounded younger and weak. Her voice belonged to someone more beaten up by men than I ever thought of being. A cry for help I could not ignore.

Ray looked startled when I came out of my bedroom fully dressed and with enough make-up to look tough and camouflage any underlying fear. "I'm going to the hospital to see Dani."

Ray's face fell. "You shouldn't be up yet," he said in a whiny voice.

"Your job is over, Ray. Go home to grandma. She's probably worried sick. You're not needed here anymore."

Ray shook his head. I couldn't begin to imagine what rattled around inside there. He looked bewildered. "I've done everything for you and now you're getting rid of me?"

His attitude shouldn't have surprised me. "I'm grateful for your help But I'm strong enough to take care of myself. You're free, Ray. Get a life. That's what I plan to do."

His face reddened. "Stop it. Why are you doing this to me?"

"I'm not doing anything to you. I'm doing for me."

For a moment, I thought Ray would break into a full blown tantrum. His voice raised an octave and cracked. "You don't have to. You've still got me. Why do you need to see Dani?"

"Because she needs *me*. I thought that's what you wanted. Shit, Ray. She called me, okay? It's my turn to be a friend and help someone else."

Ray stuck out his lower lip. "I can take care of both of you."

I put a hand on his shoulder. "No, Ray, you need to take care of yourself."

His arm came up and struck my wrist. I backed off, afraid he would punch me. His face turned purple with rage.

"You owe me. I've stolen for you. I risked jail for you."

This revelation stunned me. "What are you talking about?"

"I stole money from my grandmother to help you. Now you're throwing me out?"

"Ray, I never asked you to break any laws. You need to leave. Take whatever you brought and get out."

"What if I don't?" he challenged.

I could take him if I was completely healed. Not sure if I could now. "I'll call the cops and they'll take you home to granny."

"No, you won't," he said belligerently.

I kept my voice calm. "You really want to mess with me? Tony Corelli called a little while ago. He wanted to know who you were and why you're still here."

He looked wary. "You're lying. How could he know about me?"

"Tony had people watching my apartment. You've been seen going in and out of the building. They're not stupid. He told me to get rid of you or he'll do it himself. If I'm not out that door in ten minutes, you'll be in serious trouble."

His face turned several degrees of angst before he said, "Okay, but I'll be back. I'm not afraid of him or his men."

I smiled. "I'm sure you're not. Before you go, do you still have your grandma's money? I haven't worked in a long time. When I see Dani, I'll let her know you wish her well."

He reached into his pocket, expression turned hopeful. I almost felt sorry for him.

Almost.

૯/૭૯/૭

On the street a dark blue sedan with tinted windows flashed its lights when I came outside. My protection, I supposed. I waved and walked to the corner where I hailed a cab. I ignored the ache in my chest and the soreness in my legs. A week spent in bed hadn't worked miracles. Exercise would definitely be in my schedule.

Thirty minutes later I was in the hospital elevator. I got off on the fourth floor and found Dani's private room. She sat, propped against pillows, the purple bruises on her face a stark reminder of what had happened to her. At least the bandages were off.

She smiled and the effort made her wince.

"You look wonderful," I said.

"You still want a roommate?" she asked.

I sat on the bed and took her hands in mine. "I'll be here to pick you up as soon as the doctors say you're ready."

I knew that day could come anytime. Time to go back to work and save some money. Now I had someone who needed me.

CHAPTER 36

The following Friday Paul came into my kitchen carrying his satchel. "That's a cryin' shame about the wig, love, but I can work miracles,"

I gave him the finger. "Do your worst, Paul. I'm working tonight."

"First night back?" He stood back and appraised the present state of my hair. "You sure you're ready, love? Kind of peaked looking."

"Then do something about it. Change the way I look."

"How come you can afford me when you haven't been working? You actually save some of that bread you make?"

I closed my eyes as Paul massaged my head. "Do I ask where you get your money?"

"Yeah, you're right. I won't pry."

I thought of Ray and the C-note he gave me before he left. I should be feeling guilty for taking the money he'd stolen from his grandmother. Instead I pushed Ray out of my mind. "Is my hair hopeless?"

"You question my genius? Shame, shame on you. When I get done, you'll make all those skags you work with turn green."

With scissors in hand, Paul went to work shaping my hair.

"You are a sucker for punishment, darlin'."

"What do you mean?" I asked, my stomach tightening.

"I thought you would be anxious to get away from the business, get out of town. Someone shot at you and killed that guy in Atlantic City. You could still be a target."

"Where can I go, Paul? I have no money and no friends—except for you, Maggie, and the other girls at the bar. I need to be around people I know, who I feel comfortable with. Besides, if someone wanted me dead, they would have found me by now."

"I get you, love. Be careful, is what I'm saying."

"It's not only that," I said. "I heard from Dani. She's on the mend. I have to stick around for her. I promised she could stay with me when she got out of the hospital."

"Might be a good idea to move away from here, for both your sakes. Get a clean start."

The thought of moving drained what little energy I had left. "Need money first."

Paul put down the scissors. "Okay, since you won't take my advice and run, I'll give you another lesson free of charge."

"Oh?" I smiled. "Can't wait to hear this."

"You'll thank me one day if you ever get into real trouble."

Paul dug in his satchel and pull out a six-inch blade attached to a silver inlaid handle. "I have several of these so I'm going to lend you this one until you get your own."

"What am I going to do with that?" I wanted to laugh. "The bad guys carry guns. What do they say about carrying a knife to a gun fight?"

"Hush. I'm going to show you what you do with this."

For the next half hour, Paul taught me how to hold and throw the dagger.

"I hope you never have to use this, but it could save your life someday."

I doubted that, but I took the knife and promised to practice daily.

Paul picked up the scissors again. "Okay. You got my two cents worth. I'll shut my mouth."

Two and a half hours later, I was a blonde with lighter frosted tips, styled like the model Twiggy from London, with swirls pasted around my cheeks.

"Nobody will recognize you, doll," Paul said.

"Good."

When I arrived at the club that evening, Joe gave me a raised eyebrow, but he didn't say a word. Paul's genius extended to my costume—black mesh tights and scarlet fringe that dripped from the top of my bra to my thigh, hiding all the bruises from the accident. I was there to hustle drinks and nothing more. Joe's rules were inflexible. Until I was fully recuperated, I would not dance. My role was to act like a hooker, but withhold the action.

Maggie cornered me before I could find a bar stool. She thrust out her hip in a practiced pose. "Well, lordy, look at you. All slicked up and ready to shine." She leaned close to my ear. "I got a baggy for you. No charge."

A dime bag of pot all to myself. I'd need that later. I squeezed her hand and whispered, "Thanks."

Rachel joined us and gave me an approving grin. "Girl, you look fabulous. Paul's work, of course. Good for you. How I envy you getting to dance in Atlantic City. I've been trying to get a gig there forever. I'd even go topless."

Trixie came up behind her. "Honey, I been there. It's no big deal. Is it, Erin? I heard Charley was there. Did you see him?"

My heart might have stopped for a few seconds at the mention of Charley's name. My hands felt like ice. I took a moment before answering.

"In passing."

I moved away from them before they could ask more questions. Just the mention of Atlantic City brought Brady's death closer, made it more painful. Why couldn't I remember what happened? Because it was *my* fault.

The night dragged. I felt distant, strange, as if I were watching myself converse with strangers. All an act. I even critiqued my performance and found it lacking in enthusiasm. I glanced up now and then to see Joe checking on me. He seemed worried. Every so often he'd set a real drink in front of me.

The dark lighting worked to my advantage. My facial bruises were almost gone. I credited Paul for blending my makeup to cover what discoloration remained. The evening started slow, but old regulars wandered in and ordered drinks for me. I was able to relax after a while. To make the hours go by faster, I flirted mercilessly.

Occasionally I looked to see who was dancing. I responded as I always did to music—body swaying and foot tapping to the beat. When one guy left, another took his place. Some wanted a feel and I let them. Why the hell not? Got to make these guys happy so they'd buy more drinks. At other times, to keep myself awake, I indulged in a verbal sparring match.

A newcomer came in around ten-thirty. He took the empty seat next to me, but didn't look my way. I recognized another depressed soul as he quickly put away three whiskeys on ice.

"Buy a girl a drink?"

He swiveled on the bar stool and gave me a polite, but inquisitive appraisal. "I'm sorry. I've been rude. I've lots on my mind."

I smiled. "Want to talk about it?"

"Not really, but I will buy you that drink."

"Scotch and water. Thanks. I'm Erin."

"Vern Richland." His blue eyes seemed sad.

"Haven't seen you here before. First time?"

"No, I saw you dance once and you're incredible. Better than anyone else."

My face warmed. Usually, I discounted flattery from a customer, accepting their words as bar talk, not real. But from the beginning, Vern Richland was different. I pictured him as an accountant, disillusioned with his job. Tonight, he loosened his tie and unbuttoned his jacket as if to say, *To hell with it all, I'm going to fuck the rules.*

I didn't usually go for blonds, but the sandy shade looked good on him, particularly with the strands of gray that brushed over his temples. Better than the greasy black hair of a certain Italian in my life.

On stage Rachel was dancing to "Mustang Sally" by Wilson Pickett. My body responded and matched the rhythm.

Vern noticed and gave me an appreciative look. "You're not dancing tonight?"

"I was in an auto accident. This is my first night back."

He frowned in concern. "Seriously hurt?"

"In the hospital for a while." I shrugged, not wanting to make a big deal of it. "I'm here."

"I'm so sorry. But you look really good. You changed your hair style. I like it."

So much for "nobody will recognize you" bullshit.

I forced a smile. "Thanks for noticing."

"Hard not to notice someone so beautiful."

"Now you're making me feel self-conscious. I'll be blushing and people will wonder."

He laughed for the first time. The sound made me feel better.

He patted my hand. "Let them wonder."

He stayed until closing and promised to be back.

Joe came up to me before I left. "Who was that?"

I shrugged. "Vern somebody. Never saw him before. He's nice, but I doubt if we'll see him again." I'd heard enough broken promises.

His eyes narrowed. "You're feeling vulnerable right now. Don't get carried away with the customers. I need you to move around, see lots of people."

I gave him a short laugh. "You know me, Joe. Fuck 'em and leave 'em before they die." I swallowed at his drop-jaw expression. "Sorry. Didn't mean that. It just came out. Guess I'm feeling down about Brady."

"Are you sure you can handle this?"

I shrugged. "Don't worry so much, Joe."

Vern Richland surprised us both and kept his word. He showed up the next night.

"You seem surprised to see me," he said. "I said I'd be here."

"Everyone says that."

"Are you glad I kept my word?"

I smiled like I cared. Maybe, in a way, I did a little.

We talked and drank. I still didn't know anything new about him by the end of the night, except that he was reaching a crossroads in his life. His business no longer held a spark of interest for him. He didn't mention his home life.

The third night I kept an eye on the entrance. When he didn't arrive by ten-thirty, I grew angry. He was no different than any of the others. Couldn't be trusted. I was a fool to believe anything a customer told me.

Vern walked in the door, thirty minutes late. He scanned the room until he found me sitting with another customer.

I pretended not to see him as he sat down at the other side of the bar. I let him wait and stare at me a little while longer before I got up and slowly made my way toward him.

He apologized, said he'd been delayed by a business meeting and hoped I hadn't given up on him. I assured him that I hadn't.

"I don't watch the clock," I lied. "There are enough customers to keep me busy without worrying about one who isn't here."

He looked disappointed. "I couldn't expect you to think I'm different from the others. I know we just met, but I think you're a quite a woman."

I didn't know how to respond. Was I supposed to thank him? Feel special? I wanted to let the anger go, but I had looked for him and been disappointed. Logic be damned, I was afraid to trust him.

He ordered us drinks. By the end of the evening, I forgot why I was upset with him.

We were still on friendly terms by Friday and he hadn't missed a night yet. To my surprise, he came in earlier than usual. He looked younger and his eyes were bright, his smile wide.

"There's something different about you," I said.

"Do you like the beach?" he said.

I drew back, wary, not sure what was coming. "Yes. Why?"

"I have a very dull business meeting tomorrow. Or it would be dull except that it is in Oceanside and I'm hoping you'll come with me." He clasped my hand in both of his. "Please say yes."

I couldn't believe what I was hearing. This wasn't

the kind of invitation I had expected from him. I pulled my hand away.

His words rushed out before I could form an answer. "No strings attached, Erin. I enjoy your company. That's all. We can drive down early tomorrow. You can relax on the beach if it isn't too cold, or sip margaritas at the bar, or read a book, whatever you like to do while I attend my meeting."

"I don't know," I began.

He held up his hand to stop me. "Hear me out. We'll have a nice dinner. You like steak and lobster? The hotel has a five- star restaurant overlooking the water. I'll reserve separate rooms for us. I told you, no strings. We'll take our time driving back Sunday. I dread another business trip alone. You'd be doing me a favor."

I'd been given similar invitations by customers, but those had been suggestive and I knew their expectations from the start. That wasn't what Vern was proposing.

Still, I hesitated.

He retrieved my hand. "I know this sounds rash and last minute, but you had a terrible accident and, well, after such a traumatic experience, I thought you might enjoy a weekend relaxing and enjoying the sun and sand."

He was a customer. If I accepted, I would be breaking all the bar's rules as well as my own. But breaking rules seemed a fair trade from what I'd been doing. Others broke rules and got away with it.

Vern let go of my hand and gave me a self-effacing smile. "I know I'm not the most handsome or exciting guy you've met. All I want is a chance to enjoy your company. I want to get to know you better. I respect you. I don't expect anything more."

What more could I ask than a chance to relax and forget Atlantic City and all the rest?

"I would pay you for the work you miss here," he added.

I stiffened. "Pay me?"

He realized his mistake at once. "I'm sorry. I don't mean it like that. You told me you were out of work while you were recovering from the accident. That's the only reason I offered. I'm not buying your body. I'm trying to be fair so you won't feel pressured to stay here and work."

I felt torn. I wanted to believe him. But I had trusted before, with horrible consequences.

"Take a chance," he pleaded. "You deserve something good in your life and so do I, even if it's only for a weekend."

The thought of the beach minus gunshots and hoods won me over. "Okay," I said. "I'll go with you if Joe lets me off for the weekend."

"Want me to talk to him?" He half-rose from his seat.

"No." I laughed, feeling the tension ease.

"I will trust your persuasive powers then." A grin spread over his face. "I know it's only been a week, but I can read people. I already know you are a beautiful woman and a decent human being."

Wow. He really didn't know me. Maybe he was having a mid-life crisis. Experience taught me that most men went looking for a change in their lives when they reach their forties. But I didn't care why he wanted to spend the weekend with me. He would get what he wanted and so would I.

He put his hands on each side of my face. "I've never done this before. I'm excited. Can you tell? I can't wait until we get away from the city."

I smiled, still wondering if I was making a mistake. "Hope the weather holds up."

It had been warm and sunny all week. In another month I would be putting on fur-lined boots and coats instead of wearing a bathing suit on the beach.

"It will. I insist." He laughed. "Give me your address and I'll pick you up at nine. Is that too early?"

"In the morning?"

"Unfortunately, business meetings are in the morning. Think of it this way. You'll have more beach time under the sun."

I watched him leave. When Joe appeared in front of me, I told him I needed the weekend off. "Don't say no and please don't ask questions."

"Erin—" I could hear the warning in his voice, but I waved him off.

"I'll be back Monday night," I promised.

I hardly slept that night. What was I doing going off with a stranger? Outside the bar, I didn't know squat about Vern Richland except what he'd told me. The name could be an alias. I had no time to check up on him to see if he wasn't really a creep or, worse, working for Tony Corelli. I hadn't seen Tony since I'd come home. Johnny hadn't shown up either. I wanted to pretend Atlantic City had only been a bad dream and go on with my life.

Could I fall in love with Vern Richland, or someone like him? So different from all the men I'd been attracted to in the past? Good looking. Money in the bank. A company man in a solid business, if I believed what he told me. Everything a woman would want in a suitor. I didn't tense up when I was with him. He was easy to be with. No fights, no drama. In the few hours we'd spent talking, he made me feel better about myself.

But what could I give to a man like that?

I tossed and turned, watching the clock every hour. I finally struggled out of twisted sheets at seven and made a pot of coffee. It was a cool, sunny morning. I laid out a pair of blue slacks and a blue and a white striped jersey pullover on my bed and extracted my suitcase from the closet. I packed a bathing suit, a wrap, and a towel. The contents were sparse. I added a silk teddy and extra underwear.

Remembering at the last minute that we were going to a five-star restaurant for dinner, I contemplated my choice of dresses in the closet. Most of what I had worked well at the after-hours clubs—short, low-cut, showing lots of skin—but would not work for a respectable dinner date. I finally selected a dress I'd bought months ago and wore only once, a little black velvet number. I added the dress and matching heels to the suitcase and clicked the locks.

I showered, dressed, put on makeup, and brushed my hair. I barely had time to finish my coffee before the doorbell rang.

The sight of his ride, a '67 Vett convertible with the top down, almost made me turn back. Once I would have squealed with excitement. My boy Vern sported real money and I should be suitably impressed. But the car reminded me of Brady and his red Camaro, and I couldn't generate much more than a tight smile.

An hour later we reached the hotel Marwood, located across from the beach. Vern registered two connecting rooms. We could have been strangers as we took our suitcases to our respective rooms. I hung up my dress and changed into my bathing suit, covering up with my full-length wrap. We met in the lobby and he walked me across the street to the beach.

"See you on my break," he said and leaned toward me.

For a moment I thought he was going to kiss me. Instead, he reached for my hand and gave my fingers a squeeze.

The morning started off cool, but by mid-day the sun felt good on my bare skin. I dozed off after an hour and awoke with sweat dripping into my eyes. A quick dip in the chill water revived me. By the time the sun dried me completely, Vern joined me. He set down a picnic basket filled with fruit and cheese and a bottle of red wine. At my insistence, he removed his jacket, shoes, and socks. The lines in his face smoothed out, and he stretched his legs across the beach towel and relaxed.

"You see how good you are for me?" he said. "I couldn't wait to get out of that stuffy meeting."

I raised an eyebrow. "Doesn't sound like I'm good for business."

"The opposite," he said. "I'll go back refreshed and energized, ready to give 'em hell."

"I'm your lucky charm?" I said. "Be careful, I could get used to being your companion." I didn't say "kept woman," but that's what I was thinking.

His blue eyes shimmered, reflecting the sun and water. "Do you mean that?"

Easy there. "It's a nice thought, isn't it?" But way too early to bring up plans for the future. Time to change the subject "I'm looking forward to dinner tonight. I brought a special dress for the occasion." I picked at the cheese and popped a couple of grapes into my mouth.

He opened the bottle of wine and filled two plastic glasses. "Can't wait to see you in your dress. You'll love the view from our table." He rubbed the back of my hand with his forefinger. "How are you feeling?"

I smiled. "Warm, relaxed, sleepy."

"If you get tired out here, or too hot, you can always go back to the hotel. I'll call your room when I'm finished. Where's your key?"

I patted the pocket of my wrap. "Safe and sound."

We finished the wine and he returned to his business

meeting. The sun dipped behind a cloud and I pulled the wrap around my shoulders. I stuck it out for another hour and almost fell asleep again, but decided to take his advice and return to the hotel.

After a long hot shower, I lay across the bed nude. The sun and the wine did what it was supposed to do. I didn't wake up until I heard the knock on the door. For a moment I didn't know where I was and then I heard the key turn in the lock. I grabbed the bedspread and rolled it over me.

Vern peeked in. "Are you dressed?"

"No," I said. I wasn't sure what to do next. He had said "no strings." Who the hell was I kidding? Of course, he expected sex. Why should I be disappointed that Vern Richland was no different from any other man?

I threw off the cover, about to tell him to come in and take what he wanted. What he was paying for.

But the door closed with a thud. I heard his voice on the other side.

"Sorry. I'll wait in the lobby. Come down whenever you're dressed and we'll go eat."

I stared at the door. Had I just been rejected? Didn't he find me attractive? Or was Vern the gentleman he'd made himself out to be?

Instead of brooding, I eased off the bed and walked into the bathroom. Fifteen minutes later, with my face made up, my hair in place, and my black dress hugging my curves, I left the room to ring for the elevator.

The restaurant was classy and expensive, with a view of the ocean that left me speechless for about five seconds. We ordered lobster and steak and finished off two bottles of red wine. Sometime during dessert, he was called to the telephone. When he came back he wore a somber expression. "Do you mind if we go back to the city tonight? Something's come up."

"I don't mind. Nothing serious, I hope."

"Nothing I can't handle." He didn't elaborate. His mood became pensive. The air between us felt heavy.

The ride home was strained and awkward. He offered no explanation and I didn't press him. None of my business, I told myself repeatedly. He'd tell me when he was ready.

When we reached my apartment, he leaned over and kissed me on the cheek. "I'm so sorry, Erin. Don't be angry with me. I'll explain later."

"I'm not angry," I assured him. "If there's anything I can do—"

He shook his head. "Soon," he promised, "I'll let you know everything."

What was everything? Who had called him and changed his mood so drastically?

I let myself into my apartment, preoccupied with Vern's final words. I opened the suitcase and took out the dress. His reaction when I met him in the lobby had been one of surprise and delight. He complimented my taste and intelligence. He gave all indications that I pleased him.

The least he could have done was explain, I thought, hanging up the dress. I tossed the bathing suit and towel in the laundry basket and went into the kitchen to make coffee. I eyed the bowl of fruit on the counter. I snagged a banana and peeled it halfway. It tasted better than the dessert I left at the restaurant.

No sooner had I filled the coffee pot with water, there came a knock on the door. A wave of relief and anticipation came over me. Vern had changed his mind. He would explain and make everything right again. I smiled as I opened the door.

"You fucking bitch," Charley Rossini said.

CHAPTER 37

I slammed my body against the door, bulldozing against Charley's arm with all my strength. Charley laughed and stuck his shoe inside to prevent the door from closing. I couldn't hold on longer than a few seconds. He burst through the doorway.

I dashed toward the kitchen. "I'm calling the cops," I yelled, and scrambled for the phone.

He was too fast. He caught my arm and swung me around to face him. His expression twisted with hate as he slapped my head with his free hand. I kicked his shin. He grunted and pushed me against the counter, shoved one leg between mine and leaned his face close.

"Don't even try, bitch," he snarled. "You're dead."

I couldn't breathe. I stared at his bloodshot eyes and crazed expression. Flashing on the face I'd seen in the car racing alongside the Camaro, just before the shot that missed me and killed Brady.

He read my expression and snorted. "So, you got your memory back."

"You fucking bastard, you killed Brady."

He pinned my arms behind me. "That's right. Shouldda been you, bitch. Gonna take care of that now."

My voice croaked in desperation. "Tony's got someone watching my place. He'll be up here any second."

He smirked. "Lost your bodyguard when you took off with your new boyfriend. Tony didn't like that. Get a clue, there's no one to save you." He gripped my neck with one hand and with the other unzipped my slacks. He dipped his fingers inside my panties. "First, I'm gonna take what I missed the last time we were alone."

I brought my arms up and tried to pull his hand off my neck. He squeezed tighter and I raked his face. He grimaced and shoved two digits inside me, increasing the pressure against my throat. I tried to scream, but he smashed his open mouth against mine and bit into my lower lip. With the counter digging into my back, I fumbled for something behind me that I could use as a weapon.

I found the phone. I gripped it and swung, smashing the base against his left temple. He bellowed, freeing my lip. I reared back and spat in his face. I bashed him again then pounded at his arm until he pulled his hand out of my pants.

Blood oozed from his forehead. I brought my knee up, but he expected the move and blocked it. He roared in a rage as I twisted violently out of his reach. He caught my shirt and tried to pull me back. I picked up the bowl of fruit from the counter and let it fly.

He ducked but the bowl grazed the side of his head. He cursed and lost his balance. Apples, oranges, and bananas pelted down on him without effect. I reached for the drawer where I kept household tools and found Paul's dagger. I marked the distance to the exit, but he moved to block the way. His breath was heavy and ragged.

I feinted a move to the edge of the counter and when he took the bait, I ran like hell past him out of the kitchen and into the bedroom. I slammed the door, turning the flimsy lock.

Footsteps followed, the doorknob rattled, and then the sound of his boot kicking the door.

I raced to the window, tugged at it, but it stuck from old paint. The blade was no help. I slipped off my shoe and rammed the heel through the center. Glass shattered, falling two stories down, some pieces landing on the floor where I stood. I knocked off some of the larger shards that stuck to the window sill before Charley's boot splintered the door and he lurched inside. I swung my right leg over the window sill, trying not to put all my weight on the jagged edge. I leaned out. Two stories up and no fire escape between me and the concrete sidewalk. I glanced back at Charley, and tasted dirt. My heart pounded. He held a gun, the barrel an obscene phallic eye.

He waved the gun. "This trumps a knife any day."

I considered my chances of survival. The odds weren't on my side.

A grin split his face. "You gonna jump, bitch? Just like Johnny, huh? Wish he could see you now."

My stomach dropped. Had he been with Tony in California when Johnny was forced to jump three stories from the roof?

He must have read my mind. "Yeah, bitch, I was there."

I screamed, panic turning the volume up, hoping, praying someone would hear me. Escape seemed impossible, but I couldn't give up. Tears streamed down my cheeks as I broke glass off the window frame with my knife so I could hold on without slicing off my fingers.

"You bastard." Sharp edges of glass poked my thigh.

"Go ahead and jump," Charley said, his tone taunting. "Better than getting shot. You might not die. Maybe you'll get away. Maybe you won't end up crippled."

I glanced again at the ground as I hung on. He was right. I would be crippled—if I survived.

His grin widened. Fucker was enjoying every minute of his power, anticipating the kill.

"You'll never get away with this," I said. "Tony will find you." Empty words, I knew. I couldn't hope for rescue, but I had the knife that Charley dismissed as useless.

"Tony?" He shrugged. "He's got other worries."

"What worries?" I said to keep him talking while balancing the dagger in my hand like Paul had shown me.

"Nothing like what's gonna happen to you."

He raised the gun and I heard the click of the hammer. I didn't hesitate. I threw the knife.

My aim was off, but the blade penetrated his right shoulder. He dropped the gun on impact. His eyes went wild. He glared in disbelief at the blood.

He rushed me with a roar. He pushed my shoulders back out the window. My hand flew to Charley's shirt and held tight. The material tore but I hung on. The glass bit into my thighs as I squeezed my leg against the inside wall for purchase. With my free hand, I frantically groped along the window sill looking for more glass. I found a large shard and broke it off. With all my strength, I rammed the glass into Charley's neck. He screamed. Blood spurted. His eyes widened in shock.

My heart hammered in my ears. My breath turned ragged as I clutched at his shirt, slipping outside the window as the fabric ripped. I reached for the window frame, but Charley's blood made the wood slick and I couldn't hold on. I was falling, my hands clutching at air.

Someone shoved Charley aside and grabbed me before I cleared the window. I cried out in renewed panic as Johnny's face loomed over me. Another enemy. Without thinking, I kicked out at him, certain that he was going to finish the job Charley started. He deflected my kick and wrapped an arm around my waist. I clung to him until I was safely inside the apartment then struggled to get free.

He dropped me on the floor. Blood dripped under me, but I wasn't conscious of pain.

Johnny left me and knelt beside Charley who was moaning and reaching for the glass in his neck. By the way blood puddle under him, I must have hit an artery.

"Is he dead?" I yelled.

The moaning stopped. Johnny stood and turned around to face me. I looked at Charley. Blood still spurted from his wound. I knew I had been right. His carotid artery was severed.

"He will be," Johnny said gruffly.

With the pent-up fury that Charley had unleashed, I turned on all fours and screamed at Johnny. "Now what? You're going to kill me, you fucking bastard? You got your chance. Just try it. I'll take you down with me, you bastard, so help me God."

I crawled toward Charley's gun.

Johnny kicked the gun to the other side of the room and loomed over me. His eyes were dark and angry. "Are you crazy? I just saved your life."

I looked from him to Charley and back again. "Why?" I cried hoarsely.

Johnny was breathing hard. "If you don't know by now, I can't tell you."

"Fuck you, Johnny. You've been after me all this time. Haven't you? Answer me, dammit!"

"If I wanted you dead, you'd be dead." He shook his head and sounded calmer when he spoke again. "Couldn't let ol' Charley get away with another murder." He looked at my legs. "You're lucky you didn't sever an artery yourself. You're still bleeding."

"Don't tell me shit." I hobbled into the bathroom and sat on the edge of the tub. I ran the water and washed the blood off my legs.

Johnny followed me in. He found a roll of tape and

handed it to me. He sat on the toilet seat while I bandaged my wounds. I was glad to get away from Charley's body.

"Let me help you with that," Johnny offered.

"Get the hell away from me."

He barely suppressed a grin. "Those cuts probably won't leave scars."

"Thanks," I said, dripping sarcasm.

"Wished you'd showed this much spirit when we were together," he said.

"I did," I said. "Or did you forget?"

"No, I haven't forgotten. That's the thing about you. You hold everything in until it all turns into a big fucking deal in your head and you go a little nuts. Then you blow."

"Have me all figured out, don't you?"

"After five years with you, I've got a clue. You still want me dead?"

"If I did, you would be." But my words lacked conviction. "I'm not the same girl you knew."

"I saw that in Atlantic City. You weren't afraid of me then." His eyes swept over me. "You've grown up."

"I've dealt with men worse than you. Besides, I know what you were hiding all those years. Nico ordered the hit on you when you refused to blow someone up on his orders."

He frowned. "Who told you that?"

"Tony. Why couldn't you tell me? Because you didn't trust me."

"Because it wouldn't have been safe for you."

"Because you didn't trust me." I repeated and glanced toward the bedroom. "How did you know Charley would show up?"

"He went back to Atlantic City after he tried to shoot you. I followed him."

"Because you cared?" More sarcasm.

He didn't answer.

"What about Tony?" I said quietly.

His eyes narrowed. "What about him?"

"Did Charley do anything to him?"

"Tony can take care of himself. He's fine. He's known Charley a long time." He leaned toward me. "Why were you in Atlantic City?"

"I told you. I wanted to make sure nobody killed you."

His lips quivered, not quite a smile. "I know Nico was blackmailing Tony, saying he'd turn the mob against him for not fulfilling the hit on me. I know Nico wanted Tony's clubs. So did Charley. It was all about greed. What's the real reason you were there?"

"You won't believe me."

"Try me."

"I met Tony after I first came to Philly. I was still shaken over what I'd done to you. Anyway, I mentioned your name. I didn't know at the time he was the one you were running from. How much of a coincidence is that?" I tried to laugh, but the sound died in my throat. "He told me when we met later that he saw you in Atlantic City. He'd followed up on the little I told him. By this time, Nico had contacted him and was blackmailing him. Nico somehow found out you were still alive and that gave him leverage. Like you said, he wanted the Atlantic City clubs."

"Why would he tell you any of this?" Johnny said, clearly not convinced.

"He wanted to use me as bait to bring you out. I didn't know that or I would never have agreed. He used me. But he didn't want to kill you. I believed that. When I told him about us, told him what I did to you, he asked if I still wanted you dead. I told him no. I said I would do anything to keep you alive."

He snorted.

I leaned toward him. "I knew you were in Nico's and Charley's crosshairs. Yes, I tried to kill you once. But I wasn't going to let them do it. And I didn't want you on my conscience anymore."

Johnny stood and strolled into the bedroom.

I limped after him and avoided looking at Charley. "So you weren't looking for me all this time?"

"Why? It's evident you didn't want to be with me. You think I wanted revenge?" He turned and studied me. "I was furious as hell at first. Maybe I wanted to hurt you. But I didn't forget how you took care of me when I needed you. You loved me once. I believed that."

I nodded. Tears fell down my cheeks.

"What happens now?" I asked.

His eyes softened, but I couldn't read his thoughts.

Finally he said, "I'm going back to California. I have unfinished business there."

I tried to hide my surprise. And my relief. "Just like that? You're not worried about Tony?"

"Why? With Nico dead, he's not going to come after me."

"You're free then. No more looking back. No more running."

He smiled and nodded. "What's next for you?"

I thought about Vern Richland. "I'm not sure. I have to see a friend in the hospital first. Maybe I'll get out of this town. Or maybe I'll blackmail Tony into backing me in a nightclub of my own." I gave him a rueful look.

He chuckled. "Well, whatever you decide, I'm sure it'll be right for you."

I could breathe easier now. We looked at each other. His weathered, sun-brown skin looked more wrinkled, his blue eyes more sunken and watery. Other than looking older and more tired, he hadn't changed much in a year.

He squatted next to Charley and felt for a pulse. I shuddered. "I didn't do all that, did I?"

Johnny raised an eyebrow. "You worried?"

"Yeah. I don't want to go to jail."

"You won't. Give Tony a call. Tell him you need a cleaner."

He rose to his feet and I walked him to the door. We stood there for a moment staring at each other. There was nothing more to say. He leaned toward me and kissed me gently on the lips. A goodbye kiss.

I watched him walk out of the apartment and out of my life. It had been a year since I'd run away from him to find a new life in Philadelphia. Now I didn't have to look back either.

I went to the phone and dialed a familiar number, heard the low voice with the Italian accent.

"Tony? It's me. I need a cleanup in my apartment. How soon can you send someone?"

CHAPTER 38

The following Monday night in Dreamscape, I sipped a scotch and water and wondered if I would ever see Vern Richland again. Not sure how I felt about him or what I'd say if and when he did show up. The news had spread throughout the bars about Charley Rossini's murder and how he'd been found in a garbage bin. My first night back to work, Joe pulled me aside and asked if I knew what happened.

I shrugged and shook my head.

"Your friend Dani talked to the police," he said. "She ID'd Charley as her attacker."

"I know," I answered. "I'm picking her up from the hospital Sunday. She's going to stay with me."

He nodded, clearly not surprised. I went back to hustling drinks while looking for Vern, wondering why he hadn't been back. Maybe his problem had been more than he could handle.

I got my answer a few days later. Vern came in late, his hair disheveled and his face pale. His suit looked wrinkled, which wasn't like him. I was sitting with someone else when I saw him and decided to let him simmer a while. After all, I'd been the one waiting.

Vern drank three whiskeys in a row, just like the

night we'd met. When my customer left for the restroom, I strolled over and sat next to him. I caught the scent of Aramis.

He grasped my hand. "You're not angry with me, are you?"

"No, Vern. Why should I be?" I'd never seen him look so upset. Should I worry about his blood pressure? "It's all right. Whatever you want to tell me, I'll understand." This wasn't going to be good.

He took a deep breath and let the words rush out, "I've left my wife and five kids for you. I'm filing for divorce. I'm in love with you, Erin. I've tried to forget you, but I can't. I've been out of my head. I want you to come away with me. Tonight. Marry me."

I was so shocked I couldn't answer. "You did what?" I finally managed to get out. "You left your—your wife? You're married? Damn Vern. Five kids?"

"Please, Erin, tell me you feel the same way about me. I'm going crazy with love for you."

For one insane moment, I wanted to laugh in his face. But at the sight of his hopeful, pathetic expression, I lowered my voice. "Vern, listen to me. If I'd known you were married, I never would have agreed to spend a weekend with you. Is this why you needed to leave the hotel? Your wife found out, didn't she?"

Vern looked so miserable, I actually felt sorry for him. I took his hand. "Don't do this. Don't leave your family for me. I'm not worth it. I would make you miserable. I'm a cheat. I wouldn't be faithful. I've never been faithful. I'm not marriage material."

He put his finger against my lips and smiled. "You don't have to lie to me. I know you're just trying to make me feel better. It's all right. I will make you happy."

I shook my head. "Vern, I don't love you. You've talked yourself into this." I let go of his hand and slid off the stool. "You've got to leave now. Go back and make up with your wife. Don't come back here again."

I turned and ran for the stairs. I dashed to the dressing room and pulled the door shut, shaking so bad I could hardly stand.

Maggie burst in. "What the fuck was that all about?"

I looked at her and started laughing. I couldn't stop laughing. "Maggie, let's get high after work. I am ready to party. Break out the weed. I'm free, free for the first time in my life. And I'm going to stay that way."

THE END

About the Author

Laura Elvebak sometimes feels she has led several lives, but throughout the years her passion for reading and writing has never faltered. For the past twenty-something years, she has worked for lawyers and oil and gas executives.

Before that she held a variety of occupations, including working as waitress and even as a go-go dancer in the late sixties in Philadelphia. Born in North Dakota and raised in Los Angeles and San Francisco, she settled in Houston after living in parts of New York, New Jersey, Philadelphia, and Florida. She is happily unmarried after six attempts with men who would make fascinating characters in books but didn't succeed as husband material.

Elvebak studied writing at UCLA, USC, Rice University, and Beyond Baroque in Venice, California. After taking a directing class in Houston, she co-wrote, directed, and acted in a one-act play. She optioned three screenplays to a local production company and co-wrote a script for the 48 Hour Film Project. She is the author of the *Niki Alexander Mysteries*. *The Flawed Dance* is a stand-alone and the first to be published by Black Opal Books. The third Niki Alexander mystery will be released later in 2015 or early 2015 by Black Opal Books.

Elvebak is a member of Mystery Writers of America, Sisters-In-Crime, The International Thriller Writers, and The Final Twist Writers and has a presence on Facebook, Twitter, LinkedIn, Goodreads, and Amazon Author Central.

Her author website is http://lauraelvebak.com